Balance Power & Protection

EMPIRE OF THE LEGACIES ACADEMY
BOOK THREE

WRITTEN BY AWARD-WINNING AUTHOR

SUSAN HODDY

CHARACTERS IN THE STORYLINE

Hawk Ironclaw (Griffin)
Sully Valerith (half Griffin, half Lepidoptera Vampire, Fae)
Garrick Ironclaw (Stormclaw Aerie, Griffins leader)
Elara Ironclaw (Griffin)
Rhydian Ironclaw (Griffin)
Zephyrion Ironclaw (Griffin)
Rimmer Ironclaw (Griffin)
The Griffin Soldiers: Draven, Kael, Bennett
Elsie Brookton (Griffin)
Eryndor Ironclaw (half Griffin, half Warlock)
Malrik (Sorcerer)

Veyda (Warrior)
Drogan (Minion)
The Lepidoptera Vampires:
Queen Talitha, Princess Violette, William, Grayson, Michael, Brock, Renee, Danielle, Stephen, Christian, Kelan, Samantha, Samuel, Kiplin

Adrian Lachance (Warlock)
Stjernefrída (Mother Goddess of the stars)
Kura (Grandmother of Stjernefrída, great-grandmother of Alessia)
Alessia (Goddess of the stars, Stjernefrída's daughter)

Fae:
Aevyressa, Myrrathen, Thalara, Adeline, Danielle, Xanthia, Sully

Albinus Giordano (Human)
Xanthia Castlewood (Fae)
Eight cloaked councilors in Glittertind

Three Guardians of the River of Whispers:
Guardian of the River's Source

Guardian of the River's Flow
Guardian of the River's Destination

TJ McCrindle (Human)
Parker McCrindle (Griffin)

Lead Scientist Sebastian (Human)
Technician Jean (Human)
Dr Elias Norland (Human)
Freya Lindholm (Human)

PLACES IN THE STORYLINE

Bagnolet, France
Olden Fjord, Norway
Mibam Waterfall, Oman
Glittertind, Norway
Cowaramup, Western Australia
Gracetown, Western Australia
Bouvet Island, Norway
Utah Desert
Suytun Cenote, Mexico
Saint Lucia

ANCIENT ARTIFACTS

Twin Icefire Blades
The Golden Chalice
The Fae's Golden Ring
The Cauldron of Chaos
Ethereal Nexus Amulet
Prophecy of Balance
Blade of Severance
Starfire Crystal
Ritual of Unmaking

CHAPTER ONE

"Alessia, are you ready to go?" TJ called, rummaging through her handbag for the car keys. "We're going to be late if you don't get a wriggle on."

"Yes, *Mother*," Alessia shouted from her bedroom, rolling her blue eyes with exaggerated frustration. "I'm almost done."

She shoved the last of her university books into her bag, zipped it shut and slung it over her shoulder, before heading toward the kitchen.

"Did you sleep in again this morning?" TJ asked, as Alessia strolled into the kitchen.

"Yeah … I've been so exhausted lately," Alessia replied with a yawn. "And the weird dreams aren't helping. Things like celestial realms that I govern as a Goddess. And being able to communicate with animals and plants."

"That is strange. Sorry to hear that, sweetheart. Fortunately, they are only dreams." She handed Alessia a plate with two pieces of toast on it.

"Aww … thanks, Mum," Alessia said, taking the plate from her.

"No problem. You'll need the energy, especially with your end-of-year exams today," TJ replied.

"I'm not sure if I'm ready," Alessia admitted softly, her brow furrowing as doubt flickered in her eyes. "I've studied, I swear, but … it's overwhelming. Like there's just *too much* to hold on to, and I'm afraid I'll forget it all when it really matters."

"You'll be fine, I'm sure of it," TJ said gently, resting a reassuring hand on her daughter's shoulder. "You're smarter than you give yourself credit for. Now, come on—we'd better get going."

"Good luck today, sweetheart," Parker said, as he sat at the kitchen island bench and placed his newspaper down.

"Thanks, Dad," Alessia replied. "I'm definitely going to need it."

"See you later, babe," TJ said, slipping her bag onto her shoulder. She walked over and kissed him on the cheek.

"I'll be here," Parker replied, leaning in to her kiss.

"See you this afternoon, Dad," said Alessia, as she walked toward the carport doorway.

"See you, sweetheart," said Parker, as he watched both of them head out.

* * *

The V8 cruiser hummed along softly as TJ navigated the winding roads toward the university. Alessia sat quietly in the passenger seat, gazing out the window, her mind still buzzing with nerves.

"Did you dye some of your hair?" TJ asked, her gaze narrowing slightly when they pulled up in front of the university, as she noticed that a few strands of Alessia's hair had turned a striking shade of silver.

Alessia ran a hand through her dark brown hair, brushing the silver strands behind her ear. "No, it just kind of happened," she shrugged, a flicker of uncertainty in her eyes.

TJ leaned in a little, inspecting the silver strands more closely. "When did this start?"

"Just recently," Alessia replied. "I woke up a few days ago and they were there. It's weird, right?"

TJ's brow furrowed with concern, but she tried to mask it with a casual smile. "Well, I guess you're just getting more unique, huh?" She gave her daughter's shoulder a reassuring squeeze. "Nothing to worry about, just … keep an eye on it."

Alessia forced a smile, but inside a tiny seed of doubt began to sprout.

"Do you need anything before you go in?" TJ asked, her expression a mixture of concern and pride.

"I think I'm good," Alessia replied, with a small smile. "Just need to survive the next few hours, and then I'll be done for the year. Can't wait to get this PhD in astrophysics done and dusted."

TJ chuckled softly. "You've got this. Just remember to breathe, okay? It's only one day, one exam at a time."

Alessia nodded, trying to push the weight of the exams from her mind. Taking a deep breath, she hoped that she was ready to face whatever came next.

"I'll pick you up later," TJ said, as Alessia opened the door to get out.

"Thanks, Mum. See you soon." Alessia waved goodbye, as she made her way toward the entrance.

* * *

Alessia stood in front of a wooden door that had a sign pinned to it, that read:

EXAMS IN PROGRESS
PLEASE BE QUIET
9.30 am – 1.00 pm

Opening the door, Alessia stepped into the exam room and noticed row upon row of small tables, each paired with a chair. She quietly made her way to the back of the room, settled into a seat, and began reviewing her notes for the exam.

As a yawn escaped her, Alessia froze. Glowing runes and symbols flickered across her right forearm and hand, shimmering faintly, before spreading to her left. She frowned, shaking her head, and the strange markings vanished as quickly as they had appeared. *What the hell was that?*

Glancing around the room, she saw it had nearly filled with other students, all hunched over their notes, desperately cramming last-minute details. No one else seemed to have noticed anything out of the ordinary.

Her thoughts were interrupted as the examiner's voice rang out from the front of the room.

"Alright, quieten down, everyone," he said, his sharp gaze sweeping across the room as he waited for their attention.

"In a few minutes, I'll be handing out the exam papers. First, write your full name and today's date at the top of the page. Once the clock hits nine-thirty," he gestured to the large clock on the wall behind him, "you may begin. The exam will end promptly at one. At that time, all completed papers must be placed on my desk to be marked."

He paused briefly before continuing. "Results will be published in two weeks on the university website. You'll need your log-in ID and password to access them. Good luck to you all."

With that, he began walking between the rows of desks, placing an exam paper face down in front of each student.

When the exam began, Alessia, along with the rest of the students, turned over her paper and carefully wrote her name and the date at the top. Flipping to the first page of the questionnaire Alessia glanced at the first question. *Yep, I know this one*, she thought confidently as she scribbled down her answer.

For the next ten minutes, the pattern continued—question after question came easily to her, the answers flowing effortlessly. *Maybe I did study enough after all*, she mused with a small sense of relief.

But just as she started to settle into the rhythm, something strange happened. The glowing runes and symbols reappeared, flickering across her forearms and hands like living light. This time, however, they weren't just on her skin—they pulsed within her mind, vivid and insistent, as though they were trying to tell her something.

When the examiner's voice rang out, "Pens down," Alessia was startled back to reality. She blinked in surprise, unable to believe it was already over. Glancing around the room, she noticed other students had either finished early, or were now making their way to the front, placing their papers on the examiner's desk.

Shaking her head, she looked up at the clock. Sure enough, it read one p.m. *Far out, where did the time go?*

She glanced down at her hands and forearms, searching for the glowing symbols and runes she had seen earlier—but they were gone. *What the hell is going on?* Alessia wondered, her brow furrowing in confusion.

With a deep breath, she lowered her gaze back to the exam paper in front of her. Flipping through the pages, she realized, with surprise, that she had somehow completed the entire exam.

Alessia felt tingles of warmth coursing through her body, particularly in her hands and chest. She wondered whether it was anxiety or something else entirely—perhaps a sign of relief that her final exam was done and dusted.

Slinging her bag over her shoulder, she walked over to the examiner and placed the paperwork on his desk.

"Ah, Miss McCrindle. How do you think you did on the exam?" asked the professor, his voice warm with curiosity. He had been a great mentor to her throughout the past year at university.

"I'm not sure," Alessia replied, a hint of uncertainty in her voice. "It's all a bit of a blur. I just hope I did well. I'd really love to get a job in astrophysics."

"I'm sure you did well, dear. As I said this morning, your results will be posted in about two weeks on the university website, so you will be able to check them then," said the professor.

"Thank you. Have a good holiday, professor, and thank you for all your help throughout the year."

"You're welcome! Hope you have a good holiday, too."

Alessia smiled and walked toward the doorway.

CHAPTER TWO

A swirling vortex of light erupted at the River of Whispers, its center shimmering with hues of watery blue, while arcs of energy crackled around its edges. From the portal emerged Garrick and Elara Ironclaw, flanked by three steadfast Griffin soldiers.

"Welcome, Garrick and Elara," the Guardian of the River's Source greeted, his voice calm yet commanding as he stepped forward. Flanking him were the Guardian of the River's Flow and the Guardian of the River's Destination, their presence exuding an aura of ancient vigilance. "I believe from speaking with Kura that you have come to search for information on the child?"

"You are correct," stated Garrick, leader of the Stormclaw Aerie Griffins, as the portal closed behind him. "Lead the way!"

The Guardian of the River's Source gave a single nod to Garrick, before turning and heading toward Kura's home. The Guardian of the River's Flow and the Guardian of the River's Destination followed closely behind.

The five Griffins followed the guardians up to the house.

You will stand guard at the doorway, while we look around the house, commanded Garrick telepathically, to his three soldiers.

Yes, Sir, the three Griffin soldiers responded in unison, their voices echoing telepathically.

As Garrick and Elara walked up onto the porch, Elara said, "We are terribly sorry for your loss. Stjernefrída was a beautiful soul."

"Thank you," the Guardian of the River's Flow said solemnly. "Stjernefrída was our radiant mother, Keeper of the Celestial Vault and Weaver of Eternal Light. We will miss her dearly."

"When will Kura be returning to our realm?" asked the Guardian of the River's Destination.

"Not for a while, I'm afraid," Garrick replied as he stepped through the doorway. "She's safer with the Lepidopteras for the time being."

"Right!" said the Guardian of the River's Destination, as he looked from Garrick to the Guardian of the River's Source and the Guardian of the River's Flow.

"Do you have any idea where we can start looking for information on the child?" asked Garrick.

"Stjernefrída had a hidden chest beneath the floorboards of her bedroom, under her bed, where all such information was kept. But, when we went to retrieve it, we found that the chest was sealed with a spell and we haven't been able to open it. We are not certain, but we think Kura might be the only one left who is able to unlock it," the Guardian of the River's Source replied. He walked over to the kitchen table and indicated an ancient chest, which radiated an unnerving, otherworldly glow, as if it held secrets long forgotten.

Garrick and Elara stepped forward, their footsteps muffled against the wooden floorboards as they approached the ancient chest. The room seemed to grow quieter and the air thickened with a strange, otherworldly hum that emanated from the chest. As they neared, the unnerving glow intensified, casting long, distorted shadows across their faces.

The chest was made of dark, weathered wood, its surface cracked and worn from centuries of aging. The edges were adorned with intricate carvings, faded but still discernible, depicting ancient symbols and scenes of forgotten lore. The wood seemed to absorb the dim light around it, casting an eerie shadow that shifted with the chest's unsettling glow. Its brass hinges were tarnished and twisted, as if warped by time and the weight of the secrets it held. The top was slightly raised, as though the chest itself was breathing, exhaling a faint ethereal mist that shimmered with a dim greenish hue. At the center, an ornate lock glowed softly, an unnatural light pulsing from within, as though something alive stirred beneath its surface. The very air around the chest felt heavier, thick with a sense of dread, as if it was guarding something far more dangerous than mere memories or information.

Garrick's hand hovered over the chest and his brow furrowed in concentration. As his eyes narrowed to examine the lock, the ancient symbols etched into it seemed to pulse in rhythm with the glow. "I've never seen anything like this," he murmured. "This lock … it's tied to something more than just magic. Something far older."

"You are correct," replied the Guardian of the River's Source.

Elara stood a few paces behind Garrick, her gaze fixed on the chest, wary of its presence. Her wings shifted slightly within her back, a subconscious reaction to the growing tension in the air. "Perhaps it's better left closed?"

"Only a Goddess can open it and release the spell. Take the chest to Kura. We're certain she will be able to open it for you," said the Guardian of the River's Source.

"Right!" Garrick replied, glancing briefly at the guardian, before his attention returned to the chest. With a careful, deliberate motion, he reached forward and placed his hand on it. The glow pulsed brighter for a moment, and the temperature in the room dropped sharply, making the air feel thick and heavy.

A low, guttural growl emanated from within the chest, as if in warning. The sound reverberated through the room, its deep, rumbling tone carrying an unmistakable threat. But Garrick's resolve didn't waver. His fingers tightened around the chest, his eyes on the lock, determined to discover its secrets.

In an instant, a violent surge of energy shot out from the chest, crackling through the air. Before Garrick could react, a powerful jolt zapped through him and the chest sent him flying backward. He collided with the wall and the air was knocked from his lungs as he slid to the ground, stunned but not defeated.

Garrick's vision blurred for a moment and he gritted his teeth, struggling to push himself upright. "This thing … is not going to make it easy," he muttered under his breath, rubbing the back of his head where it had struck the wall.

Elara hurried to his side. "Are you alright?"

Garrick shook his head, his eyes still locked on the chest, which now seemed to glow even more ominously. "I'm fine. But we'll need to bring Kura here for this. Let's go." He indicated the chest, which had landed on the floor.

Elara helped her partner to his feet, then turned to face the three guardians. "Thank you. We will return with Kura."

The guardians nodded solemnly, their gazes following as Garrick and Elara made their way toward the doorway.

The three Griffin soldiers snapped to attention as Garrick and Elara stepped out onto the porch.

"We're heading to Bagnolet. Follow us," Garrick commanded.

The soldiers nodded in unison, prepared for the journey.

With a flick of her hand, Elara conjured a portal, a gateway to France, where Kura awaited.

As the portal closed behind them, the guardians of the River of Whispers faded into the surrounding forest, silently waiting for the Griffins and Kura to return.

* * *

Eryndor, who had been concealed in the shadows of the River of Whispers, stepped out from behind a tree, a wicked smile curling his lips as the weight of the new information sank in. His eyes gleamed with malice and his mind had already started to craft a dark plan. He had been lying in wait for a few days now, hoping that he could acquire information from the River of Whispers, on how to extract the chalice out of the book, now that Stjernefrída was dead.

"Hmm … A child … Stjernefrída has a child," he whispered to himself, as if savoring each word. "And Kura holds the key to unlocking the ancient chest, so that they can find the child's place of residence. My visit has certainly turned out to be valuable."

Eryndor's talons curled into a tight fist and the surge of power ignited his thoughts like a flame.

"If Stjernefrída's child is as important as they believe, then that child could be a weapon—one I'll control." A low, sinister chuckle escaped his lips, as he reveled in the thrill of victory that had not yet even been claimed.

CHAPTER THREE

The glass sliding doors of the operations room in the Gramaze mansion hissed open, drawing Violette and William's attention. Their gazes shifted as five Griffins strode purposefully into the room.

"Welcome, Garrick and Elara," William greeted warmly, stepping forward to shake Garrick's hand before turning to Elara. He had watched their arrival via portal on the operations room's security monitors and had already spoken with Garrick about the pressing matter necessitating Kura's return to the River of Whispers. "Kura should be ready in a few minutes," he assured them with a confident nod.

"Thank you, William," said Elara, shaking his hand.

"Ah, here she is now," William said, his gaze shifting, as Kura entered the operations room with a purposeful stride.

"Good evening, Goddess," Garrick said, inclining his head in a respectful bow toward her.

"Good evening," Kura began, her tone steady and commanding, as she stepped forward to stand before Garrick, Elara, Violette and William. "Before we depart for the River of Whispers to open the ancient chest, there is an important matter I need to discuss with all of you."

Garrick exchanged a quick glance with Elara before stepping forward. "Of course, Goddess," he said respectfully. "What matter requires our attention?"

"Stjernefrída's funeral and honoring the passing of a Goddess of Light and Hope," Kura replied solemnly, her voice carrying a reverence that stilled the room.

Elara's expression softened, her eyes reflecting sorrow. "Stjernefrída's loss is a great blow to us all," she said quietly. "How can we best honor her memory?"

"Now that I have prepared her body, I want to take her home to the River of Whispers, where I can perform the Rite of Eternal Light," Kura continued, her voice firm yet tinged with emotion. "It is a sacred ceremony to guide her spirit to the realm beyond and ensure her light continues to shine in the hearts of those she touched. Her legacy deserves nothing less than the highest honor we can offer."

"We can certainly help with this," Elara replied, her gaze softening as she met Kura's sorrowful eyes. "Stjernefrída's memory will be honored in the way she deserves."

"Yes, and my coven can assist with security," William added, his tone resolute. "We'll ensure the ceremony goes uninterrupted, no matter what."

"Thank you," said Kura, looking from Elara to William.

"Violette, have four members of our coven ready in the backyard within fifteen minutes," William instructed firmly. "And when they are ready, open a portal to the River of Whispers."

"Yes, Sire," Violette responded with a respectful nod. Turning to Kura, she added gently, "I will have Stjernefrída's body brought to the portal, so you may walk with her, if you wish, Goddess."

"Thank you, Princess," Kura replied, her tone warm and sincere. "That is most gracious of you."

"You're welcome," Violette replied, offering a small nod, before heading toward the doorway.

William's gaze shifted between Kura, Elara and Garrick as he spoke. "If you are in agreement, I believe we need to discuss both Stjernefrída's funeral and the guarding of the ancient chest—and the critical information it contains."

"I think that is a wise decision, William," Garrick said, his tone measured, reflecting the gravity of the situation—especially with Eryndor still at large.

"Please, take a seat," William said, gesturing toward the large table beside them. "We can discuss everything here in complete privacy."

"We need to ensure every detail is accounted for," Kura said, as she pulled out the chair. "Eryndor's presence complicates matters, especially with the ancient chest in question."

"I agree, Goddess," said William, leaning forward, resting his hands on the table. "Let's finalize our plans and ensure we're ready for what lies ahead."

The group nodded in unison, their expressions resolute. "Agreed," they said almost simultaneously, a shared determination binding them together as the weight of the task ahead settled over the room.

* * *

The three guardians of the River of Whispers stood vigilant, their postures rigid, and their eyes scanning the misty expanse. They waited in silence as a portal shimmered to life behind them and, moments later, five Griffins and five Lepidopteras emerged, with Stjernefrída's body carried gently alongside Kura. As the last figure stepped through, the portal closed behind them with a soft hum, leaving only the quiet murmur of the river's current.

"We have prepared everything, as you instructed, Goddess," said one guardian, standing at the edge where the river began.

Kura's gaze drifted over the flowing waters and she noticed how the river seemed to shimmer with an otherworldly glow, whispering softly as it wound its way toward the horizon.

"Thank you, Guardian," Kura said softly, her gaze steady and full of gratitude, as she noticed Stjernefrída's friends and the forest's elders gathered by the riverbank. She turned to Brock, who was carefully carrying Stjernefrída's body. "Please place Stjernefrída on the platform by the riverbank." She gestured toward the riverbank, where the sacred waters shimmered with an otherworldly glow. Luminous stones lined the shore, their light dancing in harmony with the soft, fluttering lanterns hanging from the tree branches above. The water's surface mirrored the starlit sky, casting an ethereal aura that enveloped the entire scene in a serene, celestial glow.

Brock nodded solemnly, his face set with reverence, as he carefully approached the small platform. With steady hands, he gently set Stjernefrída's body upon the platform, ensuring it rested peacefully among the glowing stones. His heart was heavy with the weight of the moment as he stepped back, his gaze lingering on her form.

Kura followed closely behind him, her steps quiet and deliberate. She knelt beside the platform, her fingers trembling as she unwrapped the cream woven cloth from Stjernefrída's body. The cloth, delicate and glowing faintly with an ethereal light, shimmered in the air as she unwound it. It was embroidered with intricate symbols of divine power, each stitch a reflection of Stjernefrída's eternal essence. As Kura laid the cloth aside, a soft warmth seemed to emanate from the Goddess's form, as if the warmth of life itself still clung to her.

With respect, Kura arranged the Goddess's body carefully upon the platform, her movements tender, ensuring that Stjernefrída rested perfectly in the center. As her form settled, the platform responded—its crystal surface shimmering more brightly, as if recognizing her presence. The silver and gold filigree patterns on the platform flickered gently in the air, as Kura paused, her eyes glistening with both sorrow and awe, and the cloth glowed softly—a final testament to the Goddess's power.

Soft, ethereal lights flickered from the platform like starlight, casting a serene glow across the water. As Kura gave the platform a gentle push, it began to drift downstream and the air around it was filled with a peaceful, reverent atmosphere. The sounds of the river mingled with the faint breeze, carrying the scent of lotus and herbs. This was a final, sacred journey, as Stjernefrída's essence embarked toward eternity, embraced by the river and the forces of light and transformation.

The faces of those in attendance were solemn, their expressions a mixture of grief and awe. Many, including the Griffins and Lepidopteras, stood with heads bowed, some with hands clasped in quiet prayer or offering, some with their eyes fixed upon the floating platform that carried Stjernefrída's form. A few of the elders, those who had known her in life, stood at the forefront, their faces lined with years of wisdom and sadness. Some held back tears, while others, lost in their grief, allowed them to fall freely, tracing paths down their cheeks.

With her voice soft, yet strong, Kura said,

> *Goodbye, my beloved granddaughter. You were a light in this world—bright and unwavering, like the stars that fill the heavens. The river now carries you on your final journey, but know this: you are not lost to us. You are one with the flow of life, the currents of change and the eternal spirit of the earth and sky.*

> *Though our hearts are heavy with grief, we know that your essence will never fade. It lives on in the winds that carry your whispers, in the flowers that bloom by the riverbank and in every soul whose life you touched. You were a beacon, a guide, and now you are a part of something much greater. You have returned to the river, to the source of all life, where your spirit will be forever woven into the fabric of time.*

> *We will mourn you, but we will also celebrate the beauty of your life—the*

*wisdom you shared, the love you gave and
the strength you showed even in the face of
great trials. You are our Goddess, our
Protector, and now you walk with the river
and the stars.*

*May the waters carry you swiftly and gently,
my sweet grandchild, toward the place
where light and darkness meet. You are free
now. You are eternal.*

And you are forever in our hearts.

There was no rush, no sense of urgency—just an eternal stillness, as if the passing of the Goddess had drawn time itself into a moment of suspended reverence. Every breath was deliberate, each footstep silent, and every glance toward the river held a deep respect for the journey Stjernefrída was now beginning. The air was thick with the weight of the occasion, yet there was also a sacred tranquility, as the river's current gently carried her essence toward the eternal, embraced by the forces of light and transformation. For a few minutes, a profound silence enveloped the gathering, each soul present watching as Stjernefrída slowly floated out of view, her journey now a quiet testament to her legacy.

CHAPTER FOUR

As Kura gazed down the length of the grand table, which was elegantly adorned for Stjernefrída's Feast of Light, she watched, with quiet reflection, the family and friends gathered in joyous celebration. Laughter and the clinking of glasses filled the air, as each person shared a story and smiled: a tribute to the radiant light Stjernefrída had brought into their lives, and the world beyond.

As the night came to an end, and only the Ironclaw Griffins and Gramaze Lepidoptera Vampires remained, Kura rose from her seat at the head of the table and addressed the group. "Now that we have honored Stjernefrída and celebrated her life," she said, her gaze sweeping across the table, "I wish to return home and open the ancient chest. My number one priority is to ensure the safety of my great-grandchild." Her words carried a quiet determination, resonating with the weight of her responsibility.

"I think that is a wise choice, Kura, especially since the child may be in danger," Elara said, her voice steady with concern.

Kura turned to the guardians of the river. "Stand watch while we're inside the house," she instructed, her gaze meeting each of their faces to emphasize the importance of their duty.

"Yes, Goddess," they said in unison.

"Will the three of you join me?" Kura asked, addressing Elara, Garrick and William.

They exchanged solemn glances and nodded, falling into step behind Kura as she moved away from the table and led the way toward the cabin.

Lepidopteras keep watch ... we don't want any surprises, thought William telepathically.

Yes, Sire, the four Lepidopteras replied telepathically.

Griffins, your duty is to guard us while we are inside the cabin, thought Garrick to the three Griffins telepathically.

Yes, Sir, the three Griffins replied.

* * *

Kura pushed open the cabin door and stepped inside, her movements purposeful. Without hesitation, she walked directly toward the table, where the ancient chest had rested, and noticed it lying on the floor. Picking it up, she placed it back on the table and felt its presence command the room.

Standing in front of the ancient chest, Kura's eyes traced the intricate carvings that seemed to pulse faintly with hidden power. She turned to the group, her voice calm but laced with gravity, and said, "This chest holds more than secrets; it holds a legacy, a burden, and perhaps a key to our survival." Her gaze was steady as it swept over Elara, Garrick and William. "Once I open it, there is no turning back and we need to be prepared for whatever lies within."

Elara, Garrick and William once again exchanged solemn glances and nodded in unified agreement.

Kura turned to the chest. As her fingers brushed the lock, a crackling energy surged through the room and the chest groaned, as if it was awakening from a long slumber. The chest's glow intensified, casting strange patterns on the walls and producing the faintest whisper, which was almost imperceptible, but seemed to echo in the distance, as though the chest itself was speaking.

With a final breath, and her resolve unshaken, Kura began the incantation, which she had been taught by her ancestors, many moons ago.

> *By the light of the eternal stars,*
> *And the whispers of the sacred waters,*
> *I call upon the bond of the ancients.*
> *Unveil the truths hidden within,*
> *Release the legacy bound by time,*
> *In the name of the Goddess of Light,*
> *Stjernefrída,*
> *Open, and reveal your secrets to me.*

With a soft click, the lid unsealed itself and slowly creaked open, revealing its long-guarded contents. Kura leaned closer, her breath catching as the light intensified, illuminating the treasures within.

Inside lay an orb, its surface swirling with liquid light and shadow, as though it contained the essence of the universe itself. Next to the orb was an ancient scroll, the parchment aged but intact, its ink glowing faintly with an otherworldly hue. Kura carefully unrolled it, her eyes scanning the intricate symbols and words written in the ancient tongue of the Gods.

"This … this is the Prophecy of Balance," she murmured, her voice barely above a whisper. "It speaks of a time when darkness and light must unite to save the world from destruction."

She then came across a small carved wooden amulet, which was tucked beneath a layer of protective fabric. It bore the symbol of the River of Whispers and radiated a soft warmth. Kura's heart tightened when she realized its purpose.

"This amulet … it's meant for my great-grandchild," Kura said, looking over at the others and holding it up for them to see. "It's a guardian charm, tied to the river's magic. It will protect the child from harm, but only if she chooses to embrace her destiny."

The group exchanged glances, their expressions a mix of awe and concern.

Kura closed her eyes for a moment, steadying herself. "These are the tools we need for our future," she said firmly, placing the items back in the chest for safekeeping. "But more importantly, where is the address and information on my great-granddaughter's whereabouts?"

William stood next to Kura and said, "Maybe it's hidden in the lid lining, or the bottom lining?"

Kura's brow furrowed as she glanced at William, his suggestion sparking a flicker of hope. "You might be right," she said, her voice resolute. Carefully, she began to examine the chest's interior, running her fingers over the smooth wood and intricate carvings.

William stepped closer, his sharp Vampire eyes scanning the edges. "Look there," he said, pointing to a faint seam along the bottom lining.

Kura nodded, her hands moving with precision as she pressed lightly against the seam. With a soft click, a hidden compartment revealed itself, a thin panel sliding aside to expose a folded piece of parchment.

Her breath hitched as she picked up the parchment, the paper surprisingly well-preserved, considering she knew it was twenty-two years old. Unfolding it with care, she revealed a hand-drawn map marked with a glowing rune, along with a set of coordinates and a single name: *Alessia*.

Kura's hands trembled slightly as she traced the name. "This is it," she said, her voice thick with emotion. "The path to my great-granddaughter."

You certainly picked the right name, Stjernefrída. Alessia means she is a defender and noble. Just what we will need in the River of Whispers, thought Kura.

Elara and Garrick leaned in, their expressions a mix of relief and determination. "Now we know where to start," Elara said.

Kura memorized the address and information on her great-granddaughter, folded the parchment paper carefully and placed it into her satchel, which was on the table. "We must leave immediately," she said, her resolve stronger than ever. "Every moment wasted could mean danger for my great-granddaughter."

The group exchanged solemn nods, understanding the urgency of what lay ahead. The chest had given up its secrets and now their mission was clear: find and protect the next in line to the River of Whispers throne.

Kura carefully slid the hidden compartment shut and closed the lid of the ancient chest. Turning to Elara, Garrick and William she said firmly, "Our next destination is Australia—Cowaramup, Western Australia, to be precise."

They all nodded in acknowledgment.

"Elara, can you create a portal to take us there?" asked Kura.

"Of course, Goddess. Just give me a moment," Elara replied with a nod of assurance. She stepped outside the cabin and felt the cool night air brush against her as she extended her hands forward. With a graceful motion, she pulled her arms apart and a shimmering portal materialized before her, its edges glowing faintly with pulsating energy.

Kura placed the wooden chest back under the floorboards and sealed it shut. *Keep guard of these sacred items and information, Guardians,* thought Kura telepathically.

Yes, Kura, the three guardians all replied telepathically.

"Here, Kura, let me give you a hand to put the bed back in its place," said William, walking toward her.

"Thank you, William," replied Kura, as she watched him move it with ease.

Kura, Garrick and William stepped outside, their movements purposeful as they approached the glowing portal.

Follow me, Lepidopteras, William thought, his mental voice calm but commanding. *Be prepared for anything we might encounter on the other side.*

The four Lepidoptera Vampires silently fell into step behind him, their expressions focused and resolute.

Heads up, Griffins, Garrick projected to his kin. *This portal is taking us to Australia. I want your weapons ready the moment we step through. Are we clear?*

Yes, Sir, came the unified mental response, firm and unwavering.

The three guardians of the river, who remained in the River of Whispers, watched as one by one, they all entered the portal, its shimmering energy enveloping them before it snapped shut behind the last of their party.

* * *

As the portal sealed shut behind them, a shadowed figure emerged from the forest's periphery. Eryndor stood silently, his presence menacing and deliberate. He had been lurking in the shadows, patiently observing and gathering knowledge of the child's whereabouts.

"Cowaramup, Western Australia. I'm one step closer," Eryndor muttered, his voice laced with venom. A sinister smirk curled at the corners of his lips, his gaze cold and calculating, his expression speaking volumes of the dark plans he had been carefully crafting.

CHAPTER FIVE

"Can you give me a lift to the beach, Mum?" Alessia asked, standing at the island bench, with her beach bag slung over her shoulder.

"Sure," TJ replied, placing her lunch bowl in the dishwasher. "I need to head back to work, anyway. Are you ready to leave now?"

"Yep. Just need to get a bottle of water and then I'm ready to go," replied Alessia, as she walked over to the fridge.

"Great!" said TJ, picking up her handbag and car keys off the counter. "Let's go."

* * *

Concealed behind the peppermint trees that bordered the property, Kura, Elara, Garrick, William and their soldiers watched in silence as the two women climbed into the white V8 cruiser. The engine roared to life and they observed as it rumbled past, heading toward the bitumen roadway.

The young Goddess, she is the one in the passenger seat, said Kura telepathically to everyone. *I can feel our family connection.*

Follow the car and report back to me, William instructed telepathically to his family.

The four Lepidoptera Vampires nodded to William and ran swiftly behind the dense trees, staying hidden as they trailed the cruiser. They followed TJ and Alessia to the beach in Gracetown, but stayed hidden, while they watched in anticipation.

Garrick's sharp eyes scanned the horizon as the wind whipped through the dense trees. The air hung heavy with tension, the kind that preceded a storm and his grip tightened on the hilt of his sword, the familiar weight grounding him in the moment. "Scout the property," Garrick commanded, his gaze hardening. "I want to know everything—what's happening inside the walls and outside. Do not let yourself be seen. Report back in twenty minutes."

The three soldiers nodded to their leader and their powerful wings unfurled from their backs, as they prepared to take flight. Without another word, the Griffin soldiers launched into the air, their large wings slicing through the wind with precision, and they disappeared into the sky, leaving only the soft rustling of leaves in their wake.

* * *

"Thanks, Mum," said Alessia, as they pulled up into the car park. She leaned over to give TJ a kiss on her cheek.

"You're welcome, sweetheart. I'll swing by and pick you up around three o'clock, okay?" said TJ.

"Okay. See you then," replied Alessia, opening the door.

"Bye, sweetheart," said TJ. She watched Alessia walk down to the beach, before she drove out of the car park.

Alessia walked down the many wooden steps that led to the beach, as the sun, high in the sky, cast a warm glow over the waves that gently kissed the shore. The air was filled with the salty scent of the ocean and the cheerful laughter of people enjoying their day. As she strolled along the shoreline, her feet sinking into the soft, cool sand as the waves gently lapped at the edge of the beach, Alessia found a quiet corner of the beach with plenty of space and a peaceful atmosphere, the perfect spot to unwind. Reaching into her bag, she unpacked her beach gear, carefully spreading her towel over the sand until it lay smooth and flat, then anchored her large, floral-print umbrella into the ground.

Satisfied with the setup, she turned toward the water, glancing around to see a few children building sandcastles nearby and some couples lounging under umbrellas. Taking off her clothes, to reveal a floral bikini, Alessia slowly waded into the ocean. The water lapped at her waist and the coolness eased away any remaining tension in her muscles. As she floated on her back for a while, with her eyes closed, she let the rhythm of the waves rock her gently and calm her mind.

When Alessia finally swam back to the shore and waded out of the water, she noticed a woman sitting just near her umbrella, with her legs crossed comfortably, as she gazed out at the ocean. Alessia hadn't seen her before, but something about the woman seemed warm and approachable, and also a little intriguing.

The woman noticed her looking and smiled faintly, her gesture polite but guarded.

Alessia wrung out her hair and walked up to the woman, still dripping wet, but eager to make some small talk. "Hey there!" Alessia said with a friendly wave, trying to sound casual. "I don't think we've met before. Are you new to the area?" She picked up her towel to dry herself off and wrapped it around her hips.

The young woman looked up, her face lighting up with a welcoming smile. "I am actually," she responded, her soft but pleasant voice carrying the unmistakable lilt of an American accent. "I'm Danielle. I just moved here recently."

"Nice to meet you, Danielle. I'm Alessia," she said, smiling as she sat down on the sand beside her. She wiped a few droplets of water from her arms. "So, what brings you to the beach today?"

Danielle shrugged lightly, her smile warm and open. "Just soaking in the quiet," she said. "I moved here recently, looking for a change of pace. Sometimes, a little peace and calm is exactly what you need, don't you think?"

Alessia nodded enthusiastically. "Totally! I come here whenever I need to clear my head. There's just something about the ocean that makes everything feel … calm, you know?"

"Exactly. It's like a reset button for your mind. So, are you from around here, Alessia?" asked Danielle.

"Yeah," Alessia replied, her gaze drifting toward the horizon, as a soft breeze played with her hair. "I live just a little inland from here, in Cowaramup. My parents have a property out there—it's a really beautiful spot."

They sat for a while, chatting about little things—favorite foods, music and travel destinations, before Alessia stood and stretched. "I'm going to put on some sunscreen and go for another swim. Want to join me?"

Danielle's eyes lit up at the invitation. "I'd love to! Although, full disclosure—I'm a terrible swimmer," she said with a laugh, gesturing to her outfit. "And I'm not exactly dressed for a swim."

Alessia grinned and grabbed her beach ball. "It's all good! Just wear your bra and knickers, a lot of women do that these days. And you don't have to be great at swimming to enjoy the water. Let's have some fun!"

"Okay, if you don't mind, then I'm game," replied Danielle. Standing, she took off her clothing, discarding them to the beach sand.

With that, the two of them walked toward the water, laughing and chatting as they went. Alessia had a feeling that today was the start of a new friendship and she couldn't wait to see where it would lead.

William … thought Danielle telepathically, as she entered the water, throwing the beach ball to Danielle.

Yes! thought William telepathically.

I have made friends with Alessia. What would you like me to do now? thought Danielle.

See if you can get her to take you home. At least then, we'll have someone on the inside, someone close to the family, replied William, his voice echoing in Danielle's mind like a distant whisper.

Danielle resisted the urge to react, keeping her smile warm and her demeanor easy as she continued her conversation with William, and beach ball game with Alessia.

Danielle knew that this was a delicate situation; one she needed to play just right. Trust was a fragile thing, but once earned, it could open doors that would otherwise remain firmly shut, especially when you are about to find out that you are a Goddess.

Right! Leave it with me, thought Danielle, as she threw the beach ball back to Alessia.

Christian, stay out of sight, but keep an eye on Danielle and Alessia. We can't afford any mistakes, William thought firmly, his mind reaching out to his family. *Grayson, Stephen, I want you both to return to the farm. Make sure everyone is secure there, before you leave.*

Understood, Christian replied, his voice steady, tinged with determination.

Clear as day, added Grayson, his usual easygoing demeanor replaced with focus.

Got it, Stephen confirmed.

The weight of William's orders settled over them all, as they went about the mission.

William closed his eyes for a brief moment, steeling himself. This wasn't just about protecting Danielle, who was his Lepidoptera family—Alessia's role in this was becoming more important than he'd anticipated, knowing that she would eventually become the Celestial Goddess of Light and Stars.

* * *

Twenty minutes later the three Griffin soldiers returned, landing with grace just outside the main clearing, where Garrick and the others stood waiting. Their expressions were solemn, their eyes gleaming with the sharpness of those who had seen more than they had hoped to.

"Well … what have you found out? Is there anything to be concerned about?" questioned Garrick, impatiently.

Bennett, one of the female Griffin soldiers, with silver-feathered wings, stepped forward first. "Sir," she began, her tone calm but urgent. "The property is quiet. No movement inside the house, but there are two figures patrolling the perimeter. They're armed, but we didn't get close enough to identify them."

Draven, who had extremely large, golden wings, spoke next. "We also noticed a faint glow from the eastern side of the property, near the old barn. It was … unnatural. We couldn't pinpoint the source, but it's worth investigating further."

Garrick's brow furrowed. "Unnatural? How?"

The golden-winged Griffin hesitated before responding. "It could have been magic. Something about the way the light flickered didn't sit right."

Eryndor! wondered Garrick to himself, as his brow furrowed.

Elara listened intently and exchanged a glance with Kura; both of them processing the new information.

Garrick's jaw tightened as he turned his focus back to the soldiers. "What about the inside of the house?" he asked.

Kael, whose dark wings looked like midnight, stepped forward to offer his report. "Inside, the halls are still. We found no signs of anyone entering or exiting. However, there's a door in the lower basement that appears to be locked from the inside. We didn't approach too closely, but it's worth noting."

"Right! Anything else?" Garrick pressed.

"We saw a figure in the shadows near the edge of the property, by an old oak tree. They weren't moving like the others—too deliberate. We couldn't make out their face, but their presence felt … off," replied Kael.

Garrick's eyes narrowed. "Thank you," he said, his mind already turning over the details. "We'll investigate the barn and the basement."

As the three Griffin soldiers waited for instructions from their leader, Garrick turned to Elara, Kura and William. "Something's afoot here. Let's find out what."

"I'm in agreement," William said, as he watched Grayson and Stephen return from their mission. "I think we also need to search the perimeter, don't you, Garrick?"

"Yes, I think you are correct," replied Garrick.

"Grayson, Stephen, I want you both to search the perimeter. If any of Eryndor's minions are lingering there, kill them. Keep an eye out for Hawk, though. We want him alive. Keep safe, and keep me updated," stated William.

"Yes, Sire," they both said together. They retrieved their sheathed swords and walked toward the perimeter.

"Griffins, you three stay here and guard the property," Garrick commanded, his tone firm and authoritative. "Keep a sharp eye out and let us know immediately if anyone returns to the property. Understood?"

The three Griffins exchanged glances before nodding in unison, their sharp eyes already scanning the horizon. Garrick gave them a final, approving look before turning to leave.

"We've got no time to waste. Come with me," stated Garrick, to Elara, Kura and William.

Walking side by side, the four comrades-in-arms had their weapons drawn and were ready to face whatever lay inside the barn and basement.

CHAPTER SIX

Grayson and Stephen scouted the perimeter and watched as two armed men guarded the property. "I have read their minds and I would say that they are guarding the herd of cattle from dingoes, wouldn't you?" Grayson whispered quietly, as he pointed to the cows.

"Yeah, it sure looks that way," whispered Stephen, looking into the distance.

Sire, there is no sign of a threat here at the perimeter. What would you like us to do? asked Grayson, telepathically.

Keep an eye on the grounds, while we are checking the barn and basement, commanded William.

Yes, Sire, they both said telepathically. Keeping out of sight, both Grayson and Stephen continued to scout the perimeter and grounds for any threat, while they waited for everyone else to return.

* * *

Kura placed her hand on the front doorknob and twisted it. The door clicked open with ease. "Unlocked," she muttered, a flicker of confusion crossing her face. "That's strange for a human's house. They're usually so safety conscious."

She turned to Elara, her brow raised as she shrugged. "What do you think? Careless or inviting?"

"Both. Obviously, these people are trusting, otherwise the door wouldn't be unlocked," replied Elara, as she followed Kura into the house.

"We'll work in pairs and scout the house," William stated, his voice steady and commanding. "Cover every corner, but stay alert. We don't know what we're walking into."

"Good idea. You come with me, Elara, and Kura can go with William," instructed Garrick.

With speed as their advantage, each pair quickly searched the house and regrouped in the kitchen within minutes.

"Everything seems normal here," William reported.

"Same here. I think whatever my soldiers sensed or saw was a false alarm," Garrick replied.

"I wouldn't be so certain, Garrick," Kura interjected. "You know how cunning Eryndor can be. He could be hiding in plain sight, evading us in ways we can't even perceive. Ready and waiting in the wings when we have our guard down."

"Yes, but how would he even know about Alessia, or where she lives?" Elara asked Kura, her tone laced with concern. "We are the only ones who know this information. You're only assuming he does."

"You're right, Elara," William replied thoughtfully. "But for now, we can't ignore or deny the unease we've all felt since portaling here. There's something … just beyond my sight. I can feel it lurking."

They all nodded in agreement.

Sire, there is a truck approaching the house. What would you like us to do? thought Grayson to William.

Stay put … we will deal with whoever it is, thought William.

"We have company. Let's get out of here," said William, to Elara, Kura and Garrick.

The four of them quickly exited the house via the back sliding door and waited for the male driver to walk up to the house.

* * *

"Anyone home?" Parker called as he pushed the front door open. Silence greeted him. "TJ and Alessia must still be out," he muttered to himself.

I might as well have a shower and get cleaned up. Hopefully, the girls will be back soon, thought Parker. He headed to the back of the house, into his bedroom, and began shedding his dusty clothes.

That is Alessia's adoptive father, Kura thought, her voice brushing against Elara, Garrick and William's minds. *I recognize him from the photos we saw in Alessia's bedroom earlier.*

Garrick ... heads up. A V8 cruiser is approaching the house, Draven's voice echoed in his mind.

Thank you, Draven. We've got more company. Stay hidden! Garrick directed the thought to everyone, his tone sharp and commanding, as they waited in the wings to see who was driving up to the house.

* * *

"Thank you for inviting me over for dinner, Mrs McCrindle," Danielle said, as she stepped out of the car.

"You're very welcome, dear. And please, call me TJ— Mrs McCrindle feels far too formal," TJ replied with a warm smile, slinging her handbag over her shoulder.

"Okay! Would you like some help with dinner?" Danielle offered.

"No need to worry about that, dear. I've got it covered," TJ said with a reassuring wave of her hand. "We're having sweet-and-sour pork with rice tonight. I'll let you both know when it's ready. If you'd like to freshen up, Danielle, Alessia will get you a towel."

"Yum, that sound wonderful. Thank you!" Danielle replied cheerfully.

"Come on, Danielle," Alessia said, gesturing toward the house. "I'll show you my room and then we can get cleaned up before dinner."

"Sounds good!" Danielle said, following Alessia inside the house to her bedroom. "Your Mum sure is nice."

"Yeah, she's definitely one of a kind. My Dad's pretty amazing too. I really hit the jackpot with such incredible adoptive parents," Alessia said, with a warm smile.

"Oh, so your adopted? Wow, how do you feel about that?" asked Danielle, as she walked into Alessia's bedroom.

"Doesn't faze me," replied Alessia, as she placed her beach bag on the ottoman at the end of her bed.

"That's good. Do you know who your real parents were?" asked Danielle, as she sat down on Alessia's bed.

"No, I don't have a clue. And I haven't asked either. At this stage, I don't even think about it. Mum and Dad are the only parents I've known, so I don't see the point in finding my biological parents," said Alessia, as she walked toward her walk-in wardrobe.

"Oh, right! You were saying earlier that you have just finished your university exams. What did you study, and how do you think you went with the exams?" asked Danielle.

"I have finally finished my degree in astrophysics. Took me five long, stressful years to finish it. And the exams … well, that's another story. Very stressful, but I think I did well."

"Astrophysics … you must be talented or gifted. I'm impressed," said Danielle, her eyebrows lifted.

"I'm not sure about being gifted or talented," Alessia said as she sat down on the bed beside Danielle. She hesitated for a moment, then felt an inexplicable, almost magnetic pull to confide in Danielle, even though she had only just met her today. "But the strangest thing happened during the exam. I kept seeing symbols appear on my hands, and then they would flash in my mind. And I had weird dreams before the exams … they were so vivid— visions of celestial realms where I ruled as a Goddess, and this uncanny ability to communicate with animals and plants. It all felt so … surreal.”

“That is strange. What do you think it all means?” Danielle asked, her tone carefully curious as she gauged whether Alessia was open to the idea of being a Goddess and the transformation it might entail.

“Nothing, I think.” Standing, Alessia walked toward her en suite bathroom and turned on the light. “Did you want to have a shower?”

“That would be great,” replied Danielle, standing. She walked toward the bathroom.

“There’s a fresh towel in the cupboard,” said Alessia, pointing to a cupboard under the vanity. “There’s shampoo, conditioner and body wash in the shower for you to use as well.”

“Okay, thanks!” said Danielle, walking into the en suite.

“Well, I’ll leave you to it,” said Alessia. She closed the door and walked toward her wardrobe to find something to wear.

* * *

Sire … I have made friends with Alessia and I’m staying for dinner. Is there anything you need me to find out? thought Danielle to William, as she placed her clothes on the vanity and opened the glass shower door.

Perfect! See if you can discreetly find out if the parents know anything about Alessia’s lineage, or if they are completely oblivious to the supernatural world, thought William.

Yes, Sire. Who is my backup for the night, just in case I stay over with Alessia, if she asks? thought Danielle, as she placed her head under the showerhead and closed her eyes.

Grayson, Christian and Stephen will be close by at all times. Kura refuses to leave, so she will be staying, too. Bennett, Draven and Kael will be staying as well. Since we have found nothing strange here, and there is no trace of Eryndor, the rest of us will be returning to Bagnolet for the night. But we will be back tomorrow. Take your time getting to know this family and Alessia, thought William.

Yes, Sire, thought Danielle, as she washed the shampoo out of her hair. *Sire ...*

Yes.

Do you feel that? Danielle thought to William, her mental voice edged with concern. *A strange tingling sensation, like some kind of energy in the air—it's making me uneasy.* Her Lepidoptera Vampire instincts had been on high alert all day, and the tension was starting to weigh on her.

Yes. All of us do. We are not sure what or who it is, as yet. And there is nothing obvious or in plain sight. Keep your wits about you tonight, Danielle. I want you to guard Alessia until we return, William responded, his thoughts steady, but laced with caution.

Yes, Sire, Danielle replied, her thoughts calm and resolute, as she rinsed the conditioner from her long blonde hair, letting the water cascade over her shoulders.

Trust your instincts, Danielle. If anything feels off, contact Grayson straight away. Alessia's safety is our priority, thought William.

Danielle straightened, her resolve hardening. *Understood, Sire. I won't let anything happen to her.*

A brief pause hung between them before William added, *We will be back before sunrise. Stay vigilant.*

Yes, Sire. Danielle stepped out of the shower, her senses still buzzing with the energy in the air. She grabbed a towel, her thoughts sharpening as she prepared for whatever the night might bring.

* * *

"Knock, knock," said Parker, standing in the doorway.

"Hi, Dad," said Alessia, looking up.

"How was your day, sweetheart?' asked Parker.

"Yeah, it was good. I went to the beach. Actually, I met a really nice girl there, who has moved to Cowaramup recently. You'll get to meet her soon, as she's staying for dinner. She's in the shower at the moment," replied Alessia, gesturing toward her en suite.

"Oh, right. What's her name?" asked Parker, his brow furrowing slightly with curiosity, as he walked into the room.

"Danielle. Don't worry, Dad, she's really nice," Alessia said, noticing the concern etched on his face. "She's my age, too, which is a bonus. We seem to have a lot in common."

"Right. Where is she living in Cowaramup?" asked Parker. Being a small country town, he knew most of the locals and hadn't heard of any new families moving in recently.

"I don't know. You can ask her at dinner. What's with all the questions?" asked Alessia.

"I'm wondering if I have met her parents. And for the record, I am allowed to be an overprotective parent, you know," replied Parker, smirking.

Alessia smiled warmly. "I appreciate that you care about me, Dad, I really do. But I'm old enough to make my own decisions about who I choose as a friend. Anyway, you'll meet Danielle at dinner and you'll see what I mean—she's genuinely nice."

"Okay, point taken. I'll see you later," Parker said, with a small smile. He leaned in and pressed a gentle kiss to his daughter's forehead before stepping away.

Alessia smiled and watched him walk toward the doorway.

As Parker left the room, Alessia turned toward the en suite door, hearing the faint sound of running water turn off. She smiled to herself, her thoughts drifting back to her day at the beach. There was something about Danielle, something different—almost intriguing—that she couldn't quite put her finger on.

Shaking off the thought, she busied herself tidying up her room, glancing occasionally toward the clock. Dinner wasn't far off and she hoped her Mum and Dad would warm to Danielle as quickly as she had.

CHAPTER SEVEN

"Alessia, dinner's ready!" TJ called from the kitchen.

"Coming, Mum!" Alessia shouted back. She walked over to the en suite door and gently knocked. "Hey, Danielle, you almost ready in there?" she called, her tone light and cheerful.

Danielle opened the door and emerged from the en suite. She was already dressed; her damp blonde hair was neatly combed and she had a soft smile on her face.

"Dinner's ready. Let's go eat."

"Awesome."

The two girls made their way to the dining room, where the table was already set. The aroma of sweet-and-sour pork, mingled with the warm, comforting scent of jasmine-steamed rice, made their stomachs rumble. Parker was pouring water into everyone's glasses and TJ was placing the last serving bowl on the table.

"Here they are," TJ said, with a welcoming smile as the girls entered. "Hope you're hungry, Danielle. We made plenty."

Danielle smiled back, sliding into the chair next to Alessia. "It smells amazing. Thank you so much for having me."

"Nice to meet you, Danielle." Parker nodded, his expression softening as he glanced at Danielle. "We're glad to have you here. Dig in before it gets cold."

"Thank you. Good to meet you, too," replied Danielle.

Alessia caught Danielle's eye and smiled, sensing the tension in the room beginning to ease.

"How long have you and your family been in Cowaramup, Danielle," asked Parker, as he spooned some rice onto his plate.

Danielle offered a polite smile, her response already prepared as she read their minds. "Mum and I moved here about a month ago," she replied smoothly. She'd done her homework, crafting a believable story to share with the McCrindles.

"So, it's just your mum and you, then? No brothers or sisters?" TJ asked as she settled into her chair at the table.

"Yeah, just us," Danielle replied with a small smile. She reached for the serving spoon and added a helping of sweet-and-sour pork to her plate. "It's always been the two of us, so we're pretty close."

"Does your mum work somewhere here in town?" asked TJ.

"No, she works from home," Danielle replied casually. "She's an author."

"Oh, wow, an author!" TJ said, her eyes lighting up with interest. "That's amazing. I'd love to meet her sometime."

"I'm sure she would love to meet you all, too. Mum was only saying the other day that she needs to get out of the house and meet some new people," said Danielle.

"That would be lovely, dear. Have you called your mum to let her know you're staying here for dinner?" asked TJ.

"Yeah, she's fine with it," Danielle replied with a nod. "She said she'd pick me up around nine o'clock, if that's okay?"

"Yes, that's perfectly fine with us," TJ said warmly. "And we'll get to meet her then."

Danielle smiled and continued to eat her dinner, savoring the sweet-and-sour pork flavors. The comfortable chatter around the table eased any lingering tension, making everyone feel a little more at home.

Grayson ... could you organize for Kura to pick me up at nine o'clock in a black limousine. Maybe you or Stephen could be driving it, thought Danielle, who was trying to show the McCrindle's that her family was rich, by turning up in a chauffeur driven car. *That way, Kura could meet Alessia and her adoptive parents.*

Great idea, Danielle, thought Kura. She was excited at the prospect of finally meeting her great-granddaughter.

No problem, Danielle. We will be there at nine sharp, thought Grayson, realizing that he would have to contact their Australian Lepidoptera counterparts to get a limousine, as well as clothing for him and Kura, to play the ruse that Danielle had set out.

Great! See you all then, thought Danielle.

* * *

After dinner, Alessia and Danielle helped TJ clear the table, chatting casually as they loaded plates into the dishwasher and tidied up the kitchen together.

"Want to hang out in my room for a bit? We can watch a movie, or just talk, while we wait for your mum," Alessia suggested.

"That sounds great," Danielle replied, genuinely enjoying Alessia's company.

TJ and Parker sat together in the cozy living room, just off the kitchen, exchanging a warm smile. It had been a long time since they'd seen Alessia this happy. As a child, and later as a teenager, she had always been a loner. Even now, as an adult, they often worried about how much time she spent alone.

"It's so nice to see Alessia like this," TJ said softly, her voice tinged with relief.

"It sure is," Parker agreed, his eyes following Alessia and Danielle, as they walked out of the kitchen, heading toward the back of the house.

* * *

"What type of movie do you like?" asked Alessia, as they headed to Alessia's large bedroom.

"Action, romance, crime. That sort of thing," replied Danielle, as they entered the bedroom.

"Let's have a look at what they have available on Paramount," said Alessia, as she grabbed the remote, turned the TV on and pulled up a selection of movies. After some debate, they settled on a lighthearted comedy and sprawled out on the bed.

As the movie played, their conversation drifted to deeper topics and Alessia shared stories about growing up in Cowaramup, while Danielle wove her carefully crafted tale about life with her mum.

By the time the movie ended, it was close to nine o'clock. "Your mum should be here soon," Alessia said, glancing at the clock.

Danielle nodded, glancing out the window. Right on cue, headlights swept across the driveway and a sleek black limousine pulled up. Danielle smiled to herself, pleased that Grayson had executed her plan perfectly. "Looks like she's here," Danielle said, standing up and smoothing out her clothes.

"Come on, I'll walk you out," said Alessia, standing.

As they stepped outside, a poised and elegant Kura emerged from the limousine. She offered a warm, practiced smile as Alessia and her parents joined them at the front door. "Good evening," said Kura, as she alighted from the car.

"Mum, this is TJ, Parker and Alessia McCrindle," said Danielle, smoothly gesturing to each of them. "This is my mum, Kura."

"Nice to meet you all," said Kura, holding her hand out to shake each of theirs. But as she shook Alessia's hand, she straightaway felt their connection.

When Alessia shook Kura's hand she felt a sense of warmth and a strange but comforting familiarity, as if they had known each other forever. It was an unspoken connection, one that neither of them could fully explain, but both instinctively understood.

"Nice to meet you, too, Kura," said TJ. "Would you like to come inside for a cup of tea?"

"That would be lovely. Thank you," said Kura, following them inside.

"Take a seat, Kura," offered Parker. He gestured to the table.

"Thank you," said Kura, as she walked over to the table and pulled a chair out. "And thank you for having Danielle over tonight for dinner. We will have to repay your kindness."

"Oh, there's no need. We were only too happy to have Danielle here," said TJ, as she continued to make the tea. "You have a lovely daughter."

"Thank you. Have you lived here long?" asked Kura, as she sat on the chair.

"My ancestors and family have lived here for generations," said Parker, proudly. "We're a cattle and horse farm."

Kura smiled warmly, her expression polite yet inquisitive. "That sounds wonderful. A farm must be a rewarding place to raise a family. Do you focus on breeding, or mainly on livestock for market?"

"A bit of both," Parker replied with a nod. "We've been breeding cattle for generations, and we also sell livestock to market. The horses, though—that's more of a passion for the family. Alessia's especially taken to them." He glanced at his daughter with a proud smile. "She's been riding since she could walk."

Kura's smile deepened as she turned to Alessia. "Riding since you could walk? That's impressive. Do you compete, or is it more for leisure?" she asked, her tone genuinely interested.

"Mostly for leisure," Alessia replied with a smile. "I've done a few local competitions here and there, but I prefer being out on the trails. It's so peaceful—and the bond with the horses is the best part."

Kura nodded thoughtfully. "I can imagine that must be incredibly grounding," she said. "There's something special about connecting with animals like that. Do you have a favorite horse on the farm?"

Alessia's face lit up. "Definitely! His name's Jasper. He's this gorgeous chestnut gelding with the sweetest temperament. We've kind of grown up together. He's been with us since I was a kid. He's my go-to for trail rides."

Kura smiled warmly. "Jasper sounds like a wonderful companion. Horses like that become more than just animals—they're family. Do you ever feel like he understands you, even without words?"

Parker's brow furrowed as he listened to the conversation. He couldn't help but wonder why Kura would ask such an unusual question.

"All the time," Alessia said with a soft laugh. "It's like he knows exactly how I'm feeling. If I'm upset, he's extra gentle, and if I'm happy, he's full of energy. It's like we have our own unspoken language."

Kura's expression softened. "That's a rare and beautiful connection," she said. "Animals have a way of sensing things about us that even people sometimes can't. It sounds like Jasper is more than just a horse—he's a true friend."

"He sure is," replied Alessia.

"So, Kura, I believe you are an author?" asked TJ.

"Yes, I've been writing for about ten years now. I love it," replied Kura.

"What genre do you write?" asked TJ.

"Mostly supernatural fantasy, but I do write and illustrate a few children's books, too," replied Kura.

"I love supernatural fantasy books. What type of creatures do you write about?" said Alessia.

"I usually write about Griffins, Vampires, Goddesses of the Light and Stars, Guardians, Warlocks and Fae. I also enjoy weaving in intricate ancient symbols and runes that these creatures often have. There's something magical about the way symbols can hold power and meaning," Kura replied, with a smile.

Alessia's mind wandered as Kura spoke, recalling the symbols and glowing runes that had appeared on her hands during the exams. She could still picture them clearly—how they seemed to pulse with a mysterious energy. She also thought back to the vivid dreams she'd had, where celestial realms and ancient symbols had played a significant role.

A slight shiver ran down her spine as she glanced at Danielle and she wondered if there was some connection between what she had experienced and the things Kura was describing.

Kura ... Alessia has already mentioned to me about the glowing runes and symbols that appeared on her arms and hands. It seems like her transformation may have already begun, thought Danielle

I've been listening to her thoughts and she does seem confused. The appearance of runes is often a marker of latent power awakening. We'll need to observe her closely, but gently. I don't want to overwhelm her, or frighten her, by revealing too much about our world, too soon, thought Kura.

I agree, thought Danielle. *She's already dealing with so much. Throwing everything at her at once could backfire. Maybe we should wait for her to bring it up again, let her curiosity lead the way. It might make the transition easier for her to accept.*

That's a wise approach, Kura thought in agreement. *If we let her guide the pace, she's more likely to embrace the truth when the time comes. For now, we'll keep an eye on her and offer subtle guidance when needed.*

Understood, Danielle replied. *When the time is right, we'll help her see the bigger picture.*

Alessia's eyes lit up with curiosity. "That sounds incredible! Do you create your own mythology for the symbols and runes, or do you draw inspiration from existing legends and folklore? I've always been fascinated by how stories connect symbols to power and destiny."

Kura's smile widened, clearly pleased by Alessia's interest. "A bit of both, actually. I love studying ancient myths and folklore—they're such a rich source of inspiration. But I also like to put my own spin on things, creating new symbols and meanings that tie in to the world I'm building. It's like crafting a secret language that holds the key to the story's magic."

"So, Kura, what are you currently writing?" asked Parker.

"It's called *The River of Whispers*," Kura replied, watching him closely to gauge his reaction. She hadn't been able to read his mind yet—something seemed to be blocking her and she couldn't quite put her finger on why.

Parker's expression shifted subtly, his eyes narrowing ever so slightly. "*The River of Whispers*," he repeated, his voice steady but laced with a hint of tension. "Interesting choice for a title. That's not a name you come across every day. What inspired it?" He leaned back slightly, his gaze fixed on Kura, as if trying to read more from her than her words.

"It's a place of great ancestral significance in the world I've created—a river that carries the whispers of the past, holding secrets and forgotten knowledge. The characters who encounter it are forced to confront their own truths. As for the inspiration … let's just say, it comes from places in the world where history and memory never truly fade." She paused, sensing that Parker's question went deeper than just curiosity. "Do you know of it?" asked Kura, her expression calm yet guarded.

"I've heard stories, passed down through generations. The River of Whispers has a way of calling to those who are attuned to the past. Some say it's a dangerous place, where the line between memory and reality can blur. I wouldn't be the first to get lost in its depths, if I'm being honest." He studied Kura carefully, a knowing look in his eyes. "But I'm curious how your version of it plays out," said Parker, the weight of his words heavy.

"It's a dangerous place, indeed," she acknowledged, her voice softening slightly. "Those who seek its knowledge often find themselves changed—sometimes for the better, sometimes not. The river doesn't give up its secrets easily; it tests you, makes you face your fears and desires." She leaned forward slightly, her tone dropping to a more conspiratorial pitch. "But it's also a place of great power. For those brave enough to embrace it, the river can unlock truths that would otherwise remain hidden for a lifetime. You know, I'm always on the lookout for advanced readers. Would you be willing to read my manuscript once I have finished it?" Kura's expression remained composed, though there was a flicker of intrigue in her eyes, as she wondered if Parker knew more than he was letting on.

"I would be honored to read your manuscript. It sounds intriguing, that's for sure," said Parker, his expression shifted subtly and his eyes narrowed ever so slightly.

"I suppose we should be going now. We really appreciate your kindness and hospitality," Kura remarked, getting to her feet.

"Of course. It was a pleasure having you here, Kura. I hope you enjoy the rest of your evening." Standing, Parker extended a hand, offering a firm handshake. "Safe travels."

"It was a pleasure to meet you, Kura," TJ said warmly. "Feel free to drop by anytime for a cuppa and a chat."

"I will, thank you," Kura replied with a smile. "And I'm sure our girls," she glanced at Alessia and Danielle, "will be seeing more of each other soon."

"Thank you so much for having me over for dinner, Mr and Mrs McCrindle," Danielle said gratefully.

TJ smiled warmly. "You're very welcome, my dear."

Danielle turned to Alessia and said, "I'll give you a call tomorrow and maybe we can catch up if you're free."

"Sounds like a plan," Alessia replied, leaning in for a hug.

As Kura and Danielle made their way to the car, Danielle's voice entered Kura's mind. *I feel something has changed in Alessia. When she hugged me goodbye, I sensed a supernatural presence, but it was faint—just a minor shift, I think.*

Interesting! I think there is more to this family than we know. I felt that the father knows more about the River of Whispers than he is letting on. And when he said his ancestors were on the land many years ago; well, that piqued my interest as well, said Kura telepathically. *Lucky we are sticking around to keep watch on Alessia.*

Kura and Danielle exchanged a polite smile with their hosts before stepping into the car. Grayson, who had been waiting by the door, quickly closed it behind them and made his way around to the driver's seat.

Danielle rolled down the window, her hand waving in farewell as she called out, "Goodnight, and thank you again!"

TJ, Parker and Alessia waved goodbye, their smiles warm, but tinged with a hint of longing.

As the car pulled away, Alessia raised her hand for one final wave, her gaze lingering on the glowing red taillights as they faded into the distance, disappearing into the night.

Keep a watchful eye on the house while we are gone, Lepidopteras and Griffins, thought Grayson, as he pulled out onto the bitumen roadway. *There is a threat lurking that we haven't uncovered yet.*

In unison, their telepathic voices echoed back, a chorus of resolute agreement: *Yes, we will.*

CHAPTER EIGHT

"Gather around, my minions," Eryndor commanded. His voice sliced through the cold night air as he stood on the weathered deck of a derelict ship that was anchored in the North Atlantic Ocean, shrouded by a shimmering wall of invisible wards.

As Eryndor waited for his minions to fall silent, he turned to Hawk, whose glazed eyes stared vacantly into the distance. With a sharp edge to his tone, and a smirk of disdain curling his lips, he said, "Do try to focus, Hawk. A prince with a mind so easily clouded is hardly fit for the throne—or for my plans."

Hawk's expression remained vacant, his voice flat and hollow as he spoke, "I will do as you command, Eryndor. My purpose is yours to direct." His words lacked any trace of defiance, a clear sign of the mind control gripping him.

"Your next task is to lead these minions into battle," Eryndor said, his tone commanding yet laced with a hint of warning. He stepped closer, his piercing gaze locking onto Hawk's eyes. "Listen carefully, brother," he added, emphasizing the words with a touch of mockery. "The stakes have never been higher. We are on the verge of something monumental. I will not tolerate your insubordination."

Eryndor paced slowly in front of him, the air thick with tension. "You will command them with absolute authority. Every move, every strike must be calculated. This battle is not just for victory—it's for our future. If you falter, or if you hesitate, you will not be the only one to pay the price." He stopped pacing and his eyes narrowed. "Do not forget, the power of the chalice and Alessia is in your hands now. Ensure our enemies fall. No mercy." He paused, letting the weight of his words settle. "Lead them, or I will find someone who can."

Hawk's voice was hollow, as if the mind control had stripped away any trace of his former self. He bowed his head slightly, the vacant stare still in his eyes. "Yes, Master," he replied in a flat, emotionless tone. "I will lead them. The enemies will fall." There was no defiance, no spark of rebellion, only the cold obedience of one who had no choice but to comply.

"Good boy," Eryndor said with a cruel, sarcastic smile, his eyes narrowing as he observed Hawk's empty expression. "I'm sure you'll do just fine ... as long as you remember who controls your every move." His words dripped with mock approval, with the faintest trace of amusement in his voice.

Eryndor stood at the forefront of his minions, his gaze sweeping across the group, gleaming with cold intent. "Listen up!" he began, his tone sharp and commanding. "I'll say this once, so listen carefully. I have found the farm where the great-granddaughter is living. Your task is simple: retrieve Alessia from Cowaramup and bring her back her to me, alive and unharmed."

Eryndor took a step forward and his voice grew colder. "You will leave no trace of your presence in Cowaramup. No witness. No sign of struggle. *Nothing*. You are to move silently and swiftly. If anyone stands in your way, they are to be dealt with *immediately*."

The glazed-eyed minions muttered under their breaths, their discontent palpable as they pondered the daunting task of kidnapping Alessia.

Eryndor held up a hand to silence any protest. "She must believe she is simply being taken, nothing more. We need her to feel *safe* enough to do what we ask of her, when she arrives. Am I making myself clear?"

They all nodded in agreement.

"Remember, I will be watching, and I will not tolerate failure. I have no patience for weakness. Bring her to me and we shall finally claim the power that is rightfully ours." He raised his voice slightly, as a final warning. "Remember, anyone who dares fail me will not live to regret it. Now, get yourselves ready, and make yourselves familiar with what this young woman looks like."

With a flick of his wrist, Eryndor summoned a swirling vortex of dark energy before him. The air crackled with power as a portal opened, its edges glowing with an ominous light. He turned to face his minions, his gaze unwavering.

"Go," he commanded coldly. "This portal will take you directly to the Cowaramup farm. Do not waste time; we do not have the luxury of waiting."

One by one, led by Hawk, his minions stepped forward and entered the portal without hesitation. As they passed through, Eryndor watched, his expression unreadable. The portal shimmered for a moment longer before it snapped shut, leaving the ship in silence once again.

Eryndor stood still, the weight of his plan heavy on his mind. *Soon, Alessia, you will be in my grasp and nothing will stand in my way. Nothing!*

* * *

Sully ... Hawk thought desperately as he stepped into the swirling portal and deliberately slowed his departure. The oppressive grip of Eryndor's control weakened in the void between worlds and Hawk knew this fleeting moment might be his only chance to reach out to his life partner, without Eryndor's interference.

But there was no response from Sully.

Sully ... please, forgive me. Help me! His thoughts were a plea, raw and urgent, as he clenched his jaw and shook his head, fighting with every ounce of willpower to break free from Eryndor's hold. Yet the chains around his mind tightened, trying to drag him back into submission.

Hawk! Where are you? Sully's thoughts raced as she pressed her hands to her chest, her heart pounding with both fear and hope, when she first heard his voice in her mind.

Thank the Gods you have answered my call, came Hawk's reply, his voice in her mind raw with desperation. *I am currently inside a portal, traveling to Cowaramup in Western Australia. It is the only time I can contact you without Eryndor listening to me or intervening.*

Hawk's thoughts grew heavier and were laced with dread, *Eryndor has ordered me and his minions to kidnap Alessia, Kura's great-granddaughter, and eliminate anyone guarding her. I'm trying to fight his control, but I can't hold him off for long. Sully ... I need your help. Can you stop this before it's too late?*

Sully closed her eyes and remembered the chatter that had been around the Gramaze mansion lately, about Kura and her great-granddaughter, Alessia. Her thoughts steadied, as she reached back to Hawk with fierce determination, *Hawk, listen to me. You are stronger than Eryndor's control—stronger than he will ever understand. I will do everything in my power to help you, but you must fight him from within.*

Sully's grip on her hands tightened, as her thoughts poured out, *I'll head to Cowaramup with others to help protect Alessia. Stay strong, Hawk. Hold on to me, hold on to us. You're not alone in this—I'll find a way to free you.*

Sully's tone softened slightly, but the urgency in her voice remained. *Whatever happens, don't give up. We'll end this, together.*

Thank you. I love you, Sully. I will try my best to fight this control Eryndor has over me, but I can't promise I'll succeed, Hawk's thoughts whispered, his feelings swinging between hope and despair.

I love you too, Hawk, Sully replied, her thoughts steady and filled with unwavering resolve.

As Hawk stepped out of the swirling portal, the connection between him and Sully snapped like a taut string suddenly cut. The cold air of Cowaramup hit him, but it did little to shake the oppressive weight of Eryndor's control settling back over his mind, like a suffocating fog.

His thoughts, once his own, grew distant and muddled, as the remnants of Sully's voice faded into silence. He clenched his fists, as a flicker of resistance sparked deep within him, but Eryndor's grip tightened, extinguishing it before it could take hold.

Hawk straightened and his glazed eyes scanned his surroundings, as the mission Eryndor had burned into his mind resurfaced with chilling clarity. Alessia … The Golden Chalice … No distractions … No mercy. He moved forward, his body obeying commands that were no longer his own, the brief taste of freedom already a fading memory.

* * *

Hawk … how long before you arrive? thought Sully.

There was nothing but silence.

Hawk …

Damn it … he must already be in Cowaramup. What do I do? What do I do? Sully's thoughts raced with urgency before she reached out telepathically to her Lepidoptera Vampire coven. *William, Violette, Samuel—I need your help. It's urgent!*

We hear you, Sully. Where are you? William's voice echoed in her mind, steady and calm, as he stood in the operations room with Violette and Samuel.

I'm heading to the backyard, Sully replied swiftly, her determination sharpening with each word, as she ran at Vampire speed, from her bedroom at the Gramaze mansion, to the backyard. *I need a portal created, immediately.*

Hawk has been ordered by Eryndor to kidnap Alessia, and eliminate anyone who stands in his way. He's in Cowaramup—and he's not alone. Eryndor's minions are with him.

Fuck! William's voice cut through telepathically. *We will meet you in the backyard, Sully ... All Lepidopteras who are not out on a mission, get your weapons ready and meet me in the backyard in three minutes. We have a situation!*

William felt the presence of his coven in his mind, their voices intertwining, steady and resolute, as he ran toward the backyard with Samuel and Violette.

Garrick, Elara, get ready to portal to Cowaramup. We need to protect Kura, Alessia and the McCrindles. Grayson, Stephen, Danielle and your three Griffins will be outnumbered by all of Eryndor's minions and Hawk, stated William telepathically.

We have been listening to the chatter. We are already on our way, thought Garrick, as he and Elara ran toward the back of the house.

CHAPTER NINE

Within minutes, the Gramaze Lepidoptera Vampire coven and Ironclaw Griffins had assembled in the backyard, weapons drawn, eyes hard with determination. Violette stood at the center, her hands still glowing with the power of the portal she had already conjured—a swirling rift in the air, ready to carry them all to Cowaramup. The air was thick with anticipation, each warrior brimming with the resolve to face whatever lay ahead on this mission.

Standing tall and composed at the front of the group, William addressed them. His voice was steady and commanding, laced with urgency, as his eyes scanned their faces. "We are heading to Cowaramup to stop Eryndor's plan of kidnapping Alessia, before it can unfold. Sully has confirmed that Hawk is there, and is under Eryndor's control. Our first priority is protecting Alessia, no matter the cost."

He paused, letting his words sink in. "We will not have the luxury of time. Eryndor's minions will be waiting for us and we'll be outnumbered. Our strategy is simple: we strike hard, fast and with precision. Am I making myself clear?"

The unity of their minds, all driven by the same cause, surged through him.

"Once through," William continued, his voice unwavering, "we split into two teams. Garrick, you'll lead one group to locate and protect Alessia and her family. The rest of us will engage the minions. If you must, do not hesitate to kill anyone who gets in our way, and to also protect our own. We're not just fighting for Alessia. We're fighting for control of the entire world."

With a final nod to Violette, who was staying behind with others to protect the Queen, William stepped toward the portal, his hand resting on the hilt of his sword. "Let's move. And remember, we do this together."

One by one, the Gramaze Lepidopteras and Ironclaw Griffins stepped into the portal, ready for the fight ahead.

* * *

The air was thick with anticipation as the Lepidopteras stepped out of the shimmering portal at the McCrindles farm in Cowaramup. It swirled in a vortex of deep blues and purples, that split the quiet countryside with its magical energy. Following the soldiers were the majestic figures of William, Garrick and Elara, followed by Sully and their families.

As William stepped onto the soft earth, his boots making a muted crunch in the dirt, his Lepidoptera senses felt something amiss. The hairs on the back of his neck stood on end, as his sharp eyes quickly scanned the surroundings. But all he could see for miles were the picturesque rolling hills and lush greenery of Cowaramup and its eerie silence.

"I don't like this," Sully muttered, her hand resting on the hilt of her Emberlight sword, which was a companion to the Icefire Blades. Her Griffin wings twitched inside her back and were ready for whatever was to come.

"Stay alert," Garrick commanded, his gaze narrowing as he scanned the area.

Elara's wings flared out behind her, strong and defiant, as she stood close by her partner.

Before anyone could speak again, the atmosphere shifted. Figures cloaked in dark, flowing robes materialized, slowly rising from the ground out of the mist. The air felt charged as the strange energy they radiated crackled with intent.

"Minions of Eryndor," William snarled, his eyes burning with the resolve to protect. "You're not welcome here."

These minions were twisted figures with glowing, glazed-over eyes. As they stepped forward, their hands seemed to glow with a dark magic. They were warriors who had pledged themselves to Eryndor, bound by powerful curses and shadow magic. As they raised their arms, an onslaught of jagged energy bolts shot forward, crackling through the air toward the Lepidopteras and Griffins.

Sully stood in front of everyone and her Emberlight sword deflected several blasts. "Get the fuck away from my family," she yelled, as she darted forward, striking one minion with a swift swing of her sword, the blade cutting through its dark magic with a flash of light.

The minion staggered back, howling in fury.

"We have to move fast!" Elara shouted, her voice echoing in the tension-filled air. She spread her wings and took to the sky, her talons glowing with the blue fire of her power. With a battle cry, she swooped down, slashing through the air and striking one of the minions on the ground. Her claws sank into the creature's chest, causing it to erupt in dark energy before it crumpled to the ground.

Garrick, charged forward with a roar. His wings spread wide and with his blade clutched in his talons, he hacked through the advancing minions. The fire from his blade created a searing wave of elemental energy that cut down anything in its path.

Minions were scattered, some shrieking in agony, others retreating, but none giving up easily.

William's blade sliced through the shadows, blocking incoming strikes from the remaining minions. He was a shield for the others behind him, his movements calculated and swift. With every minion that advanced, he was there to meet them head-on, no hesitation.

The minions were relentless, their eyes glinting with the dark magic of Eryndor's will. They regrouped and surrounded the group in a deadly circle of shadows and crackling energy. But with Garrick and Elara's wing advantage, William's fury, and Sully's steady aim with her sword, along with their families and soldiers, kept the minions at bay. As the battle raged on, the creatures' numbers began to thin.

"Is this all you've got?" Garrick yelled, his voice a battle cry that shook the very earth beneath them. With a final swing of his blades, a massive wave of fire erupted from the ground, cutting through the remaining minions like a storm of elemental fury.

With their forces finally broken, the few remaining minions shrieked in defeat, vanishing into the misted ground, leaving the battlefield littered with the remnants of their dark presence.

"Once they regroup, the minions will return," William said, adjusting his stance as he sheathed his sword. "Eryndor's not the type to let his minions fail him."

"Then we prepare," Garrick said, his voice firm. "We find them before they can regroup."

With the threat for the moment dealt with, the group stood tall, united by their mission, knowing that this was only the beginning of a much greater battle.

Out of the corner of her eye, Sully noticed Hawk, coming out of the McCrindles house, carrying an unconscious female. "Hawk, stop!" yelled Sully.

"You won't stop me, bitch. I have only one master: Eryndor," said a glazed-eyed Hawk.

"Stop him, NOW!" commanded William.

Faster than the eye could see, Michael, Sully and Stephen ran at Vampire speed toward Hawk.

In a blur of motion, Michael was the first to reach Hawk, his hands outstretched, trying to pry Alessia from his grasp. "Hawk, fight it!" Michael yelled, his voice laced with desperation. "This isn't you!"

But Hawk's glazed eyes remained locked on the distance, his grip tightening around Alessia, as if she were nothing more than a pawn to his twisted loyalty. "You don't understand," he snarled, his voice cold and distant. "Eryndor's will is absolute. No one can stand against it."

Sully's heart pounded as she watched her partner slip further away. She had to reach him before it was too late. With a powerful leap, she was in front of Hawk, her wings unfurling in a brilliant display of gold and blue. "Hawk, look at me!" she commanded, her voice ringing with both authority and raw emotion.

For a brief moment, his eyes flickered and a trace of the real Hawk began to break through the veil of darkness. But it was fleeting, the curse fighting back against any shred of humanity.

Stephen, who was now beside Michael, grasped Hawk's arm, attempting to break the bond that held him to the darkness. "We can help you, Hawk!" Stephen shouted. "You're not alone in this. Fight it!"

But Hawk's expression darkened and, with a growl, he threw them off with unnatural strength. "You will never win," he spat, his voice growing hollower, as the influence of Eryndor sank in deeper.

Sully, determined and unyielding, raised her Emberlight sword and pointed it toward Hawk. "I'll make you see reason, even if it takes everything I have."

Hawk's gaze sharpened, but it was unclear if it was truly him or the darkness inside him that replied, "You'll have to kill me first."

The air crackled with tension, as Hawk's words hung in the silence. His grip on Alessia tightened even further and his body trembled, with the struggle between the man he once was and the malevolent force that now controlled him.

Sully's heart twisted as she took a step forward, her hand gripping the hilt of her Emberlight sword. Her wings flared wide behind her, catching the flicker of light as she braced for whatever came next. "I don't want to fight you,

Hawk," she said, her voice soft yet firm, "but I will if it means saving you."

The moment felt like an eternity, the bond between them still there, but fraying with every passing second. Hawk's eyes flickered again, with that brief moment of recognition, but it was swallowed by the darkness.

"You can't save me," Hawk muttered, his voice strained. "You don't know what Eryndor has done to me."

"Then tell us!" Michael pleaded, stepping forward with Stephen. "Hawk, we're your friends. We can help you—please, just snap out of it."

For a moment, Hawk hesitated. His hands trembled, as the dark magic swirled around him, as if it were fighting against his will to even let go of Alessia. She remained unconscious in his arms, her face pale, but peaceful.

Sully's pulse raced, knowing that every second mattered. "Hawk, look at me! Remember who you are! Remember us!"

Something deep inside Hawk's eyes flickered—just for a heartbeat. His body stiffened and for a moment he stood still, as if torn between the two forces battling for control.

Then, as if the final thread of resistance broke, Hawk's body jerked violently, throwing Alessia forward and causing him to stumble back. The dark magic surged and his entire form seemed to ripple, consumed by the force of Eryndor's influence.

"Hawk!" Sully cried out, as she rushed to catch Alessia, pulling her out of the way, handing her to William. The others had barely enough time to react before Hawk's form shifted again—this time, it wasn't just a physical transformation. His very essence seemed to crack, breaking free of his own will.

With a loud, guttural scream, Hawk collapsed to his knees, clutching his head in agony. The magic around him surged like a storm, sparking lightning and fire into the air.

Sully's heart clenched. This was the breaking point. Either Hawk would come back to them now, or they would lose him forever.

"Hawk, please!" she shouted, rushing to his side. She knelt beside him, her hands reaching for him, feeling the tremors in his body, as the dark magic fought to consume him whole.

"Hawk!" Elara's voice suddenly rang out, her voice calm yet full of determination as she flew in, landing next to them. "You are stronger than this! We've fought beside you before, and we will do it again. Block Eryndor's hold!"

For a moment, there was nothing but silence, the storm of magic swirling in a wild fury. Then, slowly, Hawk's eyes began to clear, flickering back to their normal bourbon color. The struggle was still visible, but he was fighting and that was enough.

"Hawk?" Sully whispered, her hand gently touching his shoulder.

Hawk's breath came in shallow gasps and his voice was raw with pain. "I—I'm sorry," he croaked, his eyes darting to her, then to the others. "I … don't know how long I can fight it."

"You don't have to fight it alone," Michael said, his hand on Hawk's back, offering support. "We'll help you, every step of the way."

The air shifted and, for the first time in what felt like an eternity, the darkness surrounding Hawk began to recede. The influence of Eryndor, though still lingering, no longer had the same iron grip it once had.

Hawk took a deep breath, his body trembling as he pushed himself to his feet, still visibly struggling. "I—I don't know how to stop him," he said, his voice a mixture of guilt and frustration.

Sully, who was now standing close, looked at him with unwavering determination. "We stop him together."

Hawk smiled at Sully and leaned in to embrace her. "Thank you."

"Come on … we'll take you back to the Gramaze mansion. I am sure Talitha will be able to help you again," said Sully, hugging him back.

Hawk nodded and they watched as Elara opened a portal.

"You take Hawk back to the mansion, Sully. We need to stay here to protect the McCrindles and their farm," said William.

"Yes, Sir," said Sully, as she placed her arm around Hawk's back and walked toward the portal.

"I will go with them," stated Elara.

"Good idea. I will see you soon, my love," said Garrick. He watched Elara walk into the portal with Hawk and Sully.

"Michael, Stephen, Christian … I want you to scout the inside of the house. We need to find TJ and Parker," commanded William. But before he could finish, he heard footsteps behind him. Turning, he noticed Kura, Danielle and Grayson approaching.

"Where the fuck have you three been? We could have done with some help here," stated William, indicating all the dead minions.

"Apologies, Sire. We returned the car to our Australian counterparts and walked back. It took longer than expected. We avoided using our powers knowing it might draw attention to the farm and ourselves," said Grayson, his gaze sweeping over the scene before him.

Kura indicated the motionless body of Alessia in William's arms. "Is she …?" She gulped, hoping her thoughts were incorrect.

"No, she isn't dead … just unconscious," replied William, as he walked over to Kura.

"Danielle, I want you to go with Michael, Stephen and Christian, and search for the McCrindles," commanded William.

"Yes Sire," they all said in unison. They ran toward the house.

"Kura, will you be alright here with Alessia?" asked William.

"Yes, I will take care of the child," replied Kura. "When this is all over, I will take her back to the River of Whispers."

"Good idea," William said as he gently laid Alessia's unconscious body on the ground. He straightened, his eyes sharp and focused. "If you sense any trouble coming your way, don't hesitate to reach out to me telepathically and I'll be here immediately."

"Thank you, William," Kura said softly, as she knelt beside Alessia, then carefully settled herself next to her still form, her gaze filled with quiet determination.

"The rest of you … I want this place cleaned up," stated William, gesturing to all the dead minions. "Garrick, come with me. We need to search this property for any other minions lurking around."

"No problem," replied Garrick. He followed William to the front of the property.

CHAPTER TEN

Danielle, Michael, Stephen and Christian crept into the farmhouse through the back door, their movements were silent and deliberate, like shadows melting into the dim interior.

Danielle, Christian, you search the bedrooms and bathrooms. Stephen and I will cover the lounge, kitchen and laundry. Let's see if we can find the McCrindles, thought Michael, his mind sharp with determination.

Each Lepidoptera nodded in agreement and began their search for TJ and Parker, with an unwavering focus.

Danielle pushed the bedroom door open cautiously, the faint creak breaking the tense silence. The dim light filtering through the drawn curtains revealed a heart-stopping sight. TJ and Parker lay sprawled on the floor, their bodies motionless and unnervingly pale.

TJ's long brown hair was fanned out across the carpet and she had a crimson streak staining the corner of her temple. Her hand was outstretched as if she had been reaching for something, or someone. Parker was slumped beside her, his sandy hair matted with sweat. A dark bruise marred the side of his neck and his chest barely rose with shallow breaths.

The room was in disarray: a toppled lamp, a broken picture frame, dresser drawers pulled open and emptied, a smear of blood leading toward the doorway that hinted at a struggle. Danielle froze for a moment, her breath catching as she processed the scene, while Christian knelt beside Parker and TJ, pressing two fingers to both of their necks.

"He's alive … barely," Christian said, his voice hardly above a whisper. "Shit, TJ has no pulse."

Danielle exhaled a shaky breath, as she looked from Christian to TJ. "We need to move fast."

They're here! shouted Danielle, through her telepathic connection. *Main bedroom.*

Michael and Stephen ran toward the bedroom.

Danielle quickly knelt beside TJ, her hands trembling as she hovered them over the human woman's still form. Closing her eyes, she summoned her power and felt the familiar warmth of Lepidoptera healing energy gathering in her palms.

A faint glow radiated from her hands as she pressed them gently to TJ's temple, where blood trickled in a thin, dark line. Danielle's brow furrowed in concentration, her breathing steady, despite the mounting dread. She could feel the energy flowing into TJ's body, as she searched for wounds, seeking to repair the damage.

But TJ remained unresponsive, her body lying motionless, as if caught in a silent struggle beyond Danielle's reach.

The glow faded almost as quickly as it appeared, leaving a cold, sinking emptiness in its place. Danielle opened her eyes, panic creeping into her voice as she muttered, "Come on, TJ. Stay with me."

She tried again, her palms glowing faintly, but the energy dissipated before it could take hold. TJ's condition remained unchanged, her pale complexion a grim reminder that time was slipping away.

Christian, still crouched beside Parker, glanced up at her. "Danielle? What's happening?"

"It's not working!" Danielle snapped, her frustration and fear bubbling over. Her hands trembled as she withdrew them, clenching them into fists. "I … I don't understand. It should be working!"

Christian moved closer, placing a hand on her shoulder. "You need to stay calm. Maybe it's not her wounds, maybe it's something else blocking you."

Danielle's mind raced, torn between trying again, and the stark realization that they might be out of time. "Talitha and Violette might have the answers," she whispered, her voice wavering.

"Then let's move," Christian said firmly. "We can't lose either of them." Taking his phone out of his pocket, he called Violette.

"Yes!" said Violette, answering the call. "What can I do for you, Christian?"

"Can you create a portal. We need you to heal TJ and Parker McCrindle. Parker has a faint pulse and TJ, nothing at all," stated Christian.

"Sure. It will open in a few seconds," stated Violette, as she ran toward the backyard of the Gramaze mansion.

Sire, we are taking the McCrindles back to Bagnolet for some healing, thought Christian.

Understood. Keep me informed on how everything goes, William's voice echoed in Christian's mind.

Yes, Sire, thought Christian.

Christian and Danielle picked up the McCrindles' bodies and ran toward the front of the Cowaramup farmhouse and out the door. Within seconds, they watched a portal open. Stepping into the portal, they were enveloped by a swirling vortex of light and shadows, the air around them crackling with energy. The world blurred and shifted. With a jolt, they emerged in the backyard of the Gramaze mansion.

"Lay them down," Violette commanded, her voice calm but resolute, as she approached Christian and Danielle.

Without hesitation, they obeyed, gently lowering the McCrindles to the ground. Danielle and Christian stepped back, their eyes fixed on the Princess, with anticipation and worry etched into their faces.

Violette knelt beside the McCrindles' motionless figures, her hands glowing faintly with the soft, iridescent light of her Lepidoptera healing powers. She placed one hand over Parker's chest and the other over TJ, her focus steadfast.

Within seconds, Parker gasped sharply, his chest rising as life returned to him. Danielle let out a small sigh of relief, but it was short-lived.

"Take care of him," commanded Violette, looking at Christian.

Christian nodded to Violette and knelt next to Parker.

TJ remained still. No flicker of movement, no sign of breath. The light around Violette's hands dimmed as her expression tightened. She pressed her palms against TJ again, summoning more energy, as she started to chant an ancient Buddhist healing ritual. But the unyielding silence from TJ's body hung heavy in the air.

> *Ong Ma Lee Bae Mae Hong*
> *Ong Ma Lee Bae Mae Hong*
> *Ong Ma Lee Bae Mae Hong*

As Violette continued to chant the ancient Buddhist healing ritual, her voice steady and melodic, the Gramaze backyard transformed into a surreal tableau. The air seemed to hum in resonance with her words, each syllable rippling outward like waves on a still pond.

The backyard, usually tranquil, now glowed with a soft, otherworldly light. The grass beneath her feet shimmered as though dusted with starlight. The towering trees at the edge of the yard swayed gently, their branches moving in time with her chant, despite the absence of wind.

Golden fireflies emerged from the underbrush, their tiny bodies pulsating in sync with the rhythm of the ritual. Around Violette, a faint circle of warm amber light formed, flickering and shifting like the flame of a candle.

In the sky above, the stars seemed brighter, almost closer, and the moon cast a silvery sheen over the scene.

The air was thick with a sense of sacredness, as though the very fabric of reality was bending to her will.

The Gramaze backyard became a sanctuary of healing, a sacred space suspended between worlds, as Violette's voice wove the ancient power of the chant into the night.

Just as despair began to take hold, a faint glow emanated from TJ's chest, growing steadily brighter. Violette's eyes widened and she pulled back slightly, her hands still hovering over TJ. The light pulsed like a heartbeat, its rhythm slow at first, then gradually quickening.

TJ's body twitched, her fingers curling slightly, then she gasped a sharp, desperate inhale, as though she had been submerged underwater and finally broke the surface. Her eyes fluttered open, unfocused at first, before locking onto the worried faces surrounding her.

"TJ!" Danielle exclaimed, dropping to her knees beside her, tears of relief streaming down her face.

TJ blinked, disoriented, her voice weak but steady. "What … what happened? Where're Parker and Alessia?"

"I'm here," Parker rasped, his voice hoarse as he pushed himself to a sitting position. He reached out to clasp her hand, his grip trembling but firm. "You're okay. We're okay."

Violette let out a slow, relieved breath, her glow fading as she sat back. "It wasn't easy," she said softly, her voice tinged with exhaustion. "Something was blocking the healing … but you're both safe now."

TJ struggled to sit up, leaning heavily on Parker. Her gaze moved to Violette, gratitude shining through her fatigue. "Thank you," she whispered, her voice filled with emotion.

As the group helped the McCrindles to their feet, a strange energy lingered in the air, subtle but undeniable. TJ glanced down at her hand, where faint, shimmering marks had appeared on her skin and intricate patterns glowed briefly before fading.

"What is this?" TJ asked, holding up her hand.

Violette's eyes narrowed, her expression turning serious. "That," she said gravely, "is a mark of interference. Someone—or something—didn't want you to survive."

The words sent a chill through the group as they exchanged uneasy glances. Whatever had happened to TJ and Parker wasn't over yet.

TJ glanced at Parker. Panicked, TJ asked, "Where is Alessia?"

"At the moment, she's in Cowaramup, on your farm. She is going to be okay," stated Danielle, stepping forward to answer any questions.

"When Parker sensed someone approaching our farm, we told Alessia to hide in our walk-in robe. Is that where you found her?" asked TJ.

"I'm afraid not," Danielle replied. "She was nearly taken by one of the visitors you sensed. But, when my coven arrived at your farm, they were able to prevent it from happening."

"Coven? What the hell!" said Parker, as he glanced at TJ.

"Let's get you both inside," said Violette, gesturing to the Gramaze mansion. "You can get cleaned up in there and rest."

"Rest! We don't want to rest. We want to see our daughter," stated Parker, heatedly.

"I'm afraid that won't be possible at the moment," replied Violette, looking from Parker to TJ. "Do you both remember what happened tonight?"

"We were attacked … by some kind of creatures," TJ said, her voice trembling as she tried to piece it together. "Their eyes … they were white, glazed over. They came out of nowhere, like shadows." Her brow furrowed, struggling to comprehend the chaos she had endured.

"Is that all you remember?" Violette asked, her tone steady but probing.

TJ and Parker exchanged a brief, uncertain glance but remained silent, their hesitation speaking louder than words.

Violette's gaze sharpened as she studied them both and listened to their thoughts. "If I'm not mistaken," she said, her voice calm but tinged with authority, "You, Sir, are a Griffin, and you, Ma'am, are a human. Am I correct?"

"You are correct," Parker replied, his voice cautious, yet firm. "But what I don't understand is how you know this … and what's going to happen to us now?" His gaze locked on Violette, a mix of suspicion and unease flickering in his eyes.

"We are Vampires. That is how I know," she gestured to Danielle, Christian and herself. "I assume you've heard of Garrick and Elara Ironclaw, the leaders of the Stormclaw Griffins?"

"Yes!" Parker responded, his voice filled with recognition. "They are well-known and respected amongst my kind."

"They're close allies of our Vampire leader and our coven," Violette continued with a reassuring smile. "You're safe here. No harm will come to you. In fact, we're here to help you, and your daughter, Alessia."

"Right! … So, are we able to return to our home and collect our daughter?" asked Parker.

"Not right now. As I suggested before, why don't we get you both cleaned up and rested first," replied Violette.

"We would prefer to leave, if that is alright with you and your coven," stated Parker, as he quickly grabbed hold of TJ's hand.

"No that is not alright … You are not in Cowaramup any longer. You are in Bagnolet, France. You arrived here via an enchanted transport portal that I created. And until I have further instructions from our leader, you are not to return." Violette observed the shock on their faces, sensing their inner turmoil at being unable to check on their daughter and ensure she was safe. "Try not to worry about Alessia. She is safe with my coven."

With her Vampire gift of influencing thoughts, Danielle held out her hands to TJ and Parker, gently calming their minds. "Come … you'll be safe here."

Considering that they already knew Danielle, as Alessia's friend, they took her hands without hesitation.

"Thank you, Danielle," said TJ.

As they walked beside Danielle up the steps and into the mansion, Renee, William's life partner, appeared. "Good evening," she greeted them warmly. "I'm Renee. Welcome to our home." She gave a slight bow. "I've prepared a room for you to rest and recover. Please, follow me."

"You will be fine. Go with Renee," said Danielle, gazing from TJ to Parker. "I will see you later."

With a silent nod of agreement to Danielle, they turned and followed Renee, without question, into the house.

Danielle, Christian … William has requested that you return to Cowaramup, thought Violette, telepathically.

Yes, Violette, thought Danielle, as she watched her sister create a transport portal.

Okay! thought Christian, walking toward the portal.

* * *

TJ and Parker followed Renee inside. As they reached the room, she opened the door, revealing a king-size, four-poster bed, elegantly made up, as if for visiting dignitaries.

"There's a bathroom to freshen up, with some spare clothes inside," Renee explained, gesturing toward the right side of the room. "Next to the bed, you'll find a jug of water and two glasses. I'll return later this evening with wine and food, if you'd like?"

"Thank you, Renee. You are too generous," said TJ.

"You are welcome. Make yourselves at home," said Renee. She walked toward the doorway and closed the door behind her.

TJ sat on the bed, while Parker paced restlessly across the room.

"Sit down, Parker," she said, patting the space beside her.

"I can't," he snapped, his frustration evident. "Not when I don't know if Alessia is alright."

"These Vampires … they seem trustworthy enough," TJ said thoughtfully. "I don't think Alessia will be in any danger. In fact, I believe they could probably take better care of her than we could, especially with those glazed-eyed creatures possibly returning at any moment."

"You really believe that?" asked Parker, as he stopped pacing and sat next to TJ on the bed.

"Yes," she replied.

He shook his head. "We have kept her safe for twenty-two years, so why has this happened now?" stated Parker.

"I don't know," TJ said softly, "but I'm sure the Vampires will be able to shed some light on it. In the meantime, why don't we get cleaned up?"

"I never thought we'd have to rely on Vampires to keep our daughter safe," Parker muttered, shaking his head. "But if they can help, then maybe we should let them. It's just hard to accept, you know."

"I agree, but what other choice do we have?" TJ asked, her voice tinged with uncertainty.

"None," Parker replied, his voice steady. "We'll have to place our trust in these Vampires."

CHAPTER ELEVEN

The bluey-green portal shimmered to life in Cowaramup, its glow casting ripples of light across the ground, as Danielle and Christian stepped through, their figures emerging into the still evening air, where William stood waiting.

"How did things go with the McCrindles?" William inquired, his tone calm, yet expectant.

"All went smoothly, Sire," Danielle replied with a small nod. "Renee is looking after them, settling them into a room, so they can rest."

"Excellent," said William.

"Did you know that Parker McCrindle is a Griffin?" asked Christian, with a hint of curiosity in his voice.

"No, I didn't," William replied, considering the information. "Though, now that you mention it, that's probably a good thing. At least the McCrindles are familiar with the paranormal world."

Turning his attention to Danielle, William asked, "How are you holding up? Have you recovered from all the healing you've done over the past few hours?"

Danielle straightened slightly, her voice steady and resolute. "Yes, Sire. I'm ready and willing to assist in any way I can."

"Good," William said, his gaze shifting from Danielle to Christian. "I have a mission for you both." He paused briefly, ensuring their full attention. "Kura believes Alessia will be safer in her realm. Apparently, the ancient wards around the River of Whispers have been reawakened, so no enemy can cross them without her knowing. She's assured me that she has three guardians who can protect her, too, but I'd like the two of you to accompany Kura and Alessia to the River of Whispers. I suspect they'll need more protection than Kura can manage alone."

"When do we leave?" asked Danielle.

"Now, if you are both ready," said Kura, overhearing the conversation, as she walked toward them. "The sooner I get my great-granddaughter out of here, the better." Her protective stance spoke volumes. She hadn't strayed from Alessia's side since the attack by the minions.

"We are ready to leave," Christian said, his brow furrowed with concern, as he turned to William, "but I have a question. How are we supposed to get back to the Gramaze mansion from the River of Whispers? None of us can create portals."

"Kura will create the portal to take you back home to Bagnolet," answered William.

And if she dies, what then? We have no way to contact you either, thought Christian to William only.

Hmm ... good question. I hadn't thought about that, at all. Once you are there, I will find someone and send them to you. Does this sound okay? thought William to Christian.

Perfect. Thank you, Sire, thought Christian.

"So, are you both ready to go?" Kura asked, her gaze shifting between them.

"Ready when you are!" Danielle replied with a confident nod.

"Yes, Ma'am," Christian added, stepping forward. "Lead the way. I will carry Alessia for you." He motioned to Alessia's unconscious form lying on the ground.

Kura offered a small, appreciative smile. "Thank you, Christian. You are a true gentleman."

Kura extended her hands and her fingers moved in intricate patterns. A swirling portal materialized before them, glowing in shades of blue and silver. The air shimmered, carrying the faint sound of whispers, as if the portal itself were alive.

"Keep close," Kura instructed, stepping through first. Danielle and Christian followed, with Christian cradling Alessia's unconscious form securely in his arms.

"Stay safe," William commented, as he watched them walk into the portal.

* * *

They emerged on the other side of the portal at the River of Whispers and observed its serene waters glimmering under the twilight sky. The gentle murmur of the river echoed softly, blending with the rustle of the surrounding trees.

"Good evening, Goddess," said the Guardian of the River's Source, bowing his head slightly in respect.

"Good evening," Kura replied, her gaze sweeping over the three guardians as the portal closed behind them. "This is Christian and Danielle of the Gramaze Lepidoptera Vampires coven. They've come to help protect the young Goddess."

The three guardians inclined their heads in acknowledgment, their movements synchronized and respectful.

Christian and Danielle mirrored the gesture, their expressions solemn.

Kura gestured toward the unconscious girl in Christian's arms. "This is Stjernefrída's daughter, Alessia."

At her words, the guardians dropped to their knees in unison, lowering their heads in reverence.

"Is she alright?" asked the Guardian of the River's Source, his tone laced with concern.

"She was attacked in the human world by Eryndor's minions," Kura explained, her voice steady but edged with urgency. "She needs rest and time to heal. We must get her inside."

The three guardians rose to their feet as one.

"Your wish is our command, Goddess," said the Guardian of the River's Source. "Follow us."

They led the group along a narrow, winding path, its edges framed by soft whispers of the ancient willows.

Christian carried Alessia carefully, adjusting her in his arms to keep her comfortable. "She feels so light," he murmured, almost to himself.

"She's exhausted," Kura said over her shoulder. "The attack drained her physically and mentally. My home will provide the sanctuary she needs to recover."

As they approached Kura's home, its warm glow spilled through the windows, casting a welcoming light. The cottage stood nestled among the towering trees, exuding safety and calm.

Christian paused at the wooden steps, as Alessia stirred in his arms. Her eyelids fluttered open and her soft, weak voice broke the quiet. "Where … am I?"

Christian glanced down at her, relief washing over him. "Alessia! You're safe now. We're at Kura's home."

She blinked, her gaze unfocused and dazed. "I … I had the strangest dream … but it felt so real," she whispered.

"We'll discuss it inside," Kura said gently, as she looked over at Alessia. "For now, let's get you settled."

Recognizing Kura's face, Alessia let out a soft sigh and closed her eyes, her tense body relaxing in Christian's arms.

Christian carried her up the steps and Kura opened the door, ushering them into the cozy interior. "Place her on the couch," she directed, gesturing to a soft, green-colored sofa near the hearth.

Christian nodded and walked over to the couch and carefully laid Alessia down.

Danielle stepped inside behind them, quietly closing the door.

Guardians, remain outside and keep watch, Kura commanded telepathically. *The child must be protected at all costs. She is our future.*

The three guardians responded in unison, *yes, Goddess,* their mental voices echoing with determination. They took up their positions on the porch, standing alert and ready to defend their future Goddess from any threat.

"Here you go, my dear," Kura said, placing a pillow under Alessia's head, as she knelt beside her.

Alessia's eyes fluttered open and, with a sudden jolt, she sat up quickly, her movements filled with urgency. "Where am I?" she asked, her voice laced with confusion as her gaze darted around, taking in the unfamiliar surroundings.

"You are in my home, dear," replied Kura gently.

"In your home ... why am I here?" Alessia asked, her gaze shifting from Kura to Danielle, and then to Christian, confusion etched on her face.

"That's a long story," Kura said with a reassuring smile. "One we can save for later. For now, can I get you anything?"

"No, I don't want anything," Alessia said, her voice rising with frustration. "I want to know why I'm here."

"We brought you here to keep you safe," Danielle said calmly, sitting on the end of the couch. "What do you remember?"

Realization struck Alessia like a heavy blow, her breath catching in her throat. "My parents ... are they ...?"

Kura stood and gently pulled a chair over to the couch, sitting down in front of Alessia. "What do you remember?" she asked, her tone soft but steady.

Alessia's mind raced, but everything felt like a blur. She struggled to grasp the fragments of her memory, and her confusion deepened. "I ... I remember ... people—strange people. They came for me, I think. They were ... not normal. They had white glazed-over eyes and looked eerie. I don't know who they were, or what they wanted. I just know ... I couldn't stop them." Her voice trembled as the memory resurfaced. "I saw my parents ... they ... they were killed by them. Right in front of me, as I hid in the walk-in robe."

Tears started to stream down her face and she shook her head, looking down in a lost painful recollection. "I don't remember anything else."

Her voice faltered and she looked up at Kura, fear lingering in her eyes. "What's happening? Why were we attacked?"

Kura gently wrapped her arms around Alessia, her voice soft and soothing. "Shhh, everything will be okay. We are here for you, my dear."

Alessia leaned into Kura's embrace, clinging to her as the weight of everything overwhelmed her. She buried her face against Kura's shoulder, tears flowing freely as she cried. Her body shook with the release of all the fear and pain that she had been holding inside. "What happened to my parents? Are they at a hospital morgue or something? They're not still at the farm, are they?"

Kura slowly pulled away from Alessia, her touch gentle as she tucked a strand of dark brown hair behind Alessia's ear. She gazed into Alessia's wide, fearful blue eyes, her voice soft but firm. "My dear, your parents are still alive. They've been taken to France via one of our enchanted portals, where they'll be kept safe and guarded at all times."

Alessia blinked, disbelief flickering across her face. "They're alive?" she whispered, hope sparking in her chest for the first time since the attack. "They're in *France*?"

"Yes," said Kura.

A spark of hope ignited in Alessia's eyes. "Can I go see them?" she asked urgently, her voice almost pleading.

Kura's gaze softened, but she shook her head gently. "We need to have a chat first, my dear."

Alessia's brow furrowed, her frustration creeping in. "What about? Nothing is more important to me than seeing my parents."

"Come with me, my dear," Kura said, standing and extending her hand toward Alessia. "I want to show you something—something about our ancestry."

"Our ancestry?" Alessia hesitated for a moment, but then stood without taking Kura's hand, as curiosity began to replace her anxiety.

Guardians ... I need you to follow us throughout the River of Whispers, thought Kura.

Yes, Goddess, replied the Guardian of the River's Source, as he opened the door to the cabin.

As the door creaked open, Alessia was greeted by a towering figure who seemed carved from the essence of the river itself. His form shimmered with a translucence that reflected the rippling surface of water, his skin glowing faintly with a bluish hue, like moonlight on a still lake. His hair flowed like liquid silver, cascading down his back in waves that seemed to shift and ripple, even in the still air.

"Come with me," said Kura, as she held out her hand for Alessia to take.

"Everything will be alright, you'll see, Alessia," stated Danielle, watching the startled look on Alessia face.

Alessia frowned but, out of sheer curiosity, she decided to take Kura's hand. Her breath quickened as she glanced nervously at the three guardians, their imposing forms looming in the doorway. They stood silent and still, but their presence hummed with an energy that made her skin prickle. They were the same figures who had haunted her dreams.

Alessia tightened her grip on Kura's hand. Her palms became clammy with sweat as they walked past the three guardians.

"Come, my dear. The guardians will protect us," stated Kura.

"Protect us from what?" Alessia whispered, her voice trembling despite her attempt to sound brave. Her eyes darted to Kura, searching for an answer, but also for comfort in the midst of this strange and overwhelming encounter.

"From anyone who attacks us," stated Kura.

Alessia hesitated at the threshold of the porch, her feet reluctant to step outside where the cool air carried a faint, eerie hum, as if the world beyond was alive and watching. The guardians remained still, their glowing eyes locked on her every movement.

"I don't understand any of this," Alessia muttered, her voice barely audible. Her gaze flicked back to the guardians again, as if expecting them to suddenly spring to life. The hair on the back of her neck stood on end, as her grip on Kura's hand tightened further. Despite her fear, there was a flicker of curiosity in her eyes, a quiet resolve starting to form beneath the surface. Alessia wasn't sure what she was walking into, but Kura's calm demeanor kept her moving forward, one cautious step at a time.

Kura and Alessia walked deeper into the forest. The soft rustling of leaves around them started to hum a gentle, melodic song as Kura began to weave the ancient stories of the River of Whispers. She revealed its secrets and the mystical powers of the forest, all while gently explaining to Alessia her heritage, of how her birth mother, Stjernefrída, had once walked these lands, and of how Alessia had been adopted into the safety of humans, far from the dangers of the unknown.

Alessia walked next to Kura in stunned silence, her mind swirling as she tried to process everything Kura had told her. She had grown up with no knowledge of the paranormal world, so to suddenly learn about her true heritage, the existence of the River of Whispers, and her connection to a long-lost supernatural lineage, was disorienting.

"Wait," she said, her voice shaky, "So, you're saying … my birth mother, this Stjernefrída, was part of all this? And I … I'm connected to it? But I don't understand. How is this even possible? How can I be part of this world when I've never known any of it?"

Kura smiled gently, placing a reassuring hand on Alessia's shoulder. "I know this is overwhelming, my dear, but you are part of a legacy that has been waiting for you. I will guide you through it, step by step. You don't need to understand everything all at once. The forest, the River of Whispers—it all has a way of revealing itself to those who are ready. And you will be ready, in time."

Alessia looked down at her hands, still unsure, but something in Kura's calm presence gave her a sliver of hope. "But I don't even know where to start," she whispered.

"You've already begun," Kura replied softly. "The first step is always the hardest, but you're not alone, Alessia. We'll walk this path together."

Alessia let out a deep sigh, her mind racing to absorb everything Kura was sharing. Yet, with every word, she found herself growing more curious about her ancestry.

"Wait … so if Stjernefrída was my birth mother, and she was your granddaughter, does that mean I'm your great-granddaughter?" Alessia asked, her brows furrowing as she pieced it together.

Kura's eyes softened, a proud smile spreading across her face. "Yes, my dear. You are my great-granddaughter, and I am deeply honored to have you as part of my family."

Alessia hesitated for a moment, then admitted, "You know, when I first met you, I felt this … connection. Being around you made me feel calm, like I belonged, and, to be honest, I felt a tad jealous of Danielle, to have a lovely mother like you; that is, even though you are not really her mother."

Kura reached out, gently placing a hand on Alessia's cheek. "That connection you felt, my dear, is the bond of family. It was always there, waiting for us to find one another."

Alessia leaned in and gave her great-grandmother a warm hug. "I'm so glad you found me," she murmured. "It explains so much … like the strange dreams I've been having, and the glowing runes and symbols that have appeared on my forearms and hands before. I thought I was imagining things, because I was stressed out about my final exams. Humph … was I wrong!"

"Speaking of glowing runes and symbols," Kura said, her tone gentle but intrigued, as she pointed to Alessia's hands and arms. "It seems they're starting to manifest."

Alessia's gaze dropped to her hands and forearms, her breath catching as she saw the intricate silver-and-blue runes and symbols glowing softly against her skin. They shimmered like living light, pulsing faintly, as if in rhythm with her heartbeat.

Her voice was barely above a whisper. "They're … beautiful. But why now? What does it mean?"

"It means you are ready, my dear, to learn our craft," replied Kura.

CHAPTER TWELVE

A few hours slipped by, filled with animated discussions about Alessia's extraordinary abilities, and the potential responsibilities her role as a Goddess might demand. As they neared the cabin, Kura suddenly halted, her expression shifting to one of solemn importance.

Alessia stopped beside her, sensing the tension.

"Alessia … There's something you need to know; something I haven't told you about yet." Kura looked into Alessia eyes and her brow furrowed, "It's about an evil creature; his name is Eryndor. The attack … on you earlier at your home; it wasn't random. He sent them. He's after you."

Kura's words hung in the air, heavy and foreboding, as Alessia felt a chill run down her spine.

"Why were they after me?" questioned Alessia.

Kura paused and glanced back at the three silent guardians, who were trailing them. "Because of who you are. Eryndor believes you're the key to unlocking something he's been searching for—a Golden Chalice hidden within an ancient book."

"A chalice? From a book? That sounds … impossible," Alessia said, her brow furrowed in confusion. She had yet to grasp the full extent of what her abilities could achieve.

"Impossible for most, yes. But not for you. You've inherited a gift, Alessia—one that can pull objects from enchanted bindings. Eryndor knows this. He needs you to retrieve the chalice because he can't do it himself," replied Kura.

"What does he even want with it? I don't understand!" questioned Alessia, her steps faltering.

"The chalice isn't just any ancient artifact. It holds the power to sever the balance between life and death. Eryndor wants to use it to destroy the world we know and bring back the dead—an army to serve him. He'll stop at nothing to get it," replied Kura, watching the surprised reaction on Alessia's face.

"He … he wants to end everything? And you think *I* can help him do that?"

"Not just help—without you, he can't succeed. That's why he sent his minions to take you. He thinks he can force you to do his bidding. That's why we have to stop him, Alessia. Before it's too late."

Alessia took a deep breath. "Then we stop him. Whatever it takes." She clenched a fist by her side.

Kura's lips curved into a determined smile, her eyes steady and resolute. "You're stronger than you know, Alessia. And we're going to need every bit of that strength for what lies ahead."

As they reached the cabin, Danielle approached them. "How was your walk?"

"Enlightening, that's for sure." Alessia shook her head. "I never even knew this paranormal world existed, until today. My parents sure have kept things hidden from me."

"And for good reason. Your parents weren't just keeping you in the dark out of fear, Alessia. They knew what you're capable of—what you're destined for—and they wanted to give you a normal life for as long as they could. They knew the moment you learned the truth, your world would change forever. And it has," stated Kura.

"So, what now? How do I even begin to deal with all of this?" asked Alessia.

"You train! You learn to harness your abilities. And, most importantly, I prepare you for the fight ahead. Eryndor won't stop until he gets what he wants, and that's you. But we won't let him," stated Kura, indicating to everyone who was standing in front and behind her.

"You've got all of us now, Alessia. We'll figure this out together," said Danielle.

"Together, huh? I guess that's better than doing this alone," said Alessia.

"Strength in numbers is what we need, Alessia. And you *are* stronger than you know," stated Kura.

"And you have the Gramaze Lepidopteras and the Ironclaw Griffins on your side; they are willing to help out in any way they can," stated Christian.

Alessia gave a small nod and drew in a deep, steadying breath, trying to calm the storm of emotions swirling within her.

"I hope I can live up to everyone's expectations," Alessia said softly

"I'm sure you will. In the meantime, I have someone I want you to meet," Danielle said, gesturing toward the cabin with a slight smile. "Come inside and meet my adoptive father."

"You're adopted, too?" asked Alessia.

Danielle nodded in agreement. "Yep! My father is a warlock. His name is Adrian." Danielle held out her hand for Alessia to take.

Alessia hesitated for a moment before taking Danielle's hand, her brow furrowed in confusion. "A warlock? You're serious? So, witches and warlocks are real, too?"

Danielle chuckled softly. "Oh, very real. And my father, he's one of the best. Don't worry, he's not the scary kind. He's actually pretty amazing."

Alessia bit her lip, a mixture of curiosity and apprehension flickering in her eyes. "I feel like I've fallen into some kind of fantasy novel ... but I guess I should stop being surprised by now."

Danielle grinned, as she led Alessia toward the door. "Exactly. Welcome to the real world, Alessia—the one hiding in plain sight."

Thank you, Danielle. She needs other females, like yourself, to keep her informed and calm, thought Kura.

You're welcome. I feel Alessia and I have a lot in common, so I am only too happy to help out, thought Danielle.

Guardians ... keep watch while we are inside the cabin, thought Kura.

Yes, Goddess, said the three guardians in unison, as they stood guard outside the cabin, ready for what might eventuate.

* * *

Hmm ... interesting, Eryndor mused to himself, hidden in the shadows of a towering tree. For hours, he had silently followed Kura, Alessia and the three guardians through the dense forest, along the River of Whispers, absorbing every detail of their conversations. It was a game of patience, one he played well. *I will bide my time and wait for the child to master her craft*, he thought, his gaze lingering on the group as they disappeared into the cabin. *Then, I will return for her.*

With a swift snap of his fingers, a swirling portal materialized before him. He stepped through it, vanishing from the forest, his plans set in motion as he made his way back to the ship.

* * *

The heavy iron door creaked open and Sully stepped into the dimly lit corridor of the Gramaze mansion's cells. The air was thick with the scent of damp stone and lingering tension. She hesitated for a moment, steeling herself, before walking toward the cell at the end of the hall. *I wonder how he is today?*

Inside, Hawk sat on the cold floor, with his head in his hands. His usually sharp bourbon-colored eyes were dulled, bloodshot from exhaustion. The faint glow of the enchanted runes etched into the walls, which gave light, barely illuminated his disheveled figure.

Sully cleared her throat softly. "Hawk?"

He looked up slowly, the familiar spark of defiance flickering in his white-eyed gaze, though it was fleeting. His voice was hoarse when he spoke. "Come to gloat, Sully? Or make sure I'm still breathing?

Sully leaned against the iron bars, crossing her arms. "Neither, smart-ass. I wanted to see how you're doing now that … well, now that Talitha's started to take the mind control off you."

Hawk gave a bitter laugh and ran a hand through his unkempt hair. "How I'm doing? Let's see … I spent the last couple of months as someone else's puppet, I tried to kill two of my closest allies, and now I can't even remember half of what I've done. So, yeah, as you can plainly see, I'm doing great."

Sully winced at the sarcasm but didn't rise to the bait. "You're not the first person this has happened to, Hawk. Mind control messes with your head, but it wasn't your fault."

He stood abruptly, pacing the narrow cell like a caged animal. "Doesn't change the fact that it happened! Doesn't change the fact that I was weak enough to let it happen."

"You think this is about strength?" Sully's voice was sharp now, cutting through his self-pity. "Hawk, nobody's invincible. Not even you."

He stopped pacing, staring at her. The vulnerability in his eyes was something she hadn't seen for a while. "What if I can't come back from this? What if …" His voice cracked slightly. "What if I hurt someone again?"

Sully stepped closer to the bars, her expression softening. "You *will* come back from this. And you won't be alone. You've got people who care about you, even if you don't believe it right now."

He shook his head. "You don't get it, Sully. You're not the one with blood on your hands."

"And you're not the only one carrying scars," she shot back. "We all have our demons, Hawk. Yours just happened to come with strings attached."

There was silence for a moment, the weight of her words settling between them. Finally, Hawk sank back down onto the cold dungeon floor, his head bowed.

"Why are you here, Sully?" he muttered, his voice barely audible.

She hesitated, then spoke softly. "Because I know what it's like to feel like you've lost control. To feel like you're drowning in your own mistakes. But I also know you're stronger than this. Whether you believe it or not, you're not alone in this fight."

He looked up at her, something unreadable flickering in his expression. For the first time since she entered, there was a hint of the Hawk she knew.

"You always this stubborn?" he asked, a faint smirk tugging at the corner of his mouth.

"Only when someone's being a colossal idiot," Sully replied, a small smile breaking through her serious demeanor.

Hawk let out a quiet laugh, the sound rough but genuine. "Guess I should be glad you're here then."

She nodded. "You should. Now, get some rest. You'll need your strength if you're going to face the queen again tomorrow."

As Sully turned to leave, Hawk's voice stopped her. "Sully ... thanks."

She glanced back, her expression unreadable but her tone warm. "Anytime, Hawk. Now get some rest."

CHAPTER THIRTEEN

The air was thick with magic, alive with the scent of wildflowers, as Adeline appeared in front of the cabin. Her presence was a stark contrast to the untamed wilderness in the River of Whispers.

Her silver hair cascaded in soft waves, framing a face that seemed sculpted by moonlight itself. Delicate violet hues tinted her cheeks, and her luminous blue eyes held a gaze that was both ethereal and commanding. She wore a gown of lilac and amethyst, the fabric shimmering like starlight as she moved. Tiny butterflies, faintly glowing, flitted around her, as if drawn to her innate magic. A silver circlet adorned her forehead, and a necklace of crystalline droplets rested at her throat, catching and refracting the light in a cascade of colors.

As she approached the cabin's porch, three figures emerged from the mist—the guardians of the River of Whispers. Their forms were tall and imposing, draped in robes of deep emerald and cobalt, their features obscured by the shifting fog that seemed to cling to them.

"Adeline of the Fae Kingdom, what brings you to the River of Whispers? None cross these waters without purpose," stated the Guardian of the River's Source, his voice a deep, resonant echo.

Adeline inclined her head in a graceful bow, her voice as melodic as a lullaby. "I am honored to meet you, Guardians. I come bearing tidings from the Fae Kingdom." She extended a delicate hand, revealing a scroll sealed with the royal sigil. "This is an invitation to the crowning ceremony of our new queen."

"The crowning of a new queen? The Fae Kingdom has been without a ruler for months. Why now?" asked the Guardian of the River's Flow, stepping forward; his tone more skeptical.

Adeline met his gaze, unwavering. "The stars have aligned and the Seers have foretold her rise. Aevyressa will unite the Fae and restore balance to our realm. As protectors of this sacred river, you and your Goddess are invited to bear witness to this momentous occasion."

The Guardian of the River's Destination studied Adeline intently. "And why should we trust the words of a messenger, no matter how fair? Many have come to this river with promises and lies."

Adeline stepped closer, the butterflies around her growing brighter. "Because I speak the truth. The river itself will bear witness to my words. Its whispers do not lie. Listen, and you will hear."

The guardians exchanged glances as they listened.

"Very well, Adeline. We will deliver your message to the Goddess. If your queen is as worthy as you claim, we shall attend," stated the Guardian of the River's Source.

Adeline smiled, her beauty radiant even in the dim light. "Thank you. The Fae Kingdom awaits your presence."

With a final nod, she turned and disappeared into the mist, her form blending with the ethereal glow of the river. The whispers grew louder, carrying her name as if the river itself acknowledged her purpose.

The Guardian of the River's Source approached Kura's door and knocked softly, waiting patiently for it to open.

When the door creaked ajar, Kura stood framed in the doorway, her sharp gaze meeting the guardian. "Yes?" she asked, her tone clipped but curious.

"A delivery for you, Goddess," the guardian said, bowing slightly as he extended the scroll toward her.

Kura accepted the scroll with a nod, her fingers brushing against the intricately tied ribbon. Without hesitation, she unfurled it and her eyes scanned the elegant script within.

❉ By Royal Proclamation of the Fae Kingdom ❉

To the Esteemed Goddess Kura and the Guardians of the River of Whispers,

The stars have aligned and the ancient prophecies have spoken. You are cordially invited to witness a momentous occasion in the history of the Fae:

The Crowning Ceremony of Her Majesty, Aevyressa, Queen of the Fae, Bringer of Balance and Guardian of Light.

Date: Under the next full moon.

Time: As the first starlight graces the sky.

Location: The Crystal Glade, within the heart of the Fae Kingdom.

It is with great honor that we request your presence at this sacred event, where our realm shall celebrate the rise of our new Queen and the restoration of harmony to all enchanted lands.

This ceremony shall mark not only the ascension of our Queen, but also the unity of our kindred spirits, as the whispers of magic flow through the realms.

Attire: Ceremonial or ethereal garb (Glow enchantments are welcome, but no disruptive magics, please.)

Kindly present this invitation at the Guardian's Grove, where you shall be escorted to the Crystal Glade by our most trusted guides.

We eagerly await your presence as witnesses to this historic moment.

With the blessings of the Fae,
Myrrathen and Thalara, the Herald
On behalf of the Fae Kingdom

"Humph … interesting," Kura muttered, glancing over the invitation once more before rolling it back up. "Thank you, Guardian." She closed the door behind her and walked toward Alessia.

"Everything alright?" asked Christian, as he watched Kura place the scroll on the table.

"Looks like the Fae Kingdom has chosen a new queen. It's Elyndra's sister, Aevyressa," replied Kura. "The crowning ceremony will be at the full moon."

"Will you be attending?" asked Adrian the Warlock, overhearing the conversation.

"Why should I? The Fae Kingdom has never been a friend to our kind. They claim diplomacy now, but when has a Fae's word been worth more than the air it rides on?" replied Kura.

"Agreed! They smile while hiding a blade behind their back. If you ask me, this invitation feels like a trap," stated Christian.

"Or a distraction. Eryndor is the real threat here. He knows Alessia's potential. I wouldn't put it past him to use the Fae to weaken us," said Danielle.

"But if we could get help from the Fae Queen …" said Alessia, softly.

"It's not a help we can trust, Alessia," interrupted Adrian. "You're the Goddess of the River of Whispers now. That makes you a target for every schemer who thinks they can use your power. We're here to protect you, nothing else."

"I'm not exactly spry enough to fight off assassins. If I go, it will be to listen, to see what the Fae Queen truly wants. But that doesn't mean I'll trust her," said Kura.

"And if it's a ploy to draw you—or us—away from Alessia?" asked Adrian.

Kura's lips pressed into a thin line and her gaze drifted to Alessia. For a moment, the firelight flickered in her eyes, casting shadows of the years she'd lived and the battles she'd fought alongside Stjernefrída. "Well, then, I have no intention of leaving Alessia unprotected, not now, not ever."

Danielle gripped the hilt of her blade. "Good, because no one here is stepping out of this cabin without a damn good reason. Let the Fae wait, because we all know, Eryndor won't."

Christian crossed his arms over his chest and glanced at Adrian. "What's your take, Adrian? We can't afford to be divided on this."

"We stay united. If Kura decides to go, it's her choice, but we don't scatter ourselves thin. Alessia comes first. The Fae Queen's schemes are secondary," stated Adrian.

Kura tilted her head, a faint smile tugging at the corner of her lips. "Well said. Perhaps age hasn't dulled all my instincts. For now, the Fae can wait. We have more pressing matters to attend to."

"Thank you. All of you," said Alessia, looking at each of them.

The room fell into a thoughtful silence. The decision to stay and protect Alessia had been made, binding them all to a shared purpose, and an uncertain fate.

CHAPTER FOURTEEN

"Knock, knock," Renee called out softly, from behind the closed door. "May I come in?"

"Come in," Parker replied, rising to his feet.

"How are you settling in?" Renee asked, a warm smile on her face, as she walked into the room. She had seen on the CCTV footage that TJ and Parker had been exploring both the inside and outside of the house earlier.

"Good, thank you," TJ replied graciously. "We really appreciate your hospitality."

"When can we see our daughter?" asked Parker, his tone edged with impatience.

"Soon, I believe. But in the meantime, there is someone that we think you will want to meet," replied Renee. "Come with me."

Parker sighed heavily and rolled his eyes. "Who are we meeting?"

"Follow me and you will find out," stated Renee, as she listened to their apprehensive thoughts with her Lepidoptera Vampire ability. She walked toward the doorway and gestured for them to follow.

TJ and Parker followed Renee to the front of the two-story mansion, where they approached two closed French doors, which led into a sitting room.

Renee opened the two doors inward and turned to TJ and Parker, gesturing for them to step inside. "I will leave you with Garrick and Elara Ironclaw. I believe you already know them, Parker?"

"Thank you, yes," replied Parker, relieved to find an old friend waiting for them.

Garrick and Elara walked over to the doorway to greet them.

"Good evening, my friend," said Garrick, warmly holding out his hand. "Long time, no see."

"It certainly has been, my friend. How have you and your lovely partner been?" asked Parker, as he nodded slightly to Elara.

"We have been well," replied Garrick. "And this must be your lovely wife?"

"Yes," said Parker, turning to his wife. "TJ, this is Garrick and Elara Ironclaw. I have known them for … let's say a few hundred years."

TJ offered her hand to both Garrick and Elara and smiled politely.

"Come … let's sit. We have a lot to discuss, my friend," said Garrick, gesturing toward the elegant sitting room, which had a refined and classical design.

TJ and Parker followed Garrick and Elara into the room and took their seats across from them on a cream-colored sofa, which was accentuated by vibrant throw pillows, in shades of red, black and turquoise.

"What did you want to discuss, my friend?" questioned Parker.

"Your daughter, and our son," replied Garrick, as he looked from Parker to TJ.

"Our daughter? Your son? What is this about?" TJ asked, her voice heated, as she rose to her feet.

"Take a seat, my dear," Garrick requested, grimacing at her.

Parker tugged at TJ's hand and shook his head. "Sit, TJ. It seems we have a lot to learn."

TJ swallowed hard and sank back onto the couch.

"As you know, your daughter, Alessia, is a descendant of Stjernefrída and a Goddess of the Light and Stars," Garrick stated, studying their reaction.

"And what of it?" TJ retorted, her brow furrowing.

"Calm yourself, TJ. Let's hear him out," Parker said gently, taking her hand.

"You will do well to listen to your husband, human," Garrick said coldly, rising to his feet and walking to the window. "I'm not in the mood for your insolence."

TJ gulped hard and nodded in agreement.

"What you don't know is this: our son, Eryndor, seeks to conquer the world. He wants to destroy everything and everyone in his path. The only way he can achieve this is by binding three ancient artifacts together. And right now, he has all three." Garrick watched closely for their reactions.

"Fuck … what can we do to stop this, especially with your son now holding all three artifacts? And what does Alessia have to do with any of this?" Parker asked, a mix of concern and frustration in his voice.

"Alessia is the key Eryndor needs," Garrick replied. "She alone possesses the power to unbind spells. To complete his madness, Eryndor needs the Golden Chalice, which is hidden within the pages of an ancient book. The only other person capable of this was Stjernefrída and she is dead."

Realizing the gravity of the situation, that both their daughter and the world were at stake, Parker's voice grew steady but urgent. "What can we do?"

"We need to stop Eryndor," stated TJ.

"Yes, we do," stated Garrick, meeting Elara gaze. "But we also need to keep your daughter safe. If Eryndor takes her and forces her to do what he wants, her life, and everyone else's, will be forfeit."

"At the moment, Alessia is safe at the River of Whispers, but for how long … we can't be sure. Eryndor is cunning. It won't be long before he finds Alessia," said Elara.

"Do you know where Eryndor is hiding out, at the moment?" asked Parker.

"I believe, from speaking with William Gramaze, the owner of this mansion, and leader of the Lepidoptera Vampires, that they may have a lead. Actually, we're heading out on a mission, and we were hoping you'd join us. We could really use someone like you. Are you in?" Garrick asked.

"You can count on me. I'm not sure what we're walking into, but if you need me, I'm with you," stated Parker. He raked a hand through his sandy-colored hair.

"The sooner we act, the sooner our lives can get back to normal," stated TJ.

"Normal? My dear, what you fail to understand is Alessia has become the Goddess of the River of Whispers. That is not just a title, it's a force with the power to reshape everything we know. Her ascension is a pivotal moment in time. There is no turning back from this. Unless she chooses otherwise, Alessia will never return to the life she once knew, and she won't be returning to your farm," said Garrick.

TJ and Parker exchanged a sorrowful glance; their eyes filled with an unspoken understanding. From the moment they adopted Alessia, they had known this day might come, but they had never truly prepared for it.

As they contemplated Alessia's future, William Gramaze strode purposely into the sitting room.

"Good evening. Are you ready to go, Garrick?" asked William.

"I am," Garrick replied, nodding, "and Parker will be coming with us."

William extended his hand to Parker with a firm grip. "The more the merrier. We need as much manpower, or should I say Griffin power, as we can get."

"Where are we headed?" Parker asked William, as they shook hands.

"We believe, based on our satellite feed, that Eryndor and his minions are holed up on a derelict ship in the North Atlantic Ocean," William replied. "He thinks he's outsmarted us by casting an invisible ward, but our satellite technology is far too advanced for his illusions."

"Right! And how exactly are we supposed to capture him, if he's as powerful as you all claim?" Parker asked, his tone skeptical.

"We'll discuss that when we get there," William replied firmly. "There's a portal ready in the backyard, which will take us straight to Eryndor's location." He paused briefly before adding, "And to be clear, we're not planning to capture him. Enough of this talk. Let's move."

Parker hesitated for a moment, then nodded. Turning to TJ, he pulled her into a warm embrace. "Goodbye, my love," he said softly.

"Please … stay safe," TJ whispered, her voice trembling with emotion. "I couldn't bear to lose you, too." Her furrowed brow betrayed her sorrow as she held him close.

As Parker reluctantly pulled away from their embrace, he pressed a gentle kiss to TJ's forehead, before turning to follow William and Garrick out to the backyard.

TJ's eyes brimmed with tears, the weight of her emotions finally breaking through as they spilled down her cheeks. She stood silently, watching Parker disappear from the room.

"Don't worry, my dear," Elara said softly, placing a comforting arm around TJ's shoulders. "He will return."

"I hope so," TJ murmured, her voice thick with tears, barely audible through the ache in her chest.

CHAPTER FIFTEEN

Sully strode purposefully out of the training room, her steps echoing in the quiet hallway. With her body relaxed, but carrying the faint exhaustion of a hard morning's workout, she couldn't help but wonder what the day still had in store for her.

I wonder how Hawk is doing? she thought. Her chest tightened with worry, as she took a deep breath and swept her damp hair back behind her ears. *I miss Hawk so much. Will he ever be normal again?* Pausing in the corridor, she clenched her fists, as a familiar surge of anger twisted in her chest. *Eryndor!* The name alone was enough to ignite a fire within her. *That vile son of a bitch. I'd give anything to see him pay for what he's done.*

Her jaw tightened as she dug her nails into her palms, the sharp sting grounding her amidst the whirlwind of emotions. Flashes of the past flickered relentlessly in her mind. *Everything Eryndor has taken from us, every ounce of pain he's caused Hawk and I ...* A bitter snarl tugged at her lips. *It's like he's impossible to kill; like a cockroach crawling out of every damn corner, that has a thousand lives.*

As she continued down the hallway, toward her dorm room, Sully noticed a familiar figure in the hallway ahead, leaning casually against the wall.

Hawk! Her steps faltered in disbelief, as their eyes met.

For a heartbeat, the world stood still, as Hawk noticed her, too, and straightened, his expression soft but hesitant. He was unsure of how she would react to him, especially after all the turmoil they had endured together.

He looks different—relaxed, clear-eyed, like himself again, thought Sully. Her breath caught as she studied him, almost afraid to believe what she was seeing. The weight of her emotions crashed down all at once: *hope, relief, love.*

"Hawk!" she said quietly, almost breathless.

"It's me, Sully. Really me, this time," his voice breaking slightly.

Sully stared at him for a moment longer before suddenly rushing forward. She threw her arms around his neck and he caught her, holding her close. They clung to each other as if the world had shattered and, in that single moment, had been made whole again.

"You're really back. I thought … I thought I'd lost you, forever," said Sully, her voiced muffled against his chest. She had visited Hawk during the torment of his mind control in the past, each visit a painful reminder of the distance between them. But this time had felt like an eternity, and had been the longest and hardest to bear. Now, holding him like this, the weight of that ache finally began to lift.

"You didn't lose me; not for a second. I fought to come back. For you!" replied Hawk, pressing his cheek against her damp hair.

Without another word, Hawk leaned down and kissed her soft lips. It was slow and deep, filled with everything that they had both missed, during his time away. When they parted, they stayed close, foreheads touching, their breath blending.

"I've missed you so much, Hawk," said Sully, pulling away slowly, looking into his soulful eyes.

"I missed you, too. You were the one thing that kept me sane in the darkest moments. I kept picturing you—your voice, your smile. It's what brought me back," said Hawk. He leaned in and kissed her forehead.

Sully and Hawk stood there for a moment longer, savoring the reunion. The noise of the academy faded into the background. For the first time in what seemed like forever they both felt complete again.

* * *

The Griffins erupted from the depths of the iridescent blue portal above the North Atlantic Ocean, their powerful wings slicing through the storm-lashed skies. Upon their backs, the Lepidoptera Vampires sat poised, eyes sharp and alert, as they circled the area near the wards guarding the derelict ship. In tight formation, they drew closer, and Eryndor's invisible enchantments flickered faintly, wrapping the vessel in an ethereal glow. The ship seemed frozen in time, its dark hull veiled by the unseen barrier—a silent sentinel concealing the secrets that lay within.

I don't see anyone onboard, do you? Garrick stated telepathically, his voice calm, yet sharp.

Me neither, William responded, his tone equally focused.

I'll land on the ship's deck. Let's see what we can find, Parker added telepathically, his mind set on the mission, as he flew toward the deck, to land.

But as Parker's words echoed in their minds, the air itself seemed to tense before the ship's hull shuddered violently. A deafening blast of sound ripped through the air, and the ship erupted in a burst of fiery chaos. Flames and smoke poured from every crack, engulfing the vessel in an inferno. Wood splintered and metal groaned as the ship was torn apart, fragments flying in all directions, leaving only devastation in its wake.

The explosion had barely faded when Parker was struck by a barrage of splintered wood and jagged metal, the force of the blast sending him reeling. Mid-air, he tumbled, gasping for air, but the debris kept coming. Before he could brace himself, a sharp shard caught him across his side. Blood gushed from the wound, staining his feathers as he plunged into the icy waters below.

Parker! Garrick shouted telepathically, his mind laced with concern, as he watched what had happened.

Without hesitation, Garrick's two soldiers, Draven and Kael, flew down toward the water, their eyes sharp and focused, as they scanned every inch of the sea below. Within moments, they dove into the water after Parker.

Parker's head broke the surface of the icy-cold water with a desperate gasp. His wings felt heavy and unresponsive from the overwhelming pain of the explosion's force. He could feel his blood mixing with the seawater, and there was a bitter taste in his mouth. As his vision blurred, the world seemed to spin, but his mind was still sharp enough to know he wasn't going to last long like this.

Stay awake ... stay awake ... can't ... lose focus. TJ, Alessia, they need me ... I can't go down like this ... The mission's not over ... Eryndor ... He's still out there ... The world's still at risk ... I can't fail ... not now ... thought Parker, as he tried to stay afloat on top of the water.

Draven and Kael surfaced from the icy-cold waters below.

"We've got you, Parker. Hold on!" said Draven, gripping Parker's sodden feathers with his talons, straining to keep him above the churning water.

Parker's body felt like it was made of lead. Kael could see that every breath he took was a struggle. As he hooked his talons beneath Parker's Griffin shoulders, he heaved him out of the water and onto Draven's back. Together, they flew toward the shore. "Hold on, Parker, your family need you."

Within seconds, Draven and Kael reached the shoreline. Retracting their wings, they eased Parker onto the sand, their talons releasing him with careful control as they laid his bloodied body down with precision and care.

Garrick landed next to Parker, retracted his wings and shifted his talons back into hands. Kneeling beside him, he immediately assessed his wounds and tried to stem the flow of blood. "It's deep, but it's not fatal," Garrick muttered. "We need to get him to safety. Now!"

As William slid off the side of Rimmer's Griffin body, his mind was already working, calculating the best course of action. "We can't stay here. It's not safe. The mission still stands. Eryndor's out there, and the world's still in jeopardy. But we need to regroup, heal Parker, and find Eryndor before it's too late."

"I agree, William," said Garrick, looking across the shoreline. "I see you have already organized a portal. Thank you."

William nodded. "I have a healer ready and waiting at my home to help with Parker's wounds. So, let's get the hell out of here."

Garrick nodded in agreement. "Parker!" Garrick called, his voice low and steady, trying to rouse him. "We're going to get you back to the Gramaze mansion. Stay with us."

Parker's eyes flickered open, pain evident within them, "Eryndor … he's … still … out there," said Parker, his voice barely a whisper.

"We know," Garrick replied, his tone firm. "And we're going to stop him. Just hold on."

Parker barely acknowledged Garrick, before he fell unconscious.

Draven and Kael, now in their human forms, lifted Parker carefully and moved toward the portal gateway.

With one last look at the wreckage of the ship, William stepped through, leading the way to safety, along with the other Griffins and Lepidoptera Vampires.

* * *

Draven and Kael stepped into the Gramaze Lepidopteras' backyard, carrying Parker's limp body between them. His blood-soaked feathers left faint trails on the marble tiles of the Gramaze mansion's alfresco area. The faint scent of iron mixing with the tang of salt water lingered in the air.

"Place him on the ground," Violette commanded, her eyes focused on Parker. "What happened?" she demanded, kneeling beside him and immediately inspecting his wounds.

"The ship exploded before we could land," William said tersely. "Parker was caught in the blast and thrown into the water. He's lost a lot of blood."

Violette nodded, her hands already working. She hovered them over the deep gash in Parker's side, her magic radiating a soft lavender hue. The area seemed to quieten as her power worked its way through his body, knitting torn flesh, restoring what the explosion had damaged.

Parker groaned faintly and his eyelids fluttered, as Violette worked her magic.

"Stay still, Parker," Violette murmured softly. "You're safe now, but this will take a moment."

Parker's voice was hoarse as he struggled to speak. "I … I'm fine. Focus … on the mission …"

"Be quiet," Violette snapped gently, though her tone carried warmth. "You've done enough for now. Let me do my part."

As her hands moved with precision, the bleeding slowed and then stopped. Parker's shallow breaths began to deepen, his body visibly relaxing as the magic eased his pain and his wings retracted into his back.

"There," Violette said, sitting back on her heels. "The wound is closed, but he's not fully healed. He needs rest, and someone needs to monitor him for the next few hours."

At that moment, TJ stepped out onto the patio, her face pale with worry. "Parker!" she exclaimed, rushing to his side. "Is he going to be okay?"

"He'll be fine," Violette replied, rising to her feet. "But he needs time to recover."

TJ knelt beside him, gently brushing the damp feathers away from his face. "I'll stay with him. What can I do?"

Violette smiled faintly. "Make sure he stays hydrated and doesn't try to move too much. Men can be stubborn when they're hurt, so don't let him convince you otherwise."

Garrick stepped forward, his expression unreadable. "Draven, Kael … take Parker to their room."

The soldiers nodded, lifting Parker carefully.

Parker winced but said nothing, his eyes half-open as TJ walked beside them. As she watched him completely shift from Griffin back to human, she gently slipped her hand into his. Together, TJ walked inside with Draven and Kael, showing them the way to their room.

"I'll be fine, TJ," Parker muttered weakly.

She frowned at him. "You will be, but only if you let us help you."

As they arrived at TJ and Parker's bedroom, they settled Parker onto the bed. TJ pulled a blanket over him and perched herself on the edge, her hand never leaving his.

"I'm here, my love" she said calmly. "You're not going through this alone."

Parker managed a faint smile, his voice barely above a whisper. "Thanks, TJ … for everything."

As Draven and Kael silently left the room, Garrick waited at the doorway and said, "Get some rest. We'll regroup tomorrow and figure out how to stop Eryndor. The world's counting on us."

And with that, the room fell quiet, save for the soft sound of Parker's breathing as he drifted into much-needed sleep, with TJ by his side.

CHAPTER SIXTEEN

The warm glow of twilight bathed the Fae Kingdom in golden hues, as Kura, Alessia, Danielle and Christian emerged from a portal. Before them lay a breathtaking expanse of towering trees that shimmered with their own inner light, pathways paved with glowing crystals, and the distant silhouette of a grand palace carved into a mountain of translucent quartz.

"The Fae sure know how to throw a party. And this isn't even the celebration yet," stated Kura, her gaze darting to the floating lanterns that bobbed in the air, emitting a soft hum of melody.

Alessia's blue eyes sparkled with awe as she spun around, taking it all in. "Imagine living in a place like this. It's so … alive."

"Be careful, this kingdom is not always what it seems," advised Danielle. She had previously seen firsthand what the Fae were capable of, and the trickery they practiced.

Christian slipped his hands into his pockets. "Focus, guys! We're here for Aevyressa's crowning ceremony only. We need to be mindful that we are only visitors here."

"You are correct, Christian," stated Kura, her brow furrowed. "Even though I thought it would be customary to attend this event, and that it would be good for Alessia to make an appearance, I still think that we should keep our wits about us."

And I didn't want to antagonize the new Fae Queen by refusing to attend, especially since Alessia will soon become the Goddess of the River of Whispers and will have to deal with the Fae Kingdom one way or another throughout her life, Kura thought to herself.

The group made their way toward the palace, where an enormous crowd had gathered in the amphitheater below its steps. Fae of all shapes and sizes—some with gossamer wings, others with antlers or glowing eyes—stood in reverent silence as Aevyressa stepped forward onto a raised platform, dressed in an emerald gown that sparkled like dew in sunlight.

Elders of the Fae Kingdom, draped in ceremonial robes, encircled Aevyressa as she knelt, whispering incantations that would bind her to the land and its magic. "Aevyressa, of the royal line, do you pledge yourself to the land, its people, and the magic that binds us all?"

"With my heart and soul, I vow to protect and guide our kingdom with wisdom and strength," vowed Aevyressa.

"May the spirits of our ancestors watch over this moment, and lay their blessing upon you. May you lead with honor, grace and unyielding resolve," said the Elder. He lowered a crown of intertwined vines and gemstones, which glowed with ethereal light, onto her head as the land acknowledged her ascension.

"You may rise, Queen Aevyressa," said the Elder, as he and the other Elders stepped to the side.

Rising graciously, Aevyressa turned to face the crowd, her voice resonating clear and melodic, carried by the magic in the air. "Today, I honor the legacy of my ancestors, the dreams of my people, and the bonds that unite us with all realms. As Queen, I vow to protect this kingdom, and to guide it into a future of peace and prosperity."

The crowd erupted into cheers and a cascade of shimmering petals rained down from above.

"Now … let us celebrate," shouted Aevyressa.

The celebration began in earnest as music filled the air. Tables laden with fruits that glowed softly and goblets of sparkling nectar lined the gardens, while Fae and other noble beings danced joyfully.

Even while maintaining a sense of caution, Kura and Christian found themselves locked in a playful drinking contest with a pair of mischievous Fae twins, while Danielle wandered off to admire a fountain that appeared to be made of liquid starlight. Alessia, meanwhile, strolled through the gardens, drawn to the serene beauty of the glowing flora.

"You look troubled, dear," Aevyressa said gently, as she silently appeared beside Alessia, her gaze piercing, yet kind. The Queen's presence made Alessia feel as calm as the night sky, even if it did surprise her.

Alessia hesitated for a moment. "It's just … everything feels perfect here, like nothing could ever go wrong. It's hard to believe something so beautiful exists when … you know, the rest of the world is …" She trailed off, biting her lip.

"Perfect moments are rare," Aevyressa said, her voice laced with wisdom. "Cherish them, for they remind us what we're fighting for. But don't let them lull you into a false sense of security."

"Thank you for your wise words," said Alessia, nodding slightly to the Fae Queen.

"You are welcome, dear. I believe you are now the Goddess and Keeper of the Celestial Vault, Weaver of Eternal Light?" questioned Aevyressa, noticing the glowing runes and symbols on Alessia's hands and forearms.

"You are correct," interrupted Kura, her eyes flickering with a mixture of pride and curiosity, as she approached them. She had been listening in on their conversation. "Alessia's ascension is complete. The powers of the Celestial Vault now rest within her. The threads of light, woven into the very fabric of existence, are now hers to command." She glanced at Alessia, with a knowing smile tugging at her lips.

Alessia took a deep breath, her gaze distant for a moment as she let the weight of her new title settle. The glowing runes on her skin shimmered softly, a constant reminder of the immense power now coursing through her. She now needed to learn how to use her abilities.

"It's … overwhelming," Alessia admitted, her voice steady but laced with uncertainty. "I never imagined I would hold such power, let alone have the lives of so many entrusted to me."

Aevyressa's expression softened, her eyes full of understanding. "The light within you will guide you, Alessia. The stars themselves chose you for this path." She stepped closer, placing a gentle hand on Alessia's shoulder. "But you are not alone in this. If the Fae Kingdom can help in any way, please don't hesitate to ask."

"Thank you for your offer, but we only extend our trust to our own kind," Kura replied, her voice steady and regal, as she held her head high.

Aevyressa's gaze lingered for a moment, her expression unreadable, before she turned toward the revelry. "Very well," she said, her tone tinged with a hint of amusement. "It seems the festivities are well underway. I must make my presence known." She offered a curt nod. "Thank you for your attendance." She walked toward her guests.

Kura exchanged a knowing glance with Alessia and a quiet understanding passed between them.

As Aevyressa moved toward the heart of the celebration, the air around them seemed to shift, charged with the unspoken tension of the encounter.

Kura's expression softened and she lowered her voice, "We should remain vigilant, Alessia. The Fae may seem friendly, but their words often carry hidden meaning. Always remember: trust, especially with someone like Aevyressa, is a rare commodity."

Alessia nodded, her hand instinctively brushing the glowing runes on her skin. "Okay. I'm still trying to find my footing in all of this. It's overwhelming; everything's changing so quickly."

"Don't worry, we will face it together," Kura reassured her, her gaze firm and unyielding. "You have the Celestial Vault's light guiding you, but that doesn't mean you have to walk this path alone. Let's keep our eyes open and our hearts guarded."

Alessia looked toward the distant celebrations, the music and laughter echoing through the air. "I feel like there is much more at play here than I realize."

"You are correct, my dear," replied Kura.

Together, Kura and Alessia moved toward the fringes of the gathering, with Danielle and Christian by their sides, blending into the crowd as they kept watch on the other guests and dignitaries, ready for whatever may come next, until they returned to the River of Whispers.

CHAPTER SEVENTEEN

"Good morning, Parker and TJ," Renee greeted warmly, as she and William walked up the stairs to the alfresco area of the Gramaze mansion.

"Good morning," Parker and TJ replied in unison, offering a respectful nod to both Renee and William.

"How are you feeling today, Parker?" Renee asked, as she settled onto the cream-colored outdoor couch in front of them.

"A lot better, thank you. And I appreciate you letting me use your healer," Parker replied, leaning forward to place his empty coffee cup on the low table between them.

"You're welcome," William said, as he took a seat opposite them.

TJ's expression grew tense. "Have you heard any news about our daughter?"

William exhaled softly. "From what Kura has told me, Alessia is doing well. She's learning a lot more each day about the role she is destined to take on as Goddess of the River of Whispers."

William met Parker and TJ's gazes with quiet resolve. "As we've discussed, Alessia is next in line to ascend as the Goddess of the River of Whispers. Her great-grandmother, Kura, is far too old to take on this role. Alessia may never return to your farm. I think it's time you both start preparing yourselves for that possibility."

TJ's breath hitched, her fingers tightening around the armrest of the couch. "I know you said she might never come home, but I don't want to believe it." Her voice wavered, caught between disbelief and quiet devastation.

Parker clenched his jaw, his tanned hands pressing against his knees. "We took her in, we raised her, we *love* her. She is our daughter."

William nodded solemnly. "I know. And Alessia loves you both deeply. But this was always her destiny, whether she knew it or not."

TJ shook her head, blinking away the sting of tears. "She's just a girl, William. How can she be expected to give up everything—her family, her home—for something she never even asked for?"

"She isn't being forced," William assured them. "Kura has been guiding her, helping her understand. But the choice will ultimately be hers." He paused, letting the weight of his words settle. "And I believe, when the time comes, Alessia will do what she feels is right."

Parker exhaled sharply, rubbing a hand over his face. "And if what feels right to her is staying with us?"

William hesitated. "Then the River of Whispers will be left without its Goddess."

A heavy silence followed, broken only by the distant humming of the pool cleaner below.

"And what happens then?" asked TJ, her voice was barely above a whisper.

William looked away for a moment, his expression troubled. "Without a Goddess to guide it, the river's magic will fade. Its whispers will fall silent. And without that balance, the land it protects may begin to wither."

Parker's chest rose and fell with slow, controlled breaths. He hated this, hated the idea of Alessia being forced to choose between the life she had and the life she was meant for.

TJ reached for Parker's hand, gripping it tightly. "We need to talk to her," she said firmly. "Before any decisions are made."

William nodded. "I understand. I'll arrange for you to see her."

Parker exhaled, his shoulders stiff with tension. "Good." He stood abruptly, his chair scraping against the floor. "Because no matter what destiny says, Alessia is our daughter. And we're not letting her go without a fight." He turned to TJ, "Are we?"

Standing, TJ said, "I don't think this is our decision to make, my love. And until we can speak with Alessia, it's all speculation." She turned to William, "If you could organize for us to visit Alessia, at the River of Whispers, that would be most appreciated."

William nodded solemnly, his expression unreadable. "I understand. I'll make the arrangements. The river is a sacred place, but Alessia can meet with you there. Even if you could portal there, it will be difficult, both physically and emotionally. The River of Whispers is not just a place—it's alive, and it will test your resolve."

Parker's gaze narrowed. "We'll face whatever we have to. We're her parents. Nothing's going to keep us from her."

TJ placed a hand on his arm, her voice calm but firm. "Parker, we don't know what we're walking into. We need to approach this with an open heart, not a clenched fist."

He sighed, running a hand through his hair. "I know. But it doesn't make it any easier. This isn't just about letting go. This is about her being forced into something she didn't choose."

TJ gave him a soft but steady look. "Sometimes, our children are called to something greater than we can understand. We may not agree, but we have to respect her journey, even if it's painful."

Parker paused, his face softening as he looked at her. "I know. I just … I don't want to lose her. Not like this."

"I don't think we'll lose her," TJ said, squeezing his hand gently. "But we may have to let her go in a way we never expected."

* * *

A few days later, Parker and TJ stood before an ancient stone archway that shimmered with an iridescent glow—the portal to the River of Whispers sanctuary. The air was thick with anticipation as Lepidoptera Princess Violette placed a hand against the runes carved into the arch, activating the portal.

"This will take you directly to her," Violette said, stepping aside. "She's expecting you."

"Thank you," said Parker. He exchanged a tense glance with TJ, then squared his shoulders. "Let's go."

Stepping through the portal, they were engulfed in a rush of cool air and a faint whisper, like a thousand voices carried on the wind. When they emerged, they found themselves in a lush valley, with a winding river of crystal-blue water stretching before them. The land pulsed with an energy that was alive, in a way that was almost tangible.

And there, standing at the river's edge, was Alessia.

Her dark-brown hair seemed to gleam under the light of the setting sun, her eyes reflecting the glow of the water. She wore flowing robes embroidered with silver thread, a stark contrast to the farm clothes she once wore. But more than her attire, it was the shift in her presence that struck Parker and TJ the most—she stood taller, more confident, exuding a quiet power they had never seen before.

Alessia's face lit up with joy as she walked towards them. "Mum! Dad!"

TJ let out a broken laugh, as she rushed forward and pulled Alessia into a tight embrace. Parker followed, wrapping his arms around them both. For a moment, it was as if nothing had changed—she was just their daughter, safe in their arms.

But as Alessia pulled back, her smile faltered. "You're here because of what William told you, aren't you?" she said softly.

Parker crossed his arms. "Damn right we are."

TJ reached out, brushing a strand of hair from Alessia's face. "Sweetheart, we need to talk. About all of this." She gestured to the sanctuary, the river, the whispers in the air. "About what it means for you."

Alessia's expression turned serious. "I know. And I have so much to tell you." She took a deep breath, glancing toward the river. "But first, there's something you need to see."

She turned, leading them toward the water's edge. As Parker and TJ followed, a sense of foreboding settled over them.

Something was coming.

Something that would change everything.

As they approached the river, the gentle sound of the flowing water seemed to intensify, like the river itself was preparing to speak.

Alessia paused at the water's edge, her eyes searching the shimmering surface. "You've both heard the whispers, haven't you?" she asked quietly, almost as if she were listening for an answer from the river itself.

Parker and TJ exchanged a look. "I've heard something," Parker admitted. "But it's like nothing I've ever experienced before."

Alessia nodded. "It's the river's magic—its power. It's been calling to me, telling me things … guiding me. I can feel it in my bones, in my soul." She looked down at her glowing runes and symbols that were on her forearms and hands, flexing them as if testing the strength within them. "I was scared at first, but now I'm beginning to understand. I am the Goddess of the River of Whispers; it's my responsibility to protect it, to listen to its call."

TJ's heart ached as she watched the runes and symbols on her daughter's skin. *She is so different, yet the same.* "But Alessia … does that mean you're not coming home? You're going to stay here?"

Alessia turned to face them, her expression pained. "I don't want to leave you. I love you both more than anything." Her voice cracked slightly, betraying the raw emotion she was trying to hide. "But I can't ignore this. I can't ignore what I'm meant to do."

Parker clenched his fists, the desperation rising within him. "Is there no way for you to do both? Be our daughter, and still fulfill this … this Goddess role?"

Alessia's gaze softened, but she shook her head. "I will always be your daughter, but the river … it needs me. And I can't stay between two worlds forever. I don't know how it works yet, but when the time comes, I'll have to make a choice. This … this is my destiny. And I have to follow it."

The words hit TJ like a blow to the chest. She reached for Alessia's hands and held her hands firmly. "But what about us? What about everything we've built together? Your home … your life with us?"

"I'll never forget it, or both of you. You're my family," Alessia said, her eyes shimmering with tears. "But this—this is part of me, too. I don't know how to explain it. I've only just started to understand it myself."

As the words hung in the air, a sudden tremor passed through the ground, rippling the surface of the river. A deep, almost mournful sound echoed from within the water, like a distant voice calling for attention.

Alessia froze. "It's happening," she whispered. "I can feel it … the power is awakening."

TJ looked at Kura, who had appeared silently behind them. "What's happening?" asked TJ.

Kura glanced at Alessia, then back at Parker and TJ. "The river's magic is strengthening. The final test of her ascension is coming. She must embrace her role fully, or it may consume her—and the river itself."

A dark shadow moved across the water, a ripple in the fabric of reality itself. The wind howled and the whispers of the river grew louder, more urgent.

"It's not just about Alessia's choice anymore," Kura said. "The balance is shifting. If she doesn't take on her role as the Goddess, everything connected to the river could fall into chaos."

Parker's eyes widened as he turned to Alessia. "What do we do? How do we stop this?"

Alessia closed her eyes and the river's power swirled around her. "I don't know. But I have to try. I have to choose the river."

TJ's heart broke, but she nodded in agreement, her voice trembling. "We'll support you, no matter what. Just … don't forget where you came from. Don't forget us."

Alessia gave a small, bittersweet smile. "I never could."

With that, the river's power surged and the air around them grew heavy with magic. Something ancient, something dangerous, was awakening—and Alessia's path was set.

The river's whispers turned into a chorus, a cacophony of voices that seemed to reach into the very fabric of reality. The ground beneath them rumbled again, stronger this time, sending small tremors through the air.

Alessia stood tall, her hands lifted as though she were embracing the power swirling around her. The water at her feet began to glow, ripples of silvery-blue light emanating outward, pulsing with each beat of her heart.

Parker and TJ took a cautious step back, sensing the magnitude of the transformation that was unfolding before them. "Alessia … please," TJ whispered, her voice a mix of pleading and fear. "Don't let it take you away from us."

Alessia's eyes flickered with a deep, ethereal light. "I'm not leaving you, Mum. I'm just … becoming something more." Her voice was different now, resonating with an otherworldly echo that seemed to carry the weight of centuries. "This is what I was meant to do. But that doesn't mean I have to forget who I am, or who I was."

The whispers of the river grew louder, swirling around them like a storm, each voice distinct, filled with ancient wisdom and longing. Alessia's expression grew intense, her brow furrowing as if she was struggling to understand the flood of voices she was hearing.

The river itself seemed to rise, its waters twisting and bending unnaturally, reaching toward the sky. A bright, blinding light began to form at the center of the river's surface. Alessia's hands clenched into fists and her body vibrated with the raw power of the transformation.

"This is it," Kura said, her voice strained. "The river is calling her, testing her. She must accept the power and the role, or it will consume her."

Parker's heart raced, his protective instincts surging. "There has to be a way to stop this—something we can do to keep her safe!"

Kura shook her head gravely. "There's no stopping it now. The river chooses its next Goddess. But Alessia has a choice in how she accepts it. If she doesn't fully embrace it, she risks losing herself to it."

TJ stepped forward, her voice trembling but resolute. "Alessia, listen to me. You don't have to do this alone. We'll help you—whatever it takes. But you don't have to sacrifice everything you are."

Alessia's eyes found hers, filled with a strange clarity. "I don't want to lose myself either, Mum. But I have to trust in what's happening. I can feel it inside me. I can feel the river calling to me." She took a deep breath, her body glowing brighter now, her aura expanding, blending with the shimmering light of the river. "This isn't just a responsibility—it's part of who I am now. And I think … I think it's a part of all of us, in a way."

The river's light intensified and a wave of power surged forward, enveloping Alessia. The force of it knocked Parker and TJ back, but they held their ground, eyes locked on their daughter as the transformation took place. The air around them crackled with energy, and the whispering voices of the river seemed to merge into a single, unified roar.

For a moment, everything was still.

Then, as suddenly as it had begun, the power receded and the river's surface calmed. The bright light faded, leaving Alessia standing in the center of the water, her hair flowing around her like a halo, her eyes now glowing with an unmistakable luminescence. Her presence was overwhelming, yet serene.

"I … I did it," Alessia whispered, her voice softer now, yet carrying an unearthly echo, as she walked out of the water. "I've become the Goddess of the River of Whispers."

Parker and TJ approached slowly, awe and fear mixing in their hearts. "You're still *you*, right?" TJ asked, her voice trembling.

Alessia smiled, the warmth of her expression familiar yet different. "I am still me, Mum. But I am also … so much more. I understand now. I'm a part of this, and it's a part of me." She looked at them, her gaze filled with love and pain. "And I'm still your daughter."

Tears welled up in TJ's eyes, but she smiled through them. "We love you, Alessia. No matter who you are, no matter what you become."

Parker reached out, his strong hands resting on her shoulders. "You'll always be our girl."

Alessia nodded, her expression both proud and sorrowful. "I know. And I will never forget that. But now, I must fulfill my role. The river needs me. It's more than a duty; it's my purpose."

A low rumble passed through the ground, as if the river itself acknowledged Alessia's acceptance of her destiny. The land seemed to breathe with new life, the magic of the river strengthened by her ascension.

As they stood there, surrounded by the peaceful yet powerful flow of the river, Alessia's transformation felt complete. But an uneasy truth lingered in the air. The balance had shifted and the river's whispers, now part of her, would guide her path forward, toward a future that could never be the same again. They all knew that the true challenge had only just begun.

CHAPTER EIGHTEEN

As the sun dipped below the fiery landscape of Hanksville, Utah, the sky ignited with hues of deep crimson and violet, streaking the horizon in a breathtaking display. Suddenly, a violent ripple tore through the air, crackling like lightning and shattering the evening's tranquility, as a portal unfurled above the rugged terrain, its swirling energy distorting the fading light.

From its depths, a surge of dark energy swelled as Eryndor stepped through, his boots striking the parched earth, kicking up dust, his hooded cloak billowing around him. The Ethereal Nexus Amulet, which he wore around his neck, gleamed ominously against his chest, pulsing with an unsettling glow.

Behind him, three of his most loyal minions followed—Malrik, a gaunt sorcerer with eyes like frozen steel; Veyda, a lethal warrior with twin daggers at his hips; and Drogan, a hulking brute whose strength alone could crush bones to dust.

Eryndor surveyed their surroundings and his lips curled into a smirk. "The perfect graveyard for those who dare oppose me. This wasteland shall soon tremble beneath the power of the Cauldron of Chaos."

Veyda knelt on the sand and pressed his hand to the ground. "The earth beneath us is hollowed and riddled with passageways. It will serve well as our sanctuary."

With a sharp nod to his minion, Eryndor unleashed a pulse of spectral energy, sending a tremor rippling through the earth. As a jagged fissure cracked open before them, it revealed a hidden cavern below and, one by one, they descended into the darkness.

With a wave of his hand, Eryndor magically manufactured some torches, which hung along the cave's walls, and watched them flare to life, their eerie blue flames cast flickering shadows across the uneven rock.

In the heart of the cavern, Eryndor mystically produced a massive, ancient cauldron; its surface was etched with intricate glowing runes and symbols pulsating with malevolent power. "The time has come, my beauty."

"Place the Icefire Blades into the cauldron, Malrik," instructed Eryndor.

"Yes, Sire," Malrik replied. With a solemn gesture, he drew the Twin Icefire Blades from a blackened satchel he was carrying. As his hands steadied, he carefully lifted the lid of the cauldron and reverently placed the blades at its base inside.

"You're next, Veyda," instructed Eryndor.

"Yes, Sire." Veyda nodded and followed suit, drawing from the satchel he had been carrying the aged tome that had the Golden Chalice inside. He hesitated a moment before setting it inside the cauldron, sensing the immense power radiating from its pages.

As Eryndor watched Veyda step away from the cauldron, he indicated for Drogan to go next.

Drogan nodded and reached into a leather pouch at his waist, retrieving a small, ornate ring—the Fae's Golden Ring. As he stepped up to the cauldron and placed the ring inside, a deep, resonant hum started to echo through the chamber and the runes on the cauldron started to flare brighter as its dark magic began to stir.

With his gaze intensifying on the cauldron, Eryndor reached for the Ethereal Nexus Amulet and the magic it carried responded to him, crackling in the air like a living entity. "We only need the Golden Chalice released from this damn book, then we are complete."

"I believe, from reading the ancient laws, that the ritual cannot be performed without the blood of a Fae," said Malrik, looking at Eryndor.

Eryndor stiffened, his mind not previously knowing this, but all the while calculating. "I don't think we will be able to get close enough to the Fae Kingdom, so that is out of the equation." A slow, wicked smile spread across his face. "Danielle, Xanthia?" The names rolled off his tongue like a whispered promise of doom.

He turns to his minions, his eyes gleaming with cruel intent. "We shall make preparations to secure a Fae's blood—starting with a visit to Bagnolet, France. But first, we need to pay a visit to the River of Whispers."

A chilling silence fell over the cavern, broken only by the steady hum of dark energy emanating from the Cauldron of Chaos. Outside, the desert wind howled, carrying the promise of bloodshed to come.

* * *

The shimmering moon that reflected off the silver waters of the River of Whispers had an ethereal glow that cast long shadows across the banks. The air hummed with power, as Alessia stood near the water's edge, flanked by Kura, Danielle and Christian, trying to invoke her celestial powers. The three guardians of the river stood in a triangular formation around them all, cloaked in shifting mist as they hovered nearby—an unspoken warning to any who dared to intrude.

They all turned when a sudden gust of wind howled through the trees, and the air rippled, thickening like molten glass. Then, in a burst of dark violet energy, a portal tore open, revealing Eryndor, clad in obsidian armor, his piercing green eyes burning with cruel determination. Behind him, Malrik, Veyda and Drogan followed, their presence thick with menace. They stepped forward and the portal sealed behind them, like a mouth snapping shut.

"Ah, I see you've been expecting me. How considerate of you all to gather here," said Eryndor, sarcastically. "This will save us time. Alessia, come!" Eryndor placed his hand out front and curled his fingers into his palm, magically pulling her toward him.

Alessia fought to hold her ground with her powers, but it was futile, because Eryndor was too powerful, his strength overwhelming her.

"You should have stayed in whatever pit you crawled out of, Eryndor. She won't be going anywhere with you," stated Christian. His muscles coiled like a predator ready to strike, as he stepped toward Eryndor and his minions.

Eryndor chuckled, a sound like rusted metal grinding together. Before anyone could react, he lifted his other hand and a dark energy slithered between his fingers like liquid night. As the shadows writhed across the ground, he chanted in an ancient, guttural tongue.

"This is forbidden magic! You cannot ..." stated the Guardian of the River's Source.

"Oh, but I can," interrupted Eryndor. "And I will."

The three guardians stepped forward, trying to counter his magic, but their power barely flickered against Eryndor's powerful sorcery, as they were flung up against a tree, knocking them unconscious.

A pulse of Vampire energy exploded outward, as Christian and Danielle ran toward Eryndor and braced themselves for what was about to happen. But before they reached Eryndor, the shadows surged up and wrapped around them, turning solid, like iron shackles. The two Lepidoptera Vampires thrashed, their immense strength pushing against the restraints, but Eryndor's spell held them both upright against a dense tree.

"Let them go!" demanded Kura, her eyes wide with fear, but hands steady, as she tried to raise her own magic in a counterspell. A golden glow erupted from her fingertips, tendrils of light weaving through the darkness. For a moment, it seemed to be working—until Malrik flicked his wrist, sending a slicing wave of dark energy through Kura's spell. It shattered like glass and Kura collapsed to one knee, weakened.

Alessia's eyes blazed with divine fury. Her dark-brown hair whipped around her in an unseen wind and her skin glowed faintly with celestial power. She stood tall, her shoulders squared and her gaze burning with defiance, as she lifted her hands and summoned the celestial power of the stars and rivers combined. A shockwave rippled outward, forcing Eryndor and his minions back. "I won't be going anywhere with you, Eryndor," stated Alessia, heatedly.

"That's where you're wrong, my dear," Eryndor said, with a chilling smirk. He murmured one final incantation and the shadows beneath Alessia twisted and stretched, forming a black mirror that trapped her magic within its depths. Before she could leap away, an invisible force seized her, locking her in place. Gasping, she struggled against the unseen restraints tightening around her, swallowing her whole.

"No …" screamed Alessia. Her cries were cut short as the darkness and ground consumed her.

The ground snapped shut and the shadows dissipated, as Eryndor and his minions quickly portaled out of the River of Whispers.

As the last trace of Eryndor's magic faded, Danielle and Christian broke free.

"Shit!" said Christian, his brow furrowed with frustration.

"We are too late," stated Danielle, staring down at the empty space where the black hole had been—the same one Alessia vanished through. "Where would he have taken her?"

"I don't know," Kura admitted, as she came to stand alongside Danielle and Christian.

"We must contact William to let him know what has happened here," stated Christian.

"I agree," said Kura.

Silence fell over the riverbank, as everyone came to terms with what had happened, and Kura contacted William telepathically.

* * *

Alessia's eyes opened slowly; they felt heavy with exhaustion. Darkness loomed around her, broken only by the faint glimmer of torches on the cavern walls. Her mind fought through the lingering fog, trying to piece together where she was and how she'd gotten there. The rough bite of cold stone against her cheek sent a shiver down her spine. When she shifted, pain flared in her stiff limbs. A distant drip of water echoed through the cavern. The air was dry, yet tinged with a faint metallic scent. Blinking away the haze, she pushed herself upright, wincing as her wrists throbbed where restraints had once bound them. But they were gone now.

Where am I?

A slow clap echoed through the cave, sending another shiver down her spine.

"Finally, you're awake, Goddess!" Eryndor's voice was smooth, almost entertained. His silhouette was barely visible against the dim torchlight, his dark cloak barely brushing the ground as he stepped closer.

Alessia swallowed her unease and glared at him. "Where am I?"

"Utah, if you must know. Far from your precious River of Whispers, and even further from anyone who can save you." Eryndor smirked, crouching to meet her eyes. "Now that we have the pleasantries out of the way, let's get down to business."

Her fingers curled into fists. "What do you want?"

Eryndor straightened and gestured to a stone pedestal nearby. On it lay an ancient book, its cover worn and cracked with age. The golden markings glowed faintly, pulsing like a heartbeat. He stepped aside, giving her a full view.

"Do you know what that is?" Eryndor asked. "And do you know what's inside it?"

Alessia shook her head. "No."

His expression darkened. In one swift motion, he grabbed her by the wrist and yanked her to her feet, forcing her closer to the pedestal. "That, my dear, has something I want and only you are able to obtain it for me," stated Eryndor. "You see, you're going to open that book and take out the Golden Chalice, whether you want to or not."

Alessia gritted her teeth and tried to jerk free, but his grip was unyielding. "Humph!" Alessia stiffened. "I'm not doing this."

"Oh, but you will." His smirk widened. "Take the chalice out of the book, or else …"

She let out a bitter laugh. "Go to hell, Eryndor. I'd rather die than help you."

Eryndor sighed as if disappointed. Then, with a flick of his fingers, the torches lining the cave walls flared higher, illuminating the space fully. Alessia's stomach lurched when she saw the symbols etched into the stone surrounding them—runes of blood magic, ancient and dangerous.

"You think you have a choice?" he asked, his voice taking on an eerie calm. "If you choose to refuse me now, pain will be a remarkable motivator. I wonder how much you can endure before your resolve shatters."

Alessia refused to meet his gaze, and her breath grew shallow and uneven. *Is he bluffing? He has to be!*

Eryndor leaned in, his breath hot against her ear. "Shall we find out?"

When she remained silent, Eryndor lifted his hand and the runes in the caverns around them ignited with a blood-red glow.

A searing pain shot through Alessia's body, as though her veins were on fire. Gasping, she dropped to her knees as the agony coursed through her.

"This is only the beginning," Eryndor murmured, watching her with cold detachment. "The longer you resist, the worse it will get. Open the book, Alessia. Take the chalice out. Or you will beg me to end your suffering."

Alessia lifted her chin, defiance burning in her eyes. "I will never help you, Eryndor," she spat, her voice raw but resolute, as she forced the words out through her clenched teeth.

Eryndor smirked, his eyes cold and calculating. "You don't have a choice, Alessia," he said, his voice low and menacing. "You'll do as I say, one way or another." His gaze darkened as he stepped closer. "And if it takes breaking you to make you understand, then so be it." With a swift motion, he raised his hand and darkness enveloped her, pulling her into unconsciousness.

CHAPTER NINETEEN

"Knock, knock," William said, standing in the doorway of Parker and TJ's bedroom at the Gramaze mansion.

Parker looked up from his newspaper and noticed William. "Good evening. Come on in," he said, gesturing for him to enter. "Is there something on your mind?"

"I've got some news," William replied, stepping into the room. "Is TJ around? She needs to hear this too."

"Good evening, William. Is everything alright?" TJ asked as she emerged from the en suite bathroom.

"Good evening, TJ. Yes, everything is fine. I wanted to let you both know, from my conversation with Kura earlier today, it sounds like Alessia is settling in well. So … in saying this, I believe it's safe for you both to return to your farm and resume your lives," William said.

"Really? Thank you, William," TJ said, relief in her voice. "As much as we've appreciated your hospitality, I'd love to get back home and find some semblance of normalcy."

"What about Eryndor? Will he still be lingering around?" Parker asked, placing his newspaper on the low table in front of him.

"At this point, we're unsure where Eryndor is hiding," William replied. "However, I'll be sending two members of my coven with you for protection, until everything has settled down."

"Thank you, William. We appreciate that," said Parker, standing to shake his hand. "When will we be able to portal to our home?"

"Right now, if you are ready?" replied William, shaking his hand.

"That works for us. We can be ready in say … twenty minutes," said Parker, glancing at TJ.

TJ nodded in agreement and smiled.

"Okay! When you are ready, I will meet you in the back garden area," said William.

"Thank you, William," said TJ, as she watched him walk toward the doorway.

As TJ packed her clothes and toiletries into a backpack, she looked over at Parker and said, "I didn't realize how much I missed the farm," her voice tinged with longing. "It'll be nice to have some peace and quiet again."

Parker nodded, his expression thoughtful. "I know. But it's going to take some time to adjust, after everything that's happened, especially with Alessia not being there anymore. I sure am going to miss our girl."

"Yeah, me too," stated TJ, as she pictured Alessia's face when they visited her at the River of Whispers, a few days prior.

After Parker and TJ finished gathering their things, they made their way to the back gardens, where William was waiting, beside the swirling vortex of an open portal.

Two figures, cloaked in shadows and wearing the unmistakable insignia of the Lepidoptera Vampires, flanked William. The Vampires' butterfly tattoos on the back of their necks glowed faintly in the shifting light, their eyes sharp with alertness.

"This is Stephen and Kelan. They will accompany you," said William.

TJ raised an eyebrow as she glanced at the two Lepidopteras. "Do we really need them?"

"They will make sure you both get home safely," William replied. "Eryndor is still a threat, and I won't take any chances."

"Right!" said TJ, nodding.

Parker nodded in understanding, his fingers instinctively tightening around TJ's hand. "Better to be safe than sorry, I suppose."

"Ready?" William asked, his eyes flicking between the two of them.

Parker gave a nod. "Ready."

"Goodbye, my friends," said William, as he shook Parker's then TJ's hands. "Be safe and, please … don't hesitate to call if you need help."

"Thank you for everything," said TJ, shaking William's hand.

"Yes, thank you, my friend. We will never forget what you have done for our family," said Parker, clasping William's forearm. "And if you need me to return, to help with Eryndor, I am only too happy to help out with that."

"Thank you. I appreciate the offer," replied William. "Whenever you're ready." He gestured toward the portal.

Parker looked at TJ, his gaze steady and reassuring. "Let's go home, my love."

TJ nodded in agreement and placed her hand in his.

As Parker and TJ stepped into the portal, the air seemed to hum with power. They felt the familiar tug of the vortex pulling them through, the colors swirling in a dazzling blur around them. The sudden rush of wind and light swirled around them, but this time, they weren't alone.

As they passed through the portal their surroundings blurred, until—*snap*—it was gone and the soft, familiar scent of the farm's earthy air hit them almost immediately.

Before Parker and TJ had a chance to take a full breath of relief, the two Lepidoptera Vampires fell into defensive stances in front of them, their eyes scanning the area.

Parker's heart skipped a beat and TJ's grip on his hand tightened.

"Something's off," Stephen whispered, his eyes darting around everywhere.

Parker's senses heightened. He looked around, but the farm seemed peaceful, calm even—too calm.

Then the air shifted and a shadow appeared on the veranda of the house; a figure stepped into the clearing. Eryndor!

"Well, well," Eryndor's voice rang out, dripping with malice. "I knew you couldn't stay hidden forever."

The two Lepidoptera Vampires surged forward, eyes blazing with power, then froze mid-stride as if invisible chains had locked their limbs in place.

"What the hell do you want, Eryndor?" Kelan spat, trying to step forward despite the unseen force. "You're not welcome here."

Eryndor grinned, his eyes narrowing. "How quaint. But I don't think you're in any position to stop me."

Before either Vampire could react, Eryndor moved with blinding speed. He lunged forward, his hands flashing out. In one fluid motion, he struck both of them across the face, knocking them unconscious with an effortless precision.

TJ gasped, her eyes widening in shock. "No!"

Parker moved to step forward, but Eryndor's voice stopped him cold.

"Ah, ah," Eryndor crooned, his tone mocking. "Not so fast." With a flick of his wrist, a shadowy mist surrounded Parker and TJ.

TJ and Parker froze, held in place by Eryndor's power that twisted the air around them.

Eryndor approached slowly, savoring their fear. "You see, you were never safe. I just made it look that way," Eryndor said, his eyes gleaming with malicious delight. "You're both far too important to be left alone. And now, you'll make the perfect leverage."

"What do you want?" Parker growled, struggling against the invisible bonds holding him.

"Alessia," Eryndor spat, his grin widening. "I'm going to make her suffer. And you," he said, turning to TJ, "are going to help me make that happen."

"We would never help you hurt our daughter," stated Parker. He tried to wriggle free from Eryndor's hold, but it was to no avail.

Eryndor smirked and outstretched his hand. His shadowed tendrils wrapped around them, pulling them toward him. "Take them," he ordered to his minions, his voice filled with satisfaction.

With a sudden burst of dark energy, he portaled them both to Utah, leaving the farm behind. The quiet of the land was now shattered by the promise of more chaos. The two unconscious Vampires lay forgotten in the garden, a faint whisper of power lingering in the air.

CHAPTER TWENTY

Stephen's eyes snapped open, his Vampire senses flaring to life. Instinct took over as he leapt to his feet, his mind racing.

Eryndor ... the McCrindles. Fuck, where are they? With his Lepidoptera Vampire abilities sharpening his sight and his awareness already on heightened alert, Stephen quickly scanned the grounds, only to find that the McCrindles were gone, along with Eryndor and his minions.

"Kelan, wake up, man!" Stephen shouted, nudging him hard.

Kelan groaned, blinking up at him. "What the hell happened?" he asked, rubbing his head.

Stephen extended a hand and hauled him to his feet. "Eryndor—that's what happened. He's taken Parker and TJ. William is going to have our balls for this."

Kelan straightened, his expression hardening. "Before we call William, let's sweep the property."

"Good idea. But we stick together. No telling who's still lurking," Stephen cautioned.

"Agreed!" said Kelan.

They ran at Vampire speed throughout the house and grounds, only to find no one on the property, except for the workers.

As Kelan and Stephen stepped onto the back porch, which overlooked the whole property, Stephen took his mobile phone from his pocket and dialed William's number.

"Yes?" William's voice was sharp, answering immediately, as he sat in his office chair.

"Sire, we have a problem. When we exited the portal, Eryndor and his minions were lying in wait for us. They have taken Parker and TJ. What would you like us to do?" said Stephen.

"Fuck!" William growled, pushing to his feet, raking a hand through his hair. Taking a deep breath, he asked, "I assume you've already checked the property?"

"Yes, Sire. House, too," replied Stephen.

William clenched his jaw. "How the hell are we going to beat this bastard?"

Movement in the doorway caught William's eye. Violette stood there, listening to their conversation, her nostrils flaring in frustration, as she shook her head.

Tell them a portal is coming their way to collect them. She turned and sprinted toward the garden.

"A portal will be there in a few seconds to pick you both up. Be ready!" stated William. He hung up his phone abruptly.

"Yes, Sire," replied Stephen. He knew William didn't hear the last words he'd spoken, as the line had already gone dead.

Stephen pocketed his phone and glanced at Kelan. "You catch that?"

"Loud and clear," Kelan said. "Looks like we're in deep shit when we get back." He pointed toward the swirling portal that had appeared. "Our ride's here."

"Let's get the fuck out of here," said Stephen.

Without hesitation, they ran toward the portal at Vampire speed.

* * *

The glass doors of the operations room slid open and Stephen and Kelan stepped inside. The room was full of

Lepidoptera Vampires and several Ironclaw Griffins, all engaged in quiet conversation.

"Take a seat," William ordered, watching them enter.

"Yes, Sire," they replied in unison, quickly moving to the nearest chairs.

"Right, quieten down, everyone." William looked around the table at all of the faces.

The room fell quiet, as everyone looked to William for details of their next mission.

William turned to Brock, who was situated at the computer behind them and asked, "Have there been any sightings of them as yet?"

"Nothing, Sire. It's like they have disappeared," stated Brock, as his fingers continued their search.

"Keep searching," instructed William. He turned to Garrick, "Do you have any idea where Eryndor might be hiding?"

"No. We've torn apart every derelict ship, searched the docks and ports, even combed through the hidden inlets he's used before, but he's changed his patterns," Garrick said, frustration tightening his voice. "It's obvious he knows we're hunting him. No one's seen so much as a shadow."

"Right! Anything on the grapevine, Grayson?" asked William, to his second in charge.

Grayson gave a curt shake of his head. "No chatter, Sire."

Garrick pushed his chair back and addressed Stephen and Kelan. "Guys, when Parker and TJ were taken, did they have phones on them?" questioned Garrick.

"They could have. That is not something that we were privy to, though," said Stephen.

Garrick turned to Brock, who was still sitting at the operations room computer. "Brock … If Parker or TJ did have their mobile phone's location turned on, is there any chance you could find them from their mobile signal?" questioned Garrick.

"Yes, there is a chance, but only if there is a telecommunications tower nearby," replied Brock.

"Check that out, Brock," ordered William. He raked a hand through his hair and took a deep breath.

"Yes, Sire," Brock replied, already pulling up Parker and TJ's numbers and initiating a location search.

The room fell into silence as everyone waited for Brock to respond. The only sound in the room was the quiet tapping of Brock's fingers against the keyboard.

Brock's fingers flew over the keyboard and his eyes scanned the screen. A tense pause stretched before he exhaled sharply. "I've got something—a weak signal from TJ's mobile. It's bouncing off a tower near the Utah Desert. Not exact, but it does narrow it down." He then positioned a satellite over the area.

"The Utah Desert?" Garrick frowned. "That's a hell of a place to hide. Wide open, barely any cover."

"Unless he's underground," Grayson muttered.

William's jaw tightened. "That's a possibility. We need more intel before making a move."

Kelan leaned forward. "Sire, if we wait too long, we risk losing them. We should at least send a scout team."

"I agree. We can be in and out before Eryndor knows we're there," stated Stephen.

William drummed his fingers on the table, thinking. Then he glanced at Violette, who had been silently listening. "Thoughts?"

She crossed her arms. "A direct attack is reckless. If he's expecting us, it's a trap. But if we send in a small team under cover, we might get close enough to confirm their location, before engaging."

William nodded. "Fine. Stephen, Kelan, you'll go with Garrick and two of his best Griffins. No engaging—strictly recon. If you find them, you report back. Understood?"

"Yes, Sire," Stephen and Kelan said in unison.

Garrick, who was already standing, said, "We'll be ready in five."

As the team prepared, Violette stepped closer to William. Her voice was low, meant only for him. "And if it is a trap?" she asked quietly.

William's expression darkened. "Then we spring one of our own traps."

"Sounds like a plan … I will see you outside, in front of the portal," said Violette, confidently.

William nodded in agreement and watched her stride purposefully toward the glass sliding door.

We are certainly lucky to have you on board with us, Princess, thought William, as he remembered the days, years ago, when Violette first found out about his coven, and her lineage to Queen Talitha.

It is I who is lucky to have such a wonderful family, thought Violette, as she continued to the back gardens.

CHAPTER TWENTY-ONE

Beneath the towering red cliffs of Utah, dusk bled into night, as a bitter wind whispered secrets of ancient magic and darker intentions. Hidden deep in a labyrinthine cavern carved by time and despair, Alessia rose to her feet. The chains that had held her were now gone, and as she crept forward, every step she took was weighted with a sense of dread. The muted glow of enchanted torches revealed eerie runes etched into the stone. At the center of this macabre sanctuary lay the massive, rune-inscribed book perched upon a crumbling pedestal.

As she approached, Alessia's heart pounded in her ears. The silence was broken only by the soft scuffle of her footsteps and the distant sound of chains rattling. Uncertain and anxious, she reached for the book and its pages quivered, as if stirred by an unseen breath, as Alessia picked it up. But then, in the far recesses of the chamber, a faint sound tugged at her soul; muffled cries that sent shivers racing down her spine.

What is that? No ... it can't be ... thought Alessia, as she clutched the book to her chest.

Drawn to the sound, like a moth to a flame, she edged around a massive column draped in shadows. There, suspended in the dim light, she witnessed a sight that nearly shattered her resolve; her parents, TJ and Parker, were bound by enchanted chains, their eyes wide with fear and pleading for deliverance.

Before she could cry out, a voice as smooth and dark as the surrounding void slithered through the chamber. "Ah,

Alessia, ever so punctual. I was beginning to wonder if you would join us."

Alessia's breath caught in her throat as she stepped back, trembling. "What have you done to my parents?"

"This is all your doing, Goddess," stated Eryndor, draped in robes of midnight, with symbols of ancient malice that carried an air of malevolent grandeur. His eyes, lit with cruel amusement, swept over her with a predator's anticipation.

"Mum … Dad!"

Alessia's parents' eyes met hers, silently begging for rescue, amidst their agony.

Eryndor's lips curved into a sinister smile as he let the moment of recognition simmer in the charged air.

"Let them go. They have nothing to do with any of this," pleaded Alessia.

"Your dear parents serve a very practical purpose in our arrangement. You see, I require your unique gift—the divine power that lies dormant within you—to extract the Golden Chalice from that book," stated Eryndor, indicating the ancient book she was holding.

Alessia's defiance burned within her, even as despair clawed at her heart. "I will never serve your vile designs, Eryndor. Release them at once!"

The sorcerer's tone shifted to cold and venomous as he stepped closer and his shadow swallowed the light. "Obstinacy is a luxury you can ill afford, my dear. Refuse, and your precious parents shall suffer a fate far worse than mere chains. Choose wisely."

For a harrowing moment, the cavern seemed to hold its breath. Alessia's eyes darted between the ancient tome and her parents' pained expressions. The weight of an impossible choice pressed upon her soul. Tears welled as she whispered a heartbroken apology. "Forgive me, Guardians, Kura … I'm so sorry."

Her hands trembled as she placed one on the cover of the book. The pages whispered under her fingertips, brittle and faintly fragrant with dust and time. Alessia's breath caught in her throat as they turned to the image of the chalice, an inked drawing that seemed to shimmer in the dim light, as though alive and waiting for her gaze. She ran her fingers across the gilded illustration and the ink began to ripple like liquid. With a slow, deliberate motion, she curled her hand into a fist and pulled. The page flowed like silk and the gleaming Golden Chalice, recognizing Alessia as Stjernefrída's daughter, tore free from the parchment.

Holding it in her hand, Alessia noticed that its surface shimmered with an ethereal radiance and every engraved detail on the chalice told of a forgotten legend, and of its divine power.

Eryndor's eyes widened with a disturbing mix of triumph and adoration, as he approached the chalice, plucking it from Alessia's hands. Slowly, deliberately, his long fingers caressed its surface as if worshipping this relic from a lost era.

"Behold … the chalice of eternal luminescence," stated Eryndor, righteously holding the Golden Chalice in the air. Every curve, every delicate etching, hummed with a power beyond mortal comprehension. "How exquisite is its beauty, and now it's destined to be the key to my ascension."

All of Eryndor's minions cheered. Their voices a discordant symphony of malice and devotion, that reverberated off the cavern walls, blending with the sizzle of dark magic that now pulsed in the air.

With a ceremonious air, Eryndor turned toward the center of the chamber where the Cauldron of Chaos awaited—a monstrous, obsidian vessel surging with tumultuous energy. Resting inside it were the legendary Twin Icefire Blades, their dual natures of blistering heat and piercing frost shimmering in the low light, and the delicate Fae's Golden Ring, its luster captivating and enigmatic.

Methodically, as though performing a sacred rite, Eryndor placed the glowing chalice inside the cauldron, then arranged the Icefire Blades on either side and slipped the Fae ring into the circle of relics. The artifacts resonated in unison, their combined energies casting eerie, dancing shadows on the cavern walls. "One final piece remains—a Fae's blood—and then the path to unbridled dominion will open before me."

Alessia's anguished gaze remained fixed on her ensnared parents, while her inner world had been shattered by the realization of how deeply she had been coerced into this dark ritual. The air in the cavern crackled with imminent chaos as her heart pounded with the dual torment of loss and reluctant duty.

"Now that I've done what you asked, Eryndor, release my parents. They had nothing to do with this," Alessia demanded, tossing the ancient book to the ground.

"All in good time, my dear," Eryndor replied with a sly smile, before flicking his wrist.

A force slammed into Alessia, hurling her against the cavern wall, near her parents.

Alessia's jaw clenched as she steadied herself, pain radiating through her body from the impact. Her breath came in short, sharp gasps, but her eyes burned with unwavering determination. A trickle of blood traced a path down her temple, ignored, as she tightened her fists.

I will find a way to undo this, she vowed silently, her gaze locking onto Eryndor with defiance.

"Your rebelliousness has already been catalogued, dear Alessia. With your reluctant sacrifice, the gears of destiny have been set into motion and your world will soon learn the true meaning of chaos," Eryndor stated callously.

Alessia's inner turmoil roiled like a tempest, caught between a desperate love for her parents and the unyielding chains of coercion. In that fraught instant, every heartbeat was a silent promise of retribution and redemption, a promise that even the darkest of evils could one day be undone.

"Leave her alone! She's done what you wanted!" Parker shouted, his voice hoarse and strained, his body weak but his resolve unshaken.

Eryndor turned slowly, his eyes gleaming with cold amusement, as he strode toward Parker. "Ah, the ever-defiant father," he mused, his tone dripping with mockery. "You should be grateful, Parker. Your daughter is far more useful than I expected."

With a flick of his wrist, an invisible force slammed into Parker, sending searing pain through his body. He gasped and his muscles locked, as agony twisted through him. Eryndor stood in front of Parker, his voice a chilling whisper. "But gratitude only goes so far. Speak out of turn again and you'll regret it."

"Stop!" interrupted Alessia.

Eryndor sighed, irritation flickering across his face. "I've had enough of your interruptions."

With a flick of his hand, a surge of dark energy pulsed through the cavern. Alessia had no time to react before the force struck her, sending her crumpling to the ground, her vision fading to black.

Parker and TJ strained against the chains binding them to the wall, their breaths ragged, but they were powerless. Eryndor turned his cold gaze on them next. "You two are just as tiresome." Another wave of energy lashed out, slamming their heads back against the stone. Their bodies went slack, unconscious in an instant.

As silence settled over the cavern, Eryndor exhaled in satisfaction. "Much better!"

The cavern trembled with the surge of forbidden power as the relics pulsed in anticipation inside the Cauldron of Chaos.

In that charged silence—filled with the mingled fervor of dark minions and the simmering energy of ancient magic—the air itself seemed to bend beneath Eryndor's will. The ritual's momentum was unstoppable now. With every echo of his followers' cheers, his dominion drew nearer, the path toward chaos and conquest carved ever deeper into fate.

CHAPTER TWENTY-TWO

Eryndor stepped out of the cavern and felt the cool desert night air brush against him. The horizon burned with the last remnants of sunset, casting long shadows across the rugged landscape. His sharp gaze swept over the vast, desolate terrain before settling on Drogan, who stood waiting at the entrance, his hulking frame rigid with anticipation.

"I don't want any surprises," Eryndor said, his voice low and commanding, as he stood beside him. "Keep watch. If anyone so much as breathes out of place near this canyon, I want to know before they even realize they've been spotted."

Drogan nodded, gripping the hilt of his blade. "Yes, Sire. And if they come too close?"

Eryndor's lips curled into a smirk. "Then make sure they regret it." He cast one last glance at the desert before turning back toward the cavern. "No mistakes, Drogan. Fail me and you'll wish the desert took you first."

Without another word, Eryndor disappeared into the shadows of the cavern, leaving Drogan alone beneath the darkening sky, his sharp eyes scanning the horizon for any sign of unwelcome company.

* * *

A shimmering portal flickered open in the vast, arid Utah Desert. The scorching sunset bore down on the golden dunes and jagged red rock formations as Stephen, Kelan, Garrick and two of his finest soldiers stepped through. The moment their boots hit the sand, the portal sealed behind them, leaving nothing but the eerie silence of the open desert.

Garrick's sharp brown eyes swept across the horizon before settling on his men. "Stay alert. We're here to gather intel, nothing more. No unnecessary risks. Understood?"

Solemn nods confirmed their agreement.

"This heat is brutal. Let's move fast," Stephen said, scanning the terrain with a practiced eye. "Kelan, you ready?"

Kelan nodded and watched Garrick and his two guards transform into massive Griffins, their enormous wings stretching wide beside them.

With ease, Stephen and Kelan climbed onto the backs of the majestic Griffin creatures, gripping their thick feathered manes.

"Take flight!" commanded Garrick.

With a powerful beat of their wings, the three Griffins launched into the sky, ascending rapidly above the desert. The world below stretched endlessly, with barren rock, shifting dunes and deep crags breaking the monotony of the sand. The wind roared past them, but Stephen and Kelan maintained their balance with ease, as their senses sharpened.

After several minutes of flight, Kelan's voice cut through the rushing wind. "There! To the east!"

Stephen followed his line of sight. A cluster of jagged rock formations concealed a dark cavern mouth, barely visible in the wavering heat haze. Guarding the entrance, a lone figure stood—massive, armored and unmistakable.

"Drogan," Garrick muttered. "That's one of Eryndor's minions."

Stephen's jaw tightened. "We need to get closer. That cavern could be their hideout."

The Griffins circled high above, careful not to linger in one place too long. From their vantage point, they could make out movement—shadows flitting in and out of the cavern.

"Looks like Eryndor has a few prisoners, perhaps his minions? Parker and TJ could be down there too," stated Garrick.

Kelan exhaled sharply. "We've seen enough. If we stay too long, they'll see us."

Below them, Drogan's head snapped upward, his crimson eyes narrowing. His brute's lips curled into a snarl, as he turned and rushed into the cavern.

"Fuck, we've been made," Garrick growled, as he watched Drogan rush inside the cavern. "Time to go."

The Griffins veered sharply, angling away from the cavern, their wings beating furiously, as the team shot across the sky, pushing themselves to their limits in a desperate retreat.

The three Griffins descended onto the cracked earth of the Utah Desert, their powerful wings stirring up dust as they landed. Garrick landed first, his sharp gaze sweeping the area for any threats. His two Griffin soldiers, strong and ever-watchful, remained in place, their talons gripping the earth, as Stephen and Kelan slid off their backs.

"Everyone's accounted for!" Garrick stated, glancing at his team, as he watched his two soldier's wings retract into their backs as they resumed human form.

Stephen and Kelan nodded in agreement.

"Good. Let's get moving," commanded Garrick, as his own wings retracted into his back and he shifted into human form.

Stephen pulled out his mobile phone and dialed the Gramaze mansion's number.

"Yes!" answered William curtly.

"Sire, we need that portal to Bagnolet now," said Stephen.

Static crackled before William's voice came through. "Got you. Stand by."

A low hum filled the air as swirling light coalesced before them, expanding into a shimmering portal. Garrick turned to everyone and said, "We return together. Stay close."

One of the Griffins soldiers gave a quiet huff of agreement, shifting in place. "Lead the way, Sire."

Stephen gave a slight nod to the Griffin that had carried him. "Let's go home."

Without another word, the group moved toward the portal.

As they disappeared into the light, the world around them seemed to dissolve into the familiar, cool shadows of Bagnolet.

They emerged into the backyard of the Gramaze mansion.

Garrick walked out first, dusting the sand from his armor. Spotting William, who was waiting for them, he said, "Drogan, one of Eryndor's minions, spotted us, so I am sure, by now, he would have reported that to Eryndor. But we can confirm they have a hideout. A cavern to the east."

William exhaled. "Then we need to act fast."

Garrick's gaze hardened. "Agreed! We need a plan. And, yes, we need to act fast."

* * *

Drogan strode into the dimly lit cavern, his voice a growl as he approached Eryndor. "Sire, we have company."

Eryndor, who was perched on a jagged black stone, barely lifted his gaze. "Who?"

"Griffins and Lepidoptera Vampires. They seemed like they were scouting the area. They know we're here."

Eryndor's expression darkened. "Then we prepare to move."

Drogan cast a glance at the three prisoners—Alessia, Parker and TJ—before turning back to his master. "What about them?"

"They've served their purpose," Eryndor said coolly. "For now, we leave them." His gaze hardened. "Get everything ready. We're leaving in five minutes."

"Yes, Sire," Drogan replied, before turning sharply on his heel. He disappeared into the depths of the cavern, his footsteps echoing as he rushed to make the preparations.

CHAPTER TWENTY-THREE

The air rippled as the portal tore open, its silver-blue light illuminating the barren landscape in the Utah Desert.

The first to step through was William, his long coat billowing slightly in the hot desert wind, as his sharp, calculating eyes swept over the terrain, noting the jagged rock formations and the endless stretch of sand. "This is where you found the cavern?"

Beside him, Garrick emerged, his imposing form silhouetted against the fading sun. His brown eyes flicked toward the horizon, taking in the openness. "Yes. It's over to the east." He pointed in the direction of the open cavern where Eryndor and his minions were holed up. "This place is a death trap. There is nowhere to hide."

"I don't doubt that, Garrick. This desert sure is a rugged, barren stretch of land," William remarked.

Garrick nodded in agreement.

The portal behind them pulsed again, and the rest of their team followed—Draven, Kael, Bennett and Hawk, all Griffins, stepped onto the desert ground with steady, confident strides. The warm wind ruffled their feathers as they surveyed the barren landscape, their sharp eyes already scanning for movement, their instincts sharpening with every breath.

Behind them, the Lepidoptera Vampires emerged—Stephen, Kelan, Samuel, Kiplin and Sully, their movements silent and their keen eyes immediately searching for signs of Parker and TJ.

Kael crouched, running a gloved hand through the sand. "William, Garrick—there was movement here. Fresh tracks, but they're fading."

"Listen up!" Garrick's commanding voice cut through the air, as he scanned the faces around him. He waited until silence fell before continuing.

"Griffins, Lepidopteras—our last sighting of Eryndor and his minions was in a cavern to the east." He gestured toward the distant rock formation. "We go in together, overwhelming them with numbers. If we strike fast, we might catch them off guard. Are you ready?"

A single nod of agreement passed through the group.

"Kelan, Stephen, you stand guard here," William gestured toward the still open portal. "I don't want anyone entering this portal, without my say so. Are we clear?"

"Yes, Sire," they said in unison.

With a powerful beat of their wings, the Griffins took to the sky, while the rest of the Lepidopteras sprinted toward the open cavern at Vampire speed.

As they reached the mouth of the cavern, the air grew thick with an eerie stillness; the only sound being the faint rustling of their movement.

With his keen senses alert as he landed, Garrick shifted to human form and watched his soldiers do the same, before he signaled for the group to halt. His eyes scanned the darkened interior, but there was no sign of Eryndor or his minions. "Stay close," he whispered, his voice barely audible as they entered, moving in single file.

The walls of the cavern were jagged and hot, the ground slick with dampness. Shadows danced across the stone as their footsteps echoed softly. The deeper they ventured, the more oppressive the silence became. Not a creature stirred, not even the faintest hint of movement. It was as if the cavern had swallowed all sound, leaving only the unsettling feeling that something was amiss.

"Something's wrong. I can feel it," William muttered, glancing around with suspicion.

Garrick nodded grimly. "I feel it, too. I think they're hiding … but where?"

They pressed on, stepping carefully over loose rocks and uneven ground. The deeper they moved, the narrower the cavern became, forcing them to crouch or even crawl through some sections of tight passageways. As they rounded another bend, the flicker of torchlights in the distance caught their attention. They all moved toward it in unison, silently closing the distance.

Hidden behind a veil of shadows at the far end of the cavern, where the rock ceilings soared overhead, three figures were chained to a stone wall. The unmistakable scent of Goddess Alessia reached Garrick's nose before he even saw her. She was unconscious, her head drooping, her arms chained above her. Parker and TJ were beside her, equally motionless, their faces pale, their clothes bloodied and torn.

The sight made Garrick's blood run cold. "Alessia! Fuck what is she doing here?" Garrick's voice broke the silence, with a mix of urgency and disbelief, as he rushed to her aid.

Draven stepped forward, his sharp eyes scanning for any signs of danger. "Stay alert everyone. This could be a trap."

"We need to get them free, now," ordered Garrick. He turned to Sully and Hawk, who were standing together. "Can you help me?"

Collectively, they worked quickly, using their strength to break the chains and lower their friends to the ground. With the cavern still eerily quiet, Garrick couldn't shake the feeling that they weren't alone.

"Is she alright?" Hawk asked, kneeling beside Alessia.

"She's breathing, but unconscious," Sully said, her voice laced with concern. "Is TJ okay?" asked Sully, looking over at her lifeless body.

"She's breathing, but I think she will need some healing," replied William, looking over TJ's head wounds.

"What I want to know is, how in the hell did Alessia get here?"

"Eryndor must have kidnapped her from the River of Whispers," replied Hawk.

"Yes, I guessed as much, but that would mean that Danielle and Christian have been compromised as well. And I haven't heard from Kura," stated William. He retrieved his phone from his pocket and called the operations room at the Gramaze mansion.

"Yes, Sire," answered Brock.

"I want you to organize for someone to go to the River of Whispers via portal and see if Danielle, Christian, the guardians and Kura are alive. I think that they may have been compromised by Eryndor. Take a healer with you, too. Hurry!" commanded William.

"Shit! Yes, Sire," replied Brock. He hung up his phone and contacted Violette.

William watched Parker stir, groaning slightly. "Alessia …" he whispered hoarsely.

"Stay with them, Griffins," Garrick ordered, as his eyes scanned the darkened cavern once more. "We're not out of this yet." The silence from the cavern felt unnatural and every flicker of movement from the shadows set his nerves on edge.

Then, without warning, the ground shuddered, sending a violent tremor through the cavern. A deafening roar rumbled from the depths below and cracks snaked across the walls, as if the earth itself was tearing apart. As the vibrations intensified, shaking everything around them, a bone-jarring crack split the air from deep within the cavern's core.

"Get down!" Garrick shouted, diving toward the unconscious trio as he transformed, shielding them with his Griffin wings, as the ground shook violently.

Before anyone could react, a massive explosion ripped through the air. The cavern floor trembled as jagged rocks, dust and debris shot upward, sending the entire group into a panic. The force of the explosion sent a shockwave through the walls, causing massive cracks to appear along the cavern ceiling.

"Run!" shouted William, his voice barely audible over the chaos.

The Griffins instinctively took to the air, wings beating against the dust-filled air as they dodged chunks of falling rock from the cavern's towering ceiling. The Lepidopteras, moving with lightning speed, dashed toward the exit, their Vampire-enhanced reflexes allowing them to dodge debris and falling rocks as they sped forward.

As Garrick removed himself from the trio's bodies, Hawk lifted Alessia's limp form into his arms and raced to keep up with the others. Sully, right behind him, pulled Parker and TJ along, using her Vampire strength and speed to keep pace.

The explosion, having set off a chain reaction, tore at the walls, and the cavern started to crumble around them. Stones and rubble rained down like a deadly storm as the group fought to escape.

Garrick led the way, spreading his wings wide to shield the others from falling debris, as he pushed forward with all his might.

The exit was in sight, but the ground beneath them was unstable, crumbling as they ran.

A second, smaller explosion erupted behind them, sending a new wave of rocks tumbling from above, forcing them to dodge and duck for cover.

"We're almost there!" Garrick shouted, his voice strained. "Keep moving!"

The cavern's entrance loomed closer, but the path was quickly disappearing behind them as the explosion continued to tear apart the rock. The sound of cracking stone and collapsing walls reverberated, drowning out everything else.

They reached the mouth of the cavern just as the entire tunnel behind them gave way. The walls collapsed inward with a deafening roar, sending a massive cloud of dust into the air, nearly choking them all. As they burst into the open, they sprinted toward the safety of the distant portal, which was far from the destruction of the now-collapsed cavern.

Garrick turned, watching the once-hidden entrance crumble into rubble. His chest heaved with effort, his eyes narrowing, as the dust settled.

"We're not safe here yet," Garrick muttered, his voice low and filled with unease, as he and his soldiers shifted back into human form.

"Let's get the fuck out of here," demanded William, as he picked up Parker. "Sully … you okay to carry TJ?"

"Yes, Sir," answered Sully. She picked up TJ's body from the ground and walked toward the portal.

"I will carry Alessia through the portal," stated Hawk.

As they stepped into the portal, William's phone beeped a message. Taking it out of his pocket, he read: *Danielle, Christian, Kura and the three guardians are alive and safe.* William breathed a heavy sigh and kept walking, as he placed his phone back in his pocket and continued to carry Parker.

Despite their unscathed escape, the sense of danger still lingered, hanging thick in the air like the remnants of the explosion itself. The group knew that even though they had survived, the real battle was far from over.

CHAPTER TWENTY-FOUR

"Knock, knock," Alessia called softly, as she stood in the doorway of her parents' bedroom at the Gramaze mansion. It had been two days since the explosion and their liberation from the Utah Desert and Alessia was anxious to see her parents.

"Come in, sweetheart," TJ replied, her voice faint, but warm.

Alessia stepped inside, her gaze shifting to her father, who sat beside her mother on the bed. "How are you feeling this morning, Mum?" she asked gently.

"A lot better, thanks, sweetie," TJ said with a small smile, patting the mattress to invite Alessia to sit beside her.

Sliding onto the bed, Alessia leaned in to hug her mother. "It looks like your wounds have healed nicely," she murmured.

"Thanks to you and those incredible new powers of yours," TJ said, pulling back slightly. She squeezed Alessia's hand, her blue eyes shining with gratitude. "The pain—it's completely gone."

Alessia smiled. "That's the idea."

"You never stop amazing us, kiddo." Parker said, his voice full of pride. "You've always been strong, but this … this is something else."

Alessia glanced between them, a warmth settling in her chest. "It's part of me now. I can feel the energy moving through me, like it knows what to do."

TJ brushed a strand of hair behind Alessia's ear. "I don't want you hurting yourself in the process."

"I won't," Alessia promised, though she knew there were limits she hadn't tested yet. And if it came down to saving the people that she loved—she wasn't sure she'd stop herself from going too far.

"I believe from speaking with William this morning, that you are going to be staying here, at the Gramaze mansion, until things calm down a bit out there, or they catch Eryndor?" queried Parker.

"I sure am. And the best part … I get to spend some time with you both," Alessia said, her smile shifting between Parker and TJ. "I believe you're staying here for protection, too."

"Yes, we are," replied Parker.

"We sure are lucky to have such wonderful, caring, supernatural friends, who will always be there for us," stated Alessia.

"I agree. In all my life, I have never come across a more noble and extraordinary group than the Lepidoptera Gramaze coven. Their strength is matched only by their kindness, and their loyalty knows no bounds. We are lucky to have them, and the Ironclaw Griffins, by our side," stated Parker.

"Yes, I agree. Where is your room, sweetie?" asked TJ.

"Right next door," Alessia replied.

"Perfect. Do you have any plans for today?" TJ asked with a gentle smile, hoping to spend some time with her.

"Actually, I was planning to read some of the ancient tomes in the Gramaze library. I think they might be able to help me find answers to some of my questions," Alessia replied.

"Was that something I could help you with?" asked Parker.

Alessia smiled. "Maybe. You've always been good at spotting details that I might overlook. I'm trying to understand more about the magic tied to my abilities. An extra pair of eyes wouldn't hurt."

"Great. I can meet you there, in say … about half an hour, if you like. I need to have a shower, then help your mother, but after that, I am all yours," replied Parker.

"Sounds like a plan," said Alessia, standing. She leaned in to give them both a kiss, then walked toward the door. "See you later on."

"Bye, sweetie," said TJ.

"Bye," said Alessia.

* * *

As Alessia walked through the house and out to the back alfresco area of the Gramaze mansion, she spotted William, Renee, Garrick and Elara, Danielle and Christian, seated, and deep in conversation with Kura.

Kura's face lit up with a warm smile as Alessia approached them.

"Great-grandmother … is everything alright?" Alessia asked, curiosity flickering in her voice, as she wondered about her presence.

"Everything's fine, my dear. Actually, the Gramaze coven has asked me to stay with them for protection," She patted the seat beside her. "Come, sit. There is much we need to discuss," replied Kura.

Alessia hesitated for a brief moment, searching Kura's expression for any hint of concern. Though her great-grandmother's words were reassuring, there was a weight in her tone that suggested otherwise.

Nodding, Alessia stepped forward and took the offered seat, her gaze flickering between the others, before settling on Kura. "What's going on?" she asked, her voice steady but laced with curiosity.

"We wanted to ask you about when Eryndor and his minions captured and held you prisoner," Kura said.

"What about it?" Alessia asked cautiously.

"Did you see the three ancient artifacts he possesses? Especially the book with the Golden Chalice inside?" Garrick pressed.

Alessia swallowed hard. "Yes …"

William studied her closely, his gaze sharp. "From reading your thoughts, I can tell you're conflicted. Is there something you're not telling us?"

Alessia lowered her gaze, shame and uncertainty twisting inside her. She took a steadying breath before speaking.

"The Golden Chalice … I pulled it out of the book for Eryndor," she admitted, her voice barely above a whisper.

A heavy silence fell over the group.

"If I hadn't, Eryndor would have killed my parents," she continued, her eyes pleading for them to understand. "I couldn't let that happen. I had no choice."

Garrick's jaw tightened and William's expression darkened, but it was Kura who finally spoke, her voice calm yet laced with an undeniable weight.

"Choices made under duress still carry consequences, my dear," she said gently. "Tell us everything—what happened when you removed the chalice?"

Alessia exhaled shakily, her fingers clenching in her lap, as she prepared to relive the moment.

"I found the rune-inscribed book in the heart of a cavern, resting alone on a stone pedestal. The moment I stepped closer, it … reacted. It seemed to know I was there and who I was. Then the cover pulsed with golden light, like it had been waiting for my touch."

She glanced up, her eyes haunted. "When I picked it up, I heard distant moans echoing through the chamber. I followed the sound and found my parents. Eryndor had chained them up with powerful enchantments. Then he appeared, and gave me a choice: unlock the book or watch them die."

"When I pressed my hand to the cover, the pages burst open, flipping wildly until they stopped on an illustration of the Golden Chalice. Something deep inside my chest pulled and before I could understand what was happening, my hand sank into the page. I could feel the chalice, solid and real, inside the book. And when I pulled it free …"

She swallowed hard, dread hollowing her chest. "Eryndor took the chalice from my hand immediately and carried it over to the thing he called the Cauldron of Chaos. The moment he placed it inside; the cauldron came alive. The entire chamber trembled, as if something ancient and monstrous had just drawn breath."

"Fuck, so he has the Cauldron of Chaos, too," stated Garrick.

Alessia nodded in agreement.

"Did you see two swords and a gold ring inside the cauldron?" asked Elara.

"Yes, ma'am," replied Alessia. "I remember wondering, why he would want, or even need, those three artifacts. But then he revealed the reason."

"Did you see, or do you know if Eryndor has the Ethereal Nexus Amulet?" asked Garrick.

"I don't know … what does it look like," asked Alessia.

"The Ethereal Nexus Amulet is a delicate, silver pendant, shaped like an intricate starburst, with thin, sharp rays radiating outward. At its center, a glowing, translucent gemstone pulses with shifting colors, ranging from deep violet to a soft, ethereal blue, and it's encased in an elegant, intricate metalwork of swirling patterns," replied Garrick.

"I think I saw something like this hanging around Eryndor's neck. I can't be one hundred percent sure, though," stated Alessia, with a furrowed brow, as she pictured Eryndor and the amulet.

"Did he tell or ask you anything else?" inquired Garrick.

"That's all I can remember," Alessia replied, her gaze drifting as if replaying the events in her mind.

The air was heavy with tension once Alessia finished her story. The group was silent for a long moment, as the weight of her words hung in the air like a dark cloud. It was William who broke the silence, his sharp eyes narrowing in disbelief as the pieces began to fall into place.

"So ... Eryndor now has everything he needs," William said, his voice low, controlled, but tinged with urgency. "The chalice, the swords, the ring ... and he's holding the key to the Cauldron of Chaos. If all three artifacts are together, then ..." His words trailed off as the realization hit him. "He can end the world."

Alessia flinched at the cold truth of his statement.

"Yes," Garrick replied. "He's one step away from unleashing chaos." Garrick ran a hand through his hair and took a deep breath. "But why hasn't he done it already?" He turned to face the group, his voice laced with confusion. "Why hasn't he started his reign over the world? He has the power now. What's stopping him?"

Kura leaned forward slightly, her violet eyes reflecting a flicker of understanding. "The Cauldron of Chaos is not a tool to be wielded lightly. It's an ancient source of unimaginable power. To use it requires more than just the artifacts. There's a process, a ritual. And it's far more dangerous than Eryndor might realize."

"Is he waiting for something, or someone? Whatever it is he's planning, I'm sure he'll act sooner rather than later," stated William.

Garrick's fists clenched. "But when? The world doesn't have that much time." His voice cracked with urgency. "We have to stop him before he takes that final step. Before it's too late."

Alessia swallowed hard. "And how do we stop him? What can we do?"

"I'm afraid it's not just about stopping him," Kura said softly. "We may need to stop the very force he's trying to unleash. And that, my dear, will be no small task." She exchanged a glance with William and Garrick and then looked back at Alessia. "We may need your help again, Alessia, in ways you cannot yet understand."

Garrick shot a sharp look at Kura. "You're saying there's something else we don't know? Something about Alessia?"

Kura nodded, her gaze steady. "The artifacts are not just things to be used. They are part of a larger balance—a balance that Alessia is connected to, whether she knows it or not."

Alessia's breath hitched. "Connected? How?"

"I would say you've seen it before, Alessia—the connection between you and the chalice, the book … They called to you. But now, it's time for you to understand why. We'll help you uncover the truth, together," William said, his voice firm yet reassuring.

Garrick exhaled sharply, frustration still heavy in his chest. "But Eryndor won't wait much longer. The moment he has all the pieces in place, he won't hesitate."

Kura's expression hardened, but her voice stayed steady. "Then we must act swiftly, before he unleashes hell upon our world."

They all nodded in agreement.

CHAPTER TWENTY-FIVE

A rift split through the air and Eryndor stepped out from the depths of his otherworldly, swirling portal, inside a Mexican cenote. His dark cloak billowed slightly, as the residual energy of the portal crackled around him, casted long, flickering, eerie silhouettes upon the walls. Behind him, his minions emerged, silent as wraiths, their forms dissolving into the shadows.

As the portal snapped shut behind them, it left only the natural stillness of the cave and the hidden cenote stretched before them. The cenote's shimmering waters glowed colors of turquoise-blue hues, with hints of emerald green, and had a wide stone pathway, ancient and worn, which led to a circular platform at the center of the pool. Golden beams of sunlight streamed in from a jagged opening in the ceiling above, lighting the cavern.

Ah, there you are, my beauty, thought Eryndor, as he watched the Cauldron of Chaos materialize in front of him on the stone circular platform, and felt its immense, obsidian form pulsating with dark energy. The sheer weight of its power warped the air around it. The stolen ancient artifacts of immeasurable power still rested within its depths, under the ethereal light.

"What is this place?" asked Drogan, looking around at the stalactites hanging from the ceiling and the stalagmites rising from the floor.

Eryndor turned to see Drogan standing near him, his glazed-eyed minions lingering behind him, awaiting instruction. He lifted his chin and his voice cut through the cavern's heavy silence.

"Gather around, my minions," instructed Eryndor.

As the murmur of shuffling feet faded, Eryndor swept a hand toward the dark pool before them. "I chose this place for a reason. This cenote is more than a mere body of water—it was once a conduit to the ancient and forgotten, a sacred threshold between realms. According to the whispered legends, it possesses the power to consume and conceal artifacts of great might, shielding them from the unworthy." A slow smile curled his lips. "But more than that, the light filtering down from above will allow me to harness the cauldron's power; that is, once we have the Fae's blood."

As Eryndor's words echoed through the cavern, a ripple of anticipation spread through the gathered minions. Some murmured in hushed excitement, their voices barely above a whisper, while others clenched their fists, their eyes glinting with devotion.

Drogan bowed his head, pressing a fist to his chest in reverence. "You have chosen wisely, my lord," he intoned. "The power of the ancients will be yours."

A low, feverish chant began to rise among the minions, a rhythmic whisper of Eryndor's name, growing in intensity like a storm building on the horizon. The minions swayed slightly, their glazed eyes alight with a mix of awe and hunger, ready to serve, and ready to witness the power their master would soon command.

A smirk played on Eryndor's lips as he watched his minions revel in his words, their whispered chants growing stronger.

Real power—undeniable power—is within my grasp. Soon ... soon the world will tremble beneath it and answer to me, me only, thought Eryndor.

"Master ... we are here to serve you. What are your plans?" queried Malrik, as he approached Eryndor.

"First, we secure a Fae's blood. Only then can we awaken the cauldron's full potential," replied Eryndor, looking around at his minions. "Prepare to depart. The time for waiting is over."

The minions raised their arms triumphantly, cheering with a wicked delight.

* * *

Can't wait for this day to be over, thought Xanthia, sighing. Her mind already yearned for the end of the day. *Calculus is such a drag.* She glanced at her wristwatch and realized it was only seconds before the bell would signal the end of the school day at Lycée International. Xanthia was looking forward to getting back to the small home she shared with her father, Albinus, on the Gramaze property. They hadn't been there long and were still in the midst of unpacking.

As the bell sounded, the entire class surged toward the door, eager to leave. The professor called out after them, "Homework for tonight … page sixteen in your booklet."

Xanthia rolled her eyes and let out a heavy sigh, as she shoved her books into her bag and quickly made her way to the door.

"Hi, Xanthia," greeted Danielle, who was waiting outside the classroom, as usual, to pick her up and take her home.

"Hey," Xanthia replied, her voice a little flat.

"Everything okay?" Danielle asked, noticing her mood.

"Yeah, I'm fine," Xanthia shrugged. "That class was such a drag. And, surprise, I've got homework again tonight. I can't wait for this year to be over. I am so sick and tired of homework," she added, slinging her bag over her shoulder.

"Well, you've only got a few more days of the school year left, then after next year you're done. Have you thought about what you want to do for work, after school?" Danielle asked.

"Not really."

"I'm sure you'll figure it out when the time comes," Danielle said, offering a reassuring smile. "Anyway, let's get out of here. Your chariot awaits, milady," she added with a smirk.

Xanthia smiled, as they made their way toward the parking lot.

As they settled into the seats of the car and placed their seat belts on, Xanthia raised an eyebrow. "New ride?"

"Yeah," Danielle grinned. "It's an Aston Martin Vantage. And trust me, it drives like a dream." The engine rumbled to life as she started the car, and then drove out of the parking lot.

"Nice!" Xanthia exclaimed, taking in the sleek dash and plush leather upholstery.

"Definitely. Wait until you hear the sound system—it's wicked," Danielle said, cranking up the volume.

"Wow, that's awesome!" Xanthia shouted, over the booming music, both of them bouncing to the beat.

The afternoon sun stretched long shadows across the winding road as Danielle drove, one hand on the wheel, the other tapping rhythmically on her knee. Xanthia sat beside her, scrolling through her phone, then lowered the music when she spotted yet another assignment from her history professor.

"I swear if we get one more history assignment, I might just—" Xanthia's voice cut off when she noticed Danielle's grip on the steering wheel had tightened, her knuckles whitening.

"What's wrong?" questioned Xanthia, the pulse of their Fae empathic connection tightening in her chest. Something was off. She swallowed hard.

Before Danielle could answer, a blacked-out SUV screeched onto the road ahead of them, skidding sideways to block their path. Simultaneously, two motorbikes roared up behind them.

"Hold on!" screamed Danielle, as she slammed the car into reverse, twisting the wheel sharply to escape, but the bikers were faster. One hurled a small metallic disk onto the hood. The rune-etched device hissed and crackled with dark magic, making the engine shudder before it died completely. Steering the disabled car onto a side street, Danielle said, "I think we are in big trouble, Xanthia." She watched two glazed-eyed monsters running toward them. "These fuckers … they look like Eryndor's minions and they mean business."

"What do they want with us this time?" asked Xanthia.

"I think we are about to find out," replied Danielle. "Let's go. Stay behind me."

Xanthia nodded and they exited the car. Her Fae wings flickered inside her back, for half a second, before she cursed under her breath. "Shit, magic dampener."

Eight tall figures in dark cloaks converged on the Aston Martin from the SUV and motorbikes, all moving with eerie precision.

"Stay here!" ordered Danielle, as she lunged with supernatural speed, propelling herself forward, slamming her feet into the nearest attacker, sending him flying into the side of the SUV.

Xanthia raised her hands, her Fae magic crackling to life despite the dampening effect. Vines burst from the pavement, whipping toward the attackers who were coming straight at her.

Malrik flicked his wrist and a wave of violet energy surged forward, shattering Xanthia's vines.

Another minion launched a dart toward Danielle's neck, but she dodged it, only to have a second one strike her arm. As she tried to pull the dart out of her arm and control the attack, her vision blurred.

"Xan—get out of here!" Danielle's voice slurred, as the drug seeped into her system.

Xanthia snarled, throwing a wave of golden energy at the nearest enemy, sending them skidding across the bitumen. But then, she felt a sharp prick on her side of her neck. She gasped and her eyes grew wide as the world tilted.

Malrik caught her before she hit the ground, unconscious.

Danielle, who was trying to fight through the haze, staggered toward them, only for a final surge of magic to knock her off her feet.

Her last sight was of Xanthia's unconscious form being dragged toward the SUV, and then her head swam, as the darkness claimed her.

The minions cheered and raised their arms into the air, celebrating their victory, as Danielle and Xanthia were carried toward the SUV.

CHAPTER TWENTY-SIX

Closing the front door behind him, Albinus set his keys on the hallway stand, along with his work bag. Without pausing, he continued into the kitchen.

"Xanthia!" he called out, as he turned on the kitchen light switch.

There was only silence; the rest of the house was in complete darkness.

"Xanthia, are you home?" he called again, his voice carrying through the quiet space.

Still no answer. A frown creased his brow as he moved toward Xanthia's bedroom. He knew her routine well and this wasn't like her. Since they'd moved out of the Gramaze mansion, Danielle had been picking Xanthia up from school each afternoon, and dropping her home, to the little house at the back of the Gramaze property.

She should be here, thought Albinus.

Reaching her bedroom, Albinus flicked on the light, only to find the room was empty.

"Hmm … maybe she's at the Gramaze house?" he muttered to himself. Pulling his phone from his jacket pocket, he quickly dialed their number.

"Good evening, Albinus," William greeted, as he answered.

"Good evening, William. Sorry to disturb you, but is Xanthia over at your place?" Albinus asked, as he walked toward the backyard, to check if Xanthia was sitting outside on the patio.

"I'm not sure. Hold on a moment and I'll ask Danielle." William set his phone down.

"Thanks," Albinus replied.

Danielle ... is Xanthia here with you? thought William, telepathically.

There was no answer. *Hmm, that's strange. Christian, is Danielle here at the house, or out on a mission?* asked William, telepathically.

I haven't seen her, Sire. I thought she was at Xanthia's house, replied Christian, telepathically. *Let me see if I can contact her.*

A few moments later Christian said, *Sire ... I can't seem to locate her through our Lepidoptera connection. This isn't like her. Do you think something has happened?*

Leave it with me and I will get back to you on that, Christian, said William, telepathically.

A few minutes later, William's voice returned to the call with Albinus. "Albinus, are you still there?"

"Yes."

"Xanthia isn't here. Neither is Danielle. Christian assumed Danielle stayed with Xanthia for a while, especially since they've been spending so much time together lately."

Albinus's grip tightened on his phone. "Well, they're definitely not here. I've checked the entire house, while I waited."

A knot of unease settled in his stomach. "I feel something isn't right, William."

"Leave it with us, Albinus. I will find them, don't you worry," William assured him.

"Thank you. I will wait here in case they return," said Albinus.

"Good idea. I'll call you as soon as I have news," said William.

"Thanks, William." Albinus ended the call and set his phone on the kitchen counter.

Fuck ... We've only recently managed to get our lives back on track. Why is this happening? God, I hope nothing has happened to them, thought Albinus, the knot of nervousness tightening in his chest.

* * *

Heads up, Lepidopteras ... Danielle and Xanthia are missing. Meet me in the operations room—mission briefing starts now, William's telepathic command echoed through his coven's minds.

Moments later, the sliding glass doors to the operations room parted and William stepped inside, finding most of his coven already assembled, waiting for his arrival.

"Sire, I have instructed Brock to check the satellite feed from the time Xanthia was picked up from school by Danielle, until now. We are waiting to see what he can find," reported Grayson.

"Well done, Grayson!" William walked over to the operations room screen, his sharp gaze fixed on the display, as he waited for Brock's update.

Brock glanced up as his fingers moving swiftly over the keyboard. "So far, nothing—but I'll keep looking."

"If they don't appear on the footage, track their mobile signals," William ordered.

"Yes, Sire," Brock responded without hesitation.

William turned to the room, his expression darkening. "Right ... it appears Xanthia and Danielle are missing." His gaze snapped to Violette. "I need a portal to wherever they are."

Violette gave a swift nod. "Yes, William. It will be ready."

Before William could say more, Brock abruptly turned and said, "Sire ... you need to see this."

"Replay it."

All eyes locked onto the massive screen mounted on the wall as the footage rolled. Silence fell as they watched Xanthia and Danielle, ambushed by glazed-eyed creatures and kidnapped.

"Fuck!" William hissed, his jaw tightening. "After they were loaded into the SUV, where did they go?"

"Still working on it, Sire," Brock replied, his fingers deftly flying across the keyboard.

William's fists clenched. "Find them. NOW. I want these bastards hunted down." His voice was a low growl, laced with fury. He raked a hand through his hair, as his breathing was measured, but seething beneath the surface. "No one touches my family and walks away. Not ever. They will pay for this."

Michael stepped forward. "What are your orders in the meantime, Sire?"

William's gaze swept across the room at all the faces of his coven. "Get your combat gear on and your weapons ready. These fuckers will pay," stated William. His nostrils flared, as he let the rage settle into deadly determination.

Without a word spoken, the Lepidoptera Vampires strode out of the operations room, making their way to the combat room to arm themselves with their chosen weapons and combat gear, while William remained in the operations room with Brock, monitoring the surveillance feed.

* * *

What's going on?" Alessia asked, as she spotted Christian in the hallway, with the other Lepidopteras.

"Danielle and Xanthia have been taken by Eryndor's minions," Christian replied, his expression grim.

"Shit! Is there anything I can do to help?" Alessia asked, worry flashing across her face.

Christian placed a reassuring hand on her shoulder. "No, Goddess, but thank you for the offer. I wish I knew why ... or what Eryndor wants with two Fae."

She swallowed hard, urgency creeping into her voice. "I think I might know why. Eryndor ... I remember him saying he needed the blood of a Fae to complete his ritual. Maybe he was talking about the ritual to end the world, I am not sure." Alessia gave a small, uncertain shrug.

Christian's expression darkened. "Shit, Alessia … Why didn't you tell us this sooner? That kind of information is *critical* to our mission."

"I'm sorry … I should have seen the connection sooner. I didn't realize how important it was until you spoke about Danielle and Xanthia being taken. That's when it hit me: they're both Fae," she admitted, guilt flashing across her face.

Christian exhaled sharply. "You didn't think it was important? What … the end of the world isn't important?" Christian shook his head and pursed his lips. "We need to tell William—now." He grabbed her hand and pulled her toward the operations room.

Alessia exhaled sharply. "I really screwed up this time, didn't I?"

Christian didn't answer. His jaw was tight and his focus locked straight ahead, as they walked toward the operations room.

"Sire," Christian said, as the glass doors slid open and he stepped into the operations room with Alessia beside him.

"What?" grunted William, as he turned to face them.

"Alessia has something she urgently needs to discuss with you," replied Christian.

William's sharp gaze shifted from Christian to Alessia, his expression dark with impatience. "And that is?"

"I think I know why Eryndor's minions took Danielle and Xanthia," Alessia said, her voice tight with unease. She swallowed hard before continuing, "He needs their Fae blood for the ritual to work … to end the world." Her gaze locked onto William, dread pooling in her eyes.

"What makes you so sure of that?" William asked, his scowl deepening.

"When he held me captive, I did overhear Eryndor's conversation with one of his minions about Fae blood," answered Alessia.

"For fuck's sake, Alessia … why didn't you tell us this sooner?" William growled, his frustration clear.

"I … I didn't remember before. It only just came back to me when Christian told me Danielle and Xanthia had been taken," Alessia replied, tears welling in her eyes.

"That will be enough!" Kura declared, her voice sharp as she strode into the operations room. She could feel through her connection with Alessia that she was upset and felt remorse. "You forget, William—no matter how powerful she is, Alessia is a young woman, one who is still learning." Her words cut through the room like a blade.

"You will do well to keep your outbursts to yourself, Kura. We have more important things to worry about than your great-granddaughter's memory," stated William.

"Humph!" replied Kura, her brow furrowed, as she shook her head in repugnance. Though she bristled at his bluntness, a reluctant part of her knew he was right. Mollycoddling Alessia wouldn't change what was coming, nor would it save her from the dangers ahead.

"I don't want to state the obvious here, but I think this would explain why Eryndor hasn't used the ancient artifacts yet," said Christian, trying to bring everyone in the room back to the reason they were there.

"Yes, you are correct, Christian," said William.

"Sire … I may have a lead on Danielle's mobile phone," interrupted Brock. "It keeps going in and out of signal, though, which makes it hard to pinpoint."

"Where is it currently located?" asked William, turning to Brock.

Brock's fingers flew over the keyboard and his brows furrowed. "Looks like Mexico," he said, as his eyes flicked between data points. "I can't seem to lock in the exact location yet; still working on it."

"If you have only their general location, that would mean we need to track them physically, correct?" questioned Kura, her gaze remaining steady on the screen.

William narrowed his eyes. He was not in the mood to listen to Kura, especially when one of his family was missing. "What are you talking about?"

She met his gaze, her voice low but firm. "Fae magic. The bond between Danielle and Xanthia—it's unique, right? If we tap into that, we might be able to feel where they are."

William scoffed, though a spark of curiosity flickered in his voice. "You want to use some mystical connection to find them? Explain yourself, Kura. How exactly would that work?"

Kura's expression hardened slightly. "You've seen how powerful Fae bonds are. It's not just about their magic. There's an energy, an aura, a connection. You just have to open yourself to it."

William hesitated, but something in Kura's tone pushed him to listen. He exhaled sharply. "Fine! But if this doesn't work, we're back to square one."

"I know you already realize this, but since you don't have any leads right now, this is your best chance to find Xanthia and Danielle," said Kura.

"Agreed! But, are you on good enough terms with the Fae Queen Aevyressa to arrange a meeting and ask for help," questioned William.

Kura nodded sharply. "Leave it with me." She turned to Alessia, "Come, my dear."

"Grayson, you and I will go with Kura. Brock, while we're gone, I want you to keep trying to locate Danielle and Xanthia's phones," said William.

"Yes, Sire," replied Brock.

"In the meantime, I need to ring Albinus with an update on his daughter," said William, as he walked toward the sliding doors. "Christian, let me know if you hear from Danielle."

"Yes, Sire," said Christian.

CHAPTER TWENTY-SEVEN

The portal opened in the Fae Kingdom, with swirling hues of deep violet and sapphire, rippling like water, as William stepped through first, onto the moss-covered ground. The air was thick with the scent of wildflowers and magic, a delicate hum vibrating through the very earth beneath them. Kura followed, her sharp gaze sweeping the surrounding forest, then Alessia, with Grayson emerging last, his eyes wide at the sheer beauty of the land before them.

Kura noticed that the new Queen had redecorated since her ascension, with towering crystalline spires stretching toward the sky in the distance, their surfaces reflecting the moonlight like shards of a broken star. Luminescent plants lined the pathway leading to the Fae Queen's palace. The air around the palace pulsed with life and carried the voices of unseen spirits.

Keep your wits about you, everyone, thought William, as they approached the two formidable Fae guards at the entrance to the palace, who stood to attention, their glowing eyes fixed on the visitors.

"We have come to visit Queen Aevyressa. May we enter?" asked Kura, her head held high as she spoke, with Alessia by her side.

Without a word, the two Fae warriors stepped aside, allowing passage into the grand throne room, where Aevyressa waited.

As the door closed behind them, Kura noticed Aevyressa sitting atop a throne, which was crafted from intertwined branches of the sacred elder tree, its gnarled wood adorned with veins of purest gold. Her presence was as commanding as it was ethereal; her silver-white hair cascaded over her shoulders, her deep violet eyes holding the wisdom of centuries. She wore a gown woven from twilight and moonbeams, shimmering softly with every movement.

Flanking her were her sisters, Myrrathen and Thalara. Myrrathen stood tall, her dark emerald hair coiled in intricate braids, her expression unreadable. Thalara, the younger of the three, had an air of mischief beneath her composed exterior. Her silver-blond locks were adorned with tiny crystalline flowers that pulsed with light.

William took a step forward and bowed slightly in respect. "Queen Aevyressa, we come seeking your aid."

Aevyressa studied them for a moment, her fingers lightly tracing the armrest of her throne. "I know why you have come," she said, her voice melodic, yet firm. "Danielle and Xanthia are lost. You believe I may be able to help you find them."

Kura nodded. "Your connection to the Fae is unmatched. If anyone can sense their presence, it is you."

Aevyressa's lips curved in a knowing smile. "Flattery, while appreciated, will not sway me. My power is not freely given."

Alessia tensed beside Kura and William, but she remained calm.

"What do you want in return?" asked William.

The Queen leaned forward slightly, her gaze piercing. "I will help you, but the price of my assistance is yet to be determined."

William shifted uneasily. "So, you want us to agree to an unknown favor?"

Aevyressa inclined her head. "Yes. When I call upon you, William, you will repay this debt, whatever it may be."

A heavy silence settled over the room. William met Aevyressa's gaze, understanding the weight of such a promise. Finally, he gave a single nod. "I accept."

Aevyressa's expression remained unreadable, but a flicker of satisfaction crossed her eyes. She lifted a hand and the air around them shimmered, as she reached out with her power. The very essence of the Fae Kingdom stirred in response. "Then let us begin."

Aevyressa rose from her throne, her sisters moving aside as she extended her hands. The air crackled with raw energy as she murmured ancient words in an otherworldly tongue. Wisps of golden and violet light spiraled from her fingertips, weaving into a pulsating orb that hovered above her palms.

William, Kura, Alessia and Grayson, who stood side by side in front of Aevyressa, looked on with astonishment. The throne room dimmed and shadows twisted along the walls, as the orb expanded. Within its depths, swirling images began to form, shapes shifting into clarity.

Aevyressa's violet eyes flashed as she gasped softly. "I see them," she murmured, her voice distant. "They are beneath the earth … surrounded by water."

The vision solidified and a vast underground cavern appeared. Stone walls were covered in ancient carvings, and turquoise-blue water stretched in a perfect circle, reflecting eerie blue light from bioluminescent fungi clinging to the ceiling stalactites. From a jagged opening in the ceiling above, sunlight filtered down, onto a wide stone pathway that led to a circular platform at the center of the pool. There lay the Cauldron of Chaos.

"A cenote," Kura breathed, her brow furrowed.

Aevyressa's gaze darkened. "They are not alone." Her vision was of shadowed figures moving along the edges of the water, their forms cloaked in darkness.

"Danielle, Xanthia," said William, as he observed them both bound and unconscious, chained to the wall, with the water beneath them. "And if I'm not mistaken, Eryndor." William clenched his fists, as he watched a sinister presence lurking just beyond sight, its energy thick and malevolent. "We have to move, now."

Lowering her hands, Aevyressa allowed the vision to fade. "Suytun, Mexico…. you have your answer. I ask one thing, though."

"And that is?" William asked, his brow furrowed.

"That Eryndor is mine. Your debt will be repaid in full, Vampire," stated Aevyressa.

"That is one deal that I don't mind making, Queen Aevyressa. You have my word," replied William.

"Excellent … Now go!" said Aevyressa, waving them away.

"Thank you, Aevyressa," said Kura, as she raised her hands in the air to create a portal to take them back to the Gramaze mansion.

* * *

As they stepped out of the portal, William turned to Kura. "Thank you for your support today. It hasn't gone unnoticed. You, Alessia and the McCrindles are welcome to stay as long as needed."

Kura inclined her head in appreciation. "Your kindness is deeply valued. And if I can assist again, please don't hesitate to ask." She then turned to Alessia with a warm smile. "Come, my dear, let's go see your parents."

Alessia nodded, returning the smile as they walked side by side toward the mansion.

William shifted his focus to Grayson. "Gather the coven. We reconvene here in ten minutes to discuss our portal jump to Mexico. We're bringing Danielle and Xanthia home."

"Yes, Sire." Grayson inclined his head before vanishing toward the house with Vampire speed, heading straight for the combat room.

Brock … said William telepathically.

Yes, Sire, Brock replied.

Arrange for transport to be waiting just beyond the city limits of Valladolid, Mexico, William instructed

177

telepathically. *Have it positioned on the eastern edge, close enough for quick access, but far enough to avoid drawing attention. It needs to take us straight to the Suytun cenote when we arrive.*

Understood, Sire. I'll see to it immediately, Brock responded.

William reached into his pocket, retrieving his phone. He quickly dialed Albinus and waited for the call to connect.

"William," Albinus answered, urgency lacing his voice. "Any news?"

"We've located Xanthia and Danielle," William said. "They're being held in a cenote in Mexico. We're heading there now to bring them home. I'll keep you updated on our progress and inform you once we've returned."

"Thank the Gods," Albinus breathed in relief.

"I need to go, Albinus. We'll talk more once we return," William said.

"Understood." The line went dead as William ended the call.

Violette ... can you standby ready to create a portal to cenote in Mexico, thought William, telepathically.

Yes, Sire, mind-thought Violette, as she appeared quickly, along with William's other coven members, in front of him.

"Sire, how are we going to find the cenote, considering there are over six thousand cenotes in Mexico?" asked Michael, who had been listening in on some of the telepathic chatter going on around the Gramaze property.

"I believe, from speaking with the Fae Queen earlier, that the cenote we are looking for is called Suytun, which is about a fifteen-minute drive from Valladolid in Mexico," replied William, as he watched Violette open a portal. "Brock has informed me that apparently, Danielle's mobile phone is pinging in that location, as well."

"Right. Let's go rescue our family," said Michael. He ran toward the portal, along with William and the others from the Gramaze Lepidoptera coven, with his sword drawn.

* * *

The air around the group rippled with energy as the portal released the Vampires into the heart of Valladolid. The city's quiet streets stretched before them, bathed in the soft glow of the afternoon sun.

William stepped out first, scanning the surroundings. Behind him, Michael, Grayson, Christian and the others emerged, each moving with the quiet grace and precision that only the Lepidoptera Vampires possessed.

Kelan was the last to emerge, his gaze darting around with an unspoken curiosity. "Valladolid," he murmured, his voice barely audible. "Feels different here, doesn't it?"

"It's the energy," William replied, his tone firm but calm. "We're in the right place." He turned to look at the others. "We need to keep a low profile, just in case."

Hawk nodded, his posture already alert. "Let's make this quick, then."

William gave a short nod and looked to the others. "Let's head to the vehicle Brock organized. Grayson, take the lead."

"Yes, Sire," Grayson responded, already scanning the road ahead.

The group moved in a seamless formation toward the parking area where a sleek black passenger van waited, its engine humming quietly.

William walked around to the driver's door and the window slid down. "I believe you are our ride to the Suytun Cenote?"

The driver, who didn't speak much English, just nodded once and smiled.

Jump in Lepidopteras, thought William.

As they piled into the passenger van, the interior felt cool and still, in sharp contrast to the humid air outside.

William settled in the front passenger seat, and the others took the back, filling the space with their quiet intensity.

"Will this take long?" Kelan asked from the back, his eyes trained on the passing scenery.

"It'll take about fifteen minutes, but we can't afford any delays," William replied, his voice steady, though his thoughts were focused on the mission ahead.

The van pulled out of the city and the streets quickly gave way to the open road. Fields of green stretched in every direction, the occasional palm tree swaying in the wind. Their journey was swift and uneventful.

As they neared the outskirts of town, Grayson glanced at his GPS and said to his family, "The Suytun Cenote should be just up ahead. It's a bit off the main road, but we'll be there soon."

"Stay alert. We don't know what's waiting for us there," stated William, his eyes narrowing as he peered out the front window.

Minutes later, the car slowed and the landscape shifted. There, partially hidden by the thick trees and rocks, was the entrance to Suytun Cenote.

"We're here," Grayson said, feeling the van come to a halt.

The group stepped out of the vehicle, with their swords drawn, ready for anything that might eventuate.

William exhaled slowly, his gaze fixed on the cenote. *This is where it all ends. Let's move*, thought William, telepathically.

CHAPTER TWENTY-EIGHT

A slow, rhythmic dripping sound echoed throughout the cavernous chamber. The air was damp, yet cool, carrying the scent of minerals and moss.

Danielle's head throbbed as she stirred. Her senses were sluggish from whatever she had been drugged with, and a dull ache radiated from her arm. As she cracked open her eyes, the faint bluish glow of the filtered sunlight in the cenote illuminated the jagged ceiling. Looking at her right arm, she noticed a translucent tube snaked from her forearm, leading to a half-filled glass container, where her blood—her Fae blood—was being collected in slow, treacherous drops. *What the fuck!*

Danielle yanked the needle from her arm. Pain flared, but she shoved it aside. Swallowing back the dizziness, she turned her head and noticed Xanthia lying motionless beside her, her own arm similarly tethered to a blood collection device. *What the hell is going on here? Where are we?*

"Xanthia!" Danielle whispered sharply, shuffling over to her. She reached out and ripped the needle from Xanthia's arm. Xanthia stirred, with a weak groan. "Xanthia, wake up," Danielle urged, shaking her shoulder. "We need to get out of here. Now!"

Xanthia's blue eyes fluttered open, hazy and unfocused. "Danielle?" she murmured, trying to sit up.

"Yes, it's me. We have to move." Danielle hooked an arm under Xanthia's shoulder, helping her to her feet. Xanthia swayed, blinking sluggishly. "Try pushing through it. We can't stay here. I will try to heal you as we walk."

Xanthia nodded and inhaled sharply as awareness flooded back. "Where are we?"

"I'm not sure. No time to chat … let's go," Danielle stated, gripping her wrist. "We need to run."

Weak, but determined, they stumbled across the uneven cavern floor; water lapping at their ankles as they neared a passageway leading out.

The moment they reached the opening, shadows moved around them. Figures emerged from the darkness, blocking their escape. Eryndor stood at the center, with his slow, mocking smile and his cold, piercing gaze locking onto them.

"Leaving so soon?" Eryndor's drawled, his amusement laced with menace.

Danielle's heart pounded as she pulled Xanthia behind her. Her sharp eyes darted around the cavernous chamber looking for an escape.

Xanthia stiffened and gulped hard.

One by one, more of Eryndor's minions appeared, their eyes gleaming with predatory hunger as they stepped into the dim glow of the cavern.

"Get out of our way, fuckers," ordered Danielle, her hands curled into fists, as she felt the pulse of her Lepidoptera power stir within her.

Behind her, Xanthia's Fae energy crackled faintly, ready to unleash, though fear flickered in her blue eyes.

Eryndor smirked, tilting his head. "And waste all that precious Fae blood you have inside? No, I think not."

Xanthia wobbled, but steadied herself, and a fire ignited in her eyes. Lifting her chin, defiance etched into every line of her face, she heatedly said, "You think you've won? This is the last mistake you'll ever make. Our families will be looking for us. They won't give up until they find us, I am sure."

"Oh, but I have already won," Eryndor mused, gesturing to the filled vials of Fae blood on a nearby table.

"This will be extremely invaluable to me. I will finally be able to end this miserable world."

Danielle's breath quickened when she saw the vials. She knew that they couldn't win this fight alone, because their bodies were still sluggish and their strength had been sapped by the stolen blood. But she would at least try.

Before either Danielle or Xanthia could respond, a sudden gust of wind howled through the cenote; the torches that lined the walls flickered wildly. Shadows shifted unnaturally and a blur of movement descended from above. As a deep resonating battle cry echoed throughout the cenote, figures cloaked in darkness emerged.

William Gramaze was the first to strike, his swords flashing like silver lightning, as he lunged at Eryndor.

Eryndor barely dodged William's blade. As his smirk faded, he drew his own wickedly curved sword from its sheath. "Humph … Lepidoptera."

Grayson and Michael descended upon the minions, their blades carving through the darkness with deadly precision.

Stephen and Kelan moved in tandem, slashing through Eryndor's warriors, their attacks a whirlwind of lethal grace.

Samuel hurled his daggers with pinpoint accuracy, each blade finding its mark.

Hawk fought with raw ferocity, shifting between clawed strikes and fluid swordplay, keeping the enemy forces at bay.

Eryndor's minions' blood splattered across the stone floor, as cries of pain echoed through the cavern. The scent of sweat, iron and burnt magic thickened the air, as more minions were killed.

Danielle pushed Xanthia toward the tunnel. "Go! Now!"

Xanthia hesitated, eyes flicking between her friend and the battle raging around them. "No, I'm not leaving you."

Christian suddenly appeared at Danielle's side, his presence a shield against the chaos. "I've got you," he said firmly, standing protectively in front of Danielle and Xanthia, as a minion lunged at them. But Christian intercepted his blade and slashed through the attacker before he could reach Danielle or Xanthia.

As more minions surged forward, Danielle ducked under a wild swing, retaliating with a powerful punch and a kick of her own, sending her opponent sprawling.

Christian caught another minion's wrist mid-strike, twisting and disarming him, before delivering a devastating blow to his chest. He looked over at Danielle and said, "Great teamwork!"

Danielle's brows rose and she shook her head. "I don't think this is over with, yet."

A scream pierced the air as Xanthia was suddenly grabbed by one of Eryndor's minions. She struggled, kicking wildly, but the warrior's grip was like iron. As her panic spiked, a burst of Fae magic surged from her palms and sent a blast of energy into the warrior's chest. He staggered, but didn't let go.

Danielle struck the minion square in the chest with her boot, sending him flying backward, freeing Xanthia, who stumbled into Christian's arms.

Christian steadied her, his touch grounding and reassuring. "You're safe," he murmured, his voice fierce with protectiveness.

"Thank you," said Xanthia, looking up at him.

Eryndor snarled as William pressed him back, the clash of blades echoing through the cavern. With a powerful burst of energy, Eryndor slammed his fist into the ground and a shockwave of dark magic erupted, sending William skidding backwards.

"I grow tired of this," Eryndor muttered. He reached behind him and placed his hand on the Cauldron of Chaos. Shadows coiled and thickened, forming a swirling vortex of darkness around him. The air turned ice-cold and the torches on the wall flickered wildly, as the shadows consumed him. In a final act of defiance, he let out a sharp whistle and the limestone of the walls cracked and rumbled, as parts of the cenote's ceiling collapsed between him and William. By the time the dust cleared, Eryndor was gone.

As his remaining minions saw their leader retreat, panic spread amongst them. Some attempted to escape through hidden tunnels, but only a few managed. The rest were cut down mercilessly by the Lepidoptera Vampires, their deaths swift and brutal.

"That bastard has escaped, again," stated Michael, coming to stand beside William.

"I think we may need to speak with the Ironclaws again about what measures we can come up with to stop this fucker," replied William.

"It seems that he is always one step ahead of us," stated Michael.

William nodded to Michael in agreement and turned toward Grayson, "Collect the vials of blood," instructed William, gesturing to the table.

"Yes, Sire." Grayson ran to collect them, placing them carefully into a leather pouch at his waist.

Christian reached for Danielle's hand, his touch calming and grounding her. "Let's go."

Danielle nodded and grabbed Xanthia's hand as well. "Come on."

William and the others formed a protective barrier around Danielle and Xanthia, ensuring that no last-minute attacks took place, as they made their way toward the exit.

When they hurried through the tunnel, the torches flickered once more, the scent of blood and burnt magic lingering in the air.

"I can carry Xanthia," Kelan offered to Christian, noticing how weak she was, as she leaned heavily on Danielle, while they walked.

"That would be great. Thanks, Kelan," replied Christian.

Kelan picked Xanthia up and automatically felt her heart pounding. "Are you okay?"

"I will be, thanks to you and everyone else for saving us. I really would like to go home, though," said Xanthia, as she laid her head on his shoulder.

"Your wish is my command, milady," said Kelan, playfully.

Danielle squeezed Christian's hand, feeling the unspoken words between them—relief, determination and the understanding that this was far from over. "Thank you for coming to save us."

"Anything for you, my love," replied Christian, as he swept her up into his arms and carried her toward the exit.

As they all reached the top of the Suytun Cenote, William thought telepathically, *Let's get the fuck out of here. We will regroup once we are back at the mansion.* He ran at Vampire speed toward the waiting van and everyone followed.

Even though they had escaped and none of his family were hurt badly, or, worse yet, killed, William knew Eryndor still had the Cauldron of Chaos, with the ancient artifacts inside, and the amulet.

I wonder how long it will be before Eryndor sources a Fae's blood, to end the world, thought William to himself, as he climbed into the passenger seat of the van. *That fucker, he needs to be stopped!*

CHAPTER TWENTY-NINE

Sitting at his office desk, William took a deep breath and raked a hand through his hair. Taking his phone out of his pocket, he dialed the Ironclaws.

"Evening, William. What can I do for you, my friend?" Garrick said, as he answered the call.

"Evening, Garrick. How's things going over there?" asked William.

"Considering we still are on high alert for if and when Eryndor returns, we are good at the moment. Elara and I, however, are preparing to honor the Fjord itself. It's been over ten thousand years since the glaciers first carved these cliffs and waters, shaping a place that feels almost alive," Garrick said, his gaze lingering on the shimmering depths below.

"That certainly is a momentous occasion. Congratulations," said William.

"It sure is, but I am sure you didn't ring to talk about the celebrations. What's going on?" questioned Garrick, as he sat and looked out over the Fjord.

"Eryndor!"

Garrick's expression darkened at the mention of his adopted son's name. He leaned forward in his chair, his fingers gripping the armrests. "What has he done now?"

William exhaled sharply, his grip tightening around the phone. "Eryndor kidnapped Danielle and Xanthia."

Garrick cursed under his breath. "Why them?"

"For their Fae blood, so that he can complete the ritual to destroy the world," William said grimly. "The attack was calculated. He ambushed them on the road, drugged them and disappeared without a trace. It took us a while to find them, and we had to enlist the help of the new Fae Queen."

"Fuck!" Garrick expressed, his anger seeping to the surface. "I am sorry for the trouble he has caused your family, William. Where are Danielle and Xanthia now?"

"They're safe," William assured him. "We got to them in time. They were being held at a remote hideout in Mexico. It was heavily guarded, but we managed to extract them before he could finish whatever ritual or experiment he had planned."

Garrick let out a breath, relief flickering across his features, before they hardened into frustration. "And Eryndor?"

William's jaw clenched. "Gone. By the time we reached them, Eryndor seemed to be already two steps ahead of us, just like always. It was like he had already factored in that we might be coming."

Garrick's gaze flickered toward the window, where the distant Fjord shimmered under the moonlight. The weight of the moment settled over him, and he wondered whether they would even make it through the commemoration ceremonies he had planned. "What do you need from me?"

"Even though you have important ceremonial things to attend to, I need you here. We have to formulate a proactive and offensive plan of attack. Every second we delay gives Eryndor the upper hand," William stated.

Garrick nodded, already making up his mind. "I'll be there in thirty minutes, with a few soldiers."

"Good!" The call ended and William set the phone down. His office suddenly felt smaller, the air thick from the storm that he knew was coming. Eryndor was still out there. And next time they might not be fast enough to stop him.

"Knock, knock," said Albinus, interrupting William's thoughts.

"Come ..." answered William, watching his office door open. "Albinus ... what can I do for you?"

"I wondered if you had a spare minute or two, to discuss a few things?" asked Albinus, as he walked toward William's desk.

"I am in the middle of a security operation at the moment, but I can spare five minutes. You have my full attention, what is it you wish to discuss?" stated William, gesturing for Albinus to take a seat in front of him.

"Firstly, I wanted to say thank you for saving Xanthia's life. I am forever in your debt."

"You're welcome. Was there something else?" asked William, as he read Albinus's thoughts.

"I am wondering if the offer still stands for Xanthia and me to stay in the little house down the back of the property, full time?" asked Albinus.

"Of course, my friend. Especially after what has happened. And since you are already living there, so it would make sense," replied William.

"Thank you, William. We truly appreciate your kindness."

"You're welcome. I figure that it would give you and Xanthia a bit more privacy, too," said William, shaking his hand. "And since Xanthia is still adjusting to the Fae world, my family can help her with the transition. Wouldn't you agree?"

"Most definitely. I would also like to ask if the full-time job offer is still available?" asked Albinus.

William checked the time on his phone before giving him a small nod. "I am sure we can sort something out. But for now, I need to get going. I have a meeting in the operations room." Standing, William was already shifting back into work mode. "We'll talk more tomorrow."

Albinus got to his feet as well. "Sounds good … and again, thank you."

William clapped him on the shoulder before heading for the door with Albinus. "Anytime, my friend."

* * *

Tension thrummed through the operations room. Around the long wooden table, every face was set and serious, eyes sharp with focus as they prepared to devise a plan of attack. The air felt heavy with purpose, each mind already calculating the risks and the stakes of what lay ahead. William, who sat at the head of the table, his expression grim, was focused on the screen on the wall and the last known coordinates for Eryndor in Mexico. But after one hour of searching, there was still nothing to show. No heat signatures. No structures out of place. No trace of Eryndor.

Garrick and his soldiers occupied the seats opposite him, while William's own family and trusted warriors filled the remaining chairs.

"Still nothing," Brock muttered. "If Eryndor's hiding, he's doing it well. No satellite feed, no unusual activity—he's a ghost." Brock ran a frustrated hand through his hair.

Garrick exhaled sharply, his fingers tapping against the table. "That doesn't mean he isn't out there. He seems to be outplaying us."

"For now," William corrected, his tone firm. "But we can't afford to let him keep the upper hand. We have to assume he's planning something. Kidnapping Danielle and Xanthia wasn't just an act of desperation."

Kelan leaned forward with his arms crossed over his chest. "What if he's not just hiding? What if he's moving? Constantly shifting locations so that we can't get a lock on him?"

"That would make sense," Garrick agreed. "If he's setting something up, he won't stay in one place for long." He turned to his soldiers. "Did any of our scouts pick up unusual movement patterns? Supply lines? Anything that might indicate where he's setting up?"

"Nothing obvious," said Draven, shaking his head. "But there have been reports of sudden disappearances in remote areas—people vanishing without a trace. It could be coincidence … or it could be him, collecting resources."

William's expression darkened. "If that's true, he's gathering more than just Fae blood. He's building an army, a weapon, something big."

Griffin soldier Bennett, who had remained silent until now, leaned back in her chair. "Then we have only one option—we find him first. And we end this. No more waiting, no more playing by his rules."

A heavy silence fell over the table. No one disagreed.

William nodded. "Agreed. Eryndor must be stopped, at all costs. No matter what it takes."

Garrick met his gaze across the table, his jaw set. "Let's put an end to this."

William exhaled, glancing at the screen again. "We start with the disappearances. We investigate every lead, track every anomaly. He's slipping through the cracks, but if we push hard enough, we'll find him." He looked at Brock. "Scrap the satellites for now. Focus on ground intel. Anything out of the ordinary, no matter how small."

Brock nodded. "On it."

William turned to Garrick. "I want your best trackers sweeping every inch of where people have disappeared. If Eryndor is shifting locations, they'll find his trail."

Garrick smirked, though there was no humor in it. "Consider it done."

William pushed back his chair and stood tall. "We move immediately. This ends with Eryndor. One way or another. But remember, he must be taken alive and delivered to the new Fae Queen, to answer for the atrocities he's committed against the Fae Kingdom and the murder or the previous Fae Queen, Elyndra."

No one argued. The stakes were higher than ever before, as the Griffins and Lepidoptera marched out of the operations room, in search of Eryndor, his minions and the ancient artifacts.

CHAPTER THIRTY

In a remote research station on Bouvet Island in the south Atlantic, scientists were starting their day. "Good morning, Jean," Sebastian, the lead scientist, greeted his technician. "Have you seen the two researchers who arrived from South Georgia Island yesterday? I've searched everywhere around the base camp this morning, but can't find them."

"I believe they went out early this morning to investigate the strange magnetic anomaly on the other side of the island," Jean replied. "They haven't returned yet, though."

"Right. And why wasn't I informed about this?" Sebastian demanded.

Jean shrugged. "I couldn't tell you. Do you want me to send someone to look for them?"

"We'll wait for a few more hours," Sebastian decided, as he looked at his wristwatch. "If they're not back by lunch time, we'll call for help." He drew in a deep breath, then exhaled slowly.

"Alright, leave it to me," Jean replied. "If they don't return, I'll contact the Norwegian Coast Guard, Search and Rescue Service, for a search and rescue. Hopefully, it won't come to that."

"Good. Keep me updated," Sebastian instructed, striding away toward his lab. Despite his calm tone, a tightness in his chest hinted at the growing unease settling over the camp.

* * *

Dr Elias Norland wiped the frost from his goggles as he trudged through the deep snow, scanning the frozen terrain ahead. Fierce winds howled, biting through his thermal gear. *Must be around here somewhere.*

Behind him, his assistant, Freya Lindholm, adjusted the strap of her backpack. The bitter wind had long since robbed her cheeks of warmth, leaving them numb and raw. Each time she exhaled, a pale and ghostly mist appeared, hovering briefly before it dissolved. "Elias, are you sure this is the right area?" she asked, glancing down at the GPS, rubbing her numb fingers against the cold device. "We've got a weak satellite lock and no cell or augmentation out here and the coordinates don't match the drone feed from yesterday."

"I think whatever it was, it has shifted," Elias muttered, frustration lacing his voice. "Something's interfering with the signal. We need to—"

All of a sudden, the ground beneath them collapsed without warning. Ice and rock shattered, swallowing them whole, as they fell into an underground cavern.

Freya groaned, as she hit the hard cave floor, then tried to push herself up. "Elias? Are you okay?"

"I'm fine," replied Elias, as he reached for his head, feeling a warm trickle of blood. As he glanced around, the flickering light from his headlamp illuminated strange markings on the stone walls, which glowed faintly with ice-coated minerals.

Freya exhaled sharply when she noticed the walls. "This … isn't natural." Fumbling in her jacket, she yanked out the satellite phone to call for help, but when she pressed the power button, there was nothing. "No, no, no … It must have broken in the fall."

Elias reached for his personal locator beacon, which was inside his jacket, and flipped the cover open. Once he pressed the SOS button, a red light started to flash weakly. "The signal's weak. We need to get closer to the surface."

A profound, unsettling rumble echoed from deeper within the cave.

Freya looked at Elias with eyes wide. "I don't think we are alone down here."

"Come on," Elias got to his feet and held his hand out for her to take. "Let's see if we can find a way out of here."

Taking his hand, Freya quickly glanced ahead. "It looks like there is an opening over there," she pointed in the direction of an opening, highlighted by light shining in from above. "Maybe it will lead us outside?"

Elias nodded in agreement and they walked toward the opening.

As they walked through, Elias and Freya were immediately confronted by a large ancient cauldron adorned with intricate runes and symbols, which glowed brightly and hummed.

"Wow, what is that?" asked Freya, as she walked toward the cauldron and watched how it illuminated, its colors shifting between shades of crimson, violet and the deepest of black.

"I can't say that I have seen anything like this in my entire lifetime," said Elias, as he walked over to the cauldron. When he reached to feel the outer wall of the cauldron, he felt a small jolt of electricity go through his body and instantly retracted his hand. "What the hell is this thing?" He rubbed his hand, trying to sooth the pain.

All of a sudden, an invisible force slammed Freya and Elias against the ice wall, pinning them with a bone-jarring impact. Their feet dangled above the frozen ground, trapped in an unrelenting grip.

"Who do we have here?" Eryndor sneered, as he stood in front of Freya and Elias, reading their minds. "Ah, I see—researchers."

"Let us down," demanded Elias. "Now!"

Eryndor raised his hand and waved it at Elias, rendering him unconscious. "What are you both doing down here?" demanded Eryndor, his eyes now trained on Freya.

"We are researchers … we discovered a strange magnetic anomaly around Bouvet Island, so we thought we would come and check it out. That is all. Why are you holding us here?" asked Freya, her wide eyes glancing all around the cave for a way out.

Eryndor let out a cold chuckle, his eyes gleaming with dark amusement. "A magnetic anomaly? Is that what led you straight into my domain?" He stepped closer to Freya, tilting his head as he studied her. "Curiosity is a dangerous thing, researcher." His voice dripped with menace. "Now tell me—who else knows you're here?"

Freya swallowed hard, forcing herself to hold Eryndor's gaze. "Our team back at the base camp knows we are out here," she lied smoothly. "If we don't check in soon, they'll come looking for us." She tightened her fists, trying to ignore the pounding of her heart. "You can let us go. No one else has to get involved."

Eryndor eyes narrowed as he studied Freya's face for any hint of deception. He could hear the steady rhythm of her heartbeat—controlled, but not entirely calm. A smirk tugged at his lips. *She's lying.*

"Nice try," he drawled, stepping even closer until he loomed over her. "But I don't need your words to know the truth." He tapped his temple with two fingers. "Your mind tells me everything I need to know." His smirk darkened. "No one is expecting you anytime soon, which means I have all the time in the world to decide what to do with you." He glanced at Elias's unconscious form before returning his cold gaze to Freya. "So, tell me, researcher … do you value knowledge more than your life?"

Freya swallowed hard, her breath shallow as she struggled to keep her voice steady. "P-please … we—we didn't mean to intrude," she stammered, her eyes darting to Elias, who was still unconscious. "We were just following the readings … we didn't know anyone—anything—was down here." Her hands trembled at her sides, as she tried to think of something, anything, that might keep them alive.

"If you let us go, we won't say a word about this place. No one else has to know … I swear."

Eryndor lifted one hand, his fingers curling like the talons of a predator, as he reached toward Freya and Elias. Dark energy crackled at his fingertips, an eerie, pulsating glow casting long shadows against the icy walls. With a slow, deliberate motion, he spread his fingers wide, then clenched them into a fist.

A wave of invisible power crashed over Freya and Elias, seeping into their minds like tendrils of smoke.

Freya gasped, her body jerking as her pupils dilated. Her breath hitched, before settling into an eerily calm rhythm.

Elias shuddered, his eyes rolling back for a moment before snapping forward—vacant and obedient.

Eryndor twisted his wrist slightly and watched as their expressions smoothed into blank submission. Then, with a satisfied smirk, he flicked his fingers outward, releasing them from their invisible restraints. They landed softly on the icy floor, standing still, waiting. "Perfect," he murmured, lowering his hand. "Now, my little researchers … let's see how useful you can be.

"You belong to me, now," Eryndor said, his voice laced with dark amusement. "And you will do exactly as I command." He paced in front of them, relishing the complete control he held. "Go back to your little research team. Tell them everything is normal—no anomalies, no discoveries." He stopped and tilted his head. "And if anyone dares to dig deeper …" His smirk sharpened into something cruel. "You'll take care of them for me, won't you?"

"Your wish is our command, Master," Elias and Freya said in unison.

"Off you go," said Eryndor, gesturing toward a passage ahead.

Escort them out through the opening, thought Eryndor to a nearby minion.

Yes, Sire, thought the minion telepathically, as he walked over to Freya and Elias.

Eryndor watched Freya and Elias stare, devoid of thought or emotion, then walk with his minions toward the passage.

"Now, my beauty, it is time to get this party started," stated Eryndor, smirking as he walked over to the Cauldron of Chaos.

The cauldron pulsated as Eryndor neared with the Ethereal Nexus Amulet around his neck.

Opening a pouch that was strapped to his waist, Eryndor produced four vials of Fae blood. *And you thought you had taken every vial I had, Lepidopteras. Well, you had better think again. Now that I have what I need, I will bring this world to its knees, and you won't be able to stop me.* His sinister laugh reverberated throughout the cavern, as he stored the vials back in the pouch.

With the snowstorm raging above, and the relentless winds howling across the icy surface of Bouvet Island, Eryndor's voice cut through the cold air, to his minions. *Stand guard outside. No one is to enter this cavern. Do I make myself clear?*

Yes, Master! his minions responded in unison; their voices tinged with obedience.

Eryndor's eyes narrowed as he watched them hesitate. "What are you waiting for?" he growled, his command sharp, to the ones still inside the cave. He watched his minions scramble to obey, disappearing into the storm without a word.

Beneath the frozen ground, hidden in the heart of the cavern deep under the snow, Eryndor stood alone, his cloak fluttering, as he hovered above the ancient cauldron. The air was thick with frost, the only warmth coming from the dark energy pulsing in the room. Removing the lid of the cauldron, he revealed the three ancient artifacts—the Twin Icefire Blades, the Golden Chalice, and the Fae's Golden Ring—lying inside, worn by time, but brimming with power. They were relics that were key to the destruction he sought.

Eryndor unhooked the Ethereal Nexus Amulet from around his neck. Its dark gem gleamed in the dim light of the cavern. As he held it over the cauldron for a long moment, Eryndor felt the power of the artifacts calling to him like a magnet. With deliberate care, he placed the Ethereal Nexus Amulet on top of the artifacts and watched the cauldron pulsate.

With a swift motion, Eryndor reached into the folds of his pouch and withdrew the four vials of Fae blood—their crimson contents swirling ominously inside.

"This is it," he whispered to himself, his breath misting in the air.

The blood of the Fae, rare and potent, would be the catalyst he needed. He opened the first vial; the hiss of the breaking seal sounded like a promise of destruction.

As he poured the blood into the cauldron, it merged with the glowing artifacts, the liquid sizzling upon contact. When the cauldron began to tremble, and the air around it pulsed with power, Eryndor opened the second vial, pouring it in, and then the third; each addition caused the hum filling the chamber to deepen. The cold, desolate cavern seemed to come alive with growing energy, as though the world itself was waiting for the ritual to unfold.

When the final vial of Fae blood was empty, Eryndor's eyes flashed with madness, as he replaced the lid. Raising his hands above the cauldron, his voice low and steady, he began to chant in an ancient, forgotten tongue.

> *By the blood of the Fae, and the Nexus might,*
> *Let this world be swallowed by endless night.*
> *From the deepest earth to the heavens high,*
> *The world shall crumble, and none shall*
> *survive.*

The air thickened, crackling with dark magic. The cauldron's light grew brighter, blinding in its intensity. The cavern walls shook, snow and ice falling from the ceiling, as if the earth itself was reacting to the ritual.

Eryndor's grin spread wider and his voice rose in power with each word. "The world will burn, and from the ashes, I will forge a new order. One that bows only to me. I alone will rise to rule what remains."

The cauldron erupted with a flash of blinding light toward the sky and the ground beneath Eryndor's feet trembled violently. His sinister laugh echoed throughout the cavern, rising in pitch and cruelty, as the ritual neared its climax. The forces of destruction were unleashed and, with them, Eryndor's reign of terror had begun.

CHAPTER THIRTY-ONE

An urgent beeping noise on the large screen pulled William's attention away from the strategy table. He turned to Brock, who was already scanning the incoming transmission. "What is happening?"

"It's a distress signal," Brock confirmed, typing rapidly on his laptop. "A Norwegian research team on Bouvet Island activated their emergency beacon. The signal's weak—barely transmitting. I'll see if I can find anything by satellite."

Garrick leaned in, his arms crossed over his chest. "Could be a malfunction. Or it could mean they're in serious trouble."

William's jaw tightened. "Bouvet Island … Is that one of the places where some of your Norwegian people have disappeared?"

"It sure is," replied Garrick.

"This can't be a coincidence!" William turned to Grayson and Michael. "Get a team ready. We leave immediately."

"Yes, Sire," they both said, as they ran out of the operations room, toward the combat room of the Gramaze mansion, to retrieve weapons.

Stephen studied the screen. "Hang on, if Eryndor is there, this could be a trap."

"Doesn't matter," William said firmly. "People's lives are at stake. And if Eryndor is after something on that island, we need to stop him before he gets it."

"Let's move," said Garrick, to his soldiers. "Every second counts."

Lepidopteras ... we have a new mission. We meet in the backyard in five minutes. Violette, I need a portal created to Bouvet Island, thought William telepathically.

Any Lepidopteras who weren't out on a mission scrambled to their feet and ran toward the back of the house.

Already on it, William, thought Violette telepathically. She, and the others, had been listening to their chatter.

* * *

As Violette conjured the portal, the Gramaze Lepidopteras and Ironclaw Griffins positioned themselves on either side, with their weapons in hand. Every one of them understood the gravity of the mission. If Eryndor was indeed hiding on Bouvet Island, with the Cauldron of Chaos, and the ancient artifacts, this would be a do-or-die operation, with fatalities inevitable.

"Everyone ready?" asked William, as he glanced around at each of their faces.

They all nodded in agreement. The group stood ready, their hearts racing, with their hands gripped on their weapons, determined to reach their destination.

"Let's go!" instructed Garrick, gesturing toward the portal, which shimmered in front of them, a swirling mass of light and energy, its edges crackling with power.

But as William's foot was about to cross the threshold, the portal snapped shut with a violent force, which unleashed a shockwave that hurled every Lepidoptera and Griffin backward, crashing them to the ground.

"What the fuck ..." said William, quickly rising to his feet. "Violette, what just happened?"

"I don't know, William," replied Violette, trying to collect her thoughts, as she rose to her feet.

"Everyone alright?" asked William, glancing around at the Lepidopteras and Griffins.

They all nodded in agreement.

William ... Violette ... the wards are down around the mansion and academy. What is going on? thought Queen Talitha, from her basement room.

We don't know what has happened. We are about to find out, thought William telepathically.

"Violette, are you able to open another portal?" asked William.

Violette placed both hands out front and tried to open another portal, but there was nothing. "What is going on? I don't understand why it's not working."

The air around them vibrated with a deafening sound, like the world itself was breaking apart.

"What the hell is that?" asked Garrick, who was now standing next to William and Violette, with his soldiers behind him.

"Sire!" Grayson gestured toward the sky above them, which had darkened, with swirling storm clouds, as though something ancient and malicious was awakening. "Eryndor?"

A chill ran through the air and the faintest whisper of darkness brushed against everyone's mind.

"I believe you're right, Grayson," Garrick said, his voice heavy with realization. "I would say that my son has found the Fae blood he was searching for, and he's already begun his reign."

"Everyone inside, NOW!" yelled William, above the noise.

All Lepidopteras out on missions—you are to return to the mansion immediately, thought William to his family telepathically, as he and everyone ran toward the operations room.

"Let's go, Griffins," demanded Garrick.

* * *

As William watched the last of his family enter the operations room, he said loudly, "Listen up!" He glanced around the room at each of the faces standing before him, waiting for the room to quieten. "Violette … where are you?"

"Here!" stated Violette, who was standing at the back of everyone, as she lifted her hand in the air.

William looked in her direction. "I want you to take care of our Queen and everything and everyone at the academy."

"Yes, William," replied Violette.

"Hawk, Sully, Kiplin, Samuel, Elsie, Michael, Kelan and Samantha, you will be going with Violette, to watch over Queen Talitha and the academy," instructed William, as he spotted each of them in the crowded room.

They all nodded in agreement and walked toward the sliding doors, following Violette into the hallway, to discuss a plan on keeping the academy and the mansion safe from any attacks.

William turned to Brock, who was sitting at the operations room computer. "Brock … what have you got on the satellite feedback? Anything?"

Brock shook his head. "Nothing … I can't even get the internet to work. It seems the world has been cut off from all telecommunications, even though at this stage, the power is still on."

William raked a hand through his hair. "Shit!"

"I have an idea. Since you're the communications expert around here, Brock, do you happen to know if you have a telegraph at the mansion?" Garrick asked.

"We do," Brock said, trying to remember where it was stored. "Good idea. It may be old tech, but it'll keep us connected and I'm betting our counterparts are already thinking the same thing."

"Can I leave that in your capable hands, Brock?" asked William.

Brock rose to his feet. "Yes, Sire." He walked toward the sliding doors then ran at Vampire speed down to the basement.

"We need to get to Bouvet Island. Now!" stated Garrick, as he clenched his fists, frustration flickering in his eyes.

"How? Obviously, the portals no longer work, and it's too far to fly, even for us," stated Kael, with hands on his hips. "And I'm sure Eryndor knows we will be coming."

"How in the hell are we going to get to Bouvet Island, when we don't have a portal to travel? With telecommunications down I would expect that all planes have been grounded too," stated Grayson, his mind racing.

"That's enough …" stated William gruffly, looking at Grayson and Kael. "The only way we are going to be able to travel to Bouvet Island is the old-fashioned way, by foot. And at this stage … and let me make myself clear … we are not even sure that this is the place that Eryndor is holed up, are we?"

"I can answer that, Sire," Brock replied, as he stepped back into the operations room, with the telegraph in hand. "When I brought up satellite images of Bouvet Island, I spotted Eryndor's minions escorting two humans through the snow on foot. When I traced their footprints back to the source, I saw a strange light emanating from beneath the snow, just before the internet and satellite feeds cut out. So, I'd say you're right to assume that Eryndor is on Bouvet Island."

"I have an idea … could we travel via the ancient ley lines?" Bennett called out.

"Ley lines?" said Garrick, his brow furrowed. "Those things are ancient and unstable. They've been dormant for centuries, if not millennia. Even if we could find one, we'd have to do it manually, and that's risky."

"I've heard of the ley line pathways hidden beneath the earth," stated Stephen. "There's one near a place called the Hollow of Winds, just north of Olden, that is used to access Bouvet Island. It might be our only shot."

"We've also got the old roadways. They're tunnels beneath Europe, hidden from the mortal world, which are used by the ancient ones. They're far from ideal, but they could get us to Norway faster," said Bennett.

"You mean the underworld passages? They're fraught with danger, and would take us through areas where we might attract attention from Eryndor's spies. But …" Garrick hesitated, then nodded. "If we move quickly and quietly, that might be our best option."

"How long do you think it will take, Garrick?" asked William.

"Honestly, it may take us three days. Longer, if we run into trouble," replied Garrick.

"The sooner we get to Bouvet Island to stop Eryndor, the better," stated William.

Garrick's eyes darted toward the map, which was up on the operations room wall, to where the route to Olden was marked in red. "The quickest route is through the hidden caverns beneath the Alps, into the tunnels under Norway. They're known only to the old ones. No mortal or others know of them, and we should be safe from Eryndor's eyes."

"Great! Sounds like a plan. Let get moving." William looked at Garrick with determination in his eyes.

"Brock … Once you have the telegraph set up, I want you to contact our counterparts and let them know what is happening," instructed William.

"Yes, Sire," replied Brock.

"Grayson, I want you to go and see Lamia and get together some blood supplies and food for everyone to take on this mission," instructed William.

"Yes, Sire," replied Grayson.

"Alright … everyone else … make sure you're fully armed for this mission," William commanded. "We meet outside in five minutes. Prepare yourselves, because we have got a long road ahead of us and we will be coming across Antarctic weather conditions."

CHAPTER THIRTY-TWO

The air was thick with the scent of ancient magic, crackling with malevolent energy. Eryndor's haunting eyes gleamed with cruel delight, his hunger for power intensifying as he approached the Cauldron of Chaos.

"My wondrous beauty," Eryndor muttered with smug arrogance.

The cavern trembled softly at the sound of his voice, resonating with the dark power pulsing from the ancient relics within. Jagged runes carved into the icy floor glowed ominously, feeding on the energy that seeped from the cauldron.

Eryndor extended a hand toward it, his fingertips barely grazing the sinister mist rising from its depths. As he touched it, the seething shadows stilled, swirling into a mirrored surface that gleamed with an unnatural clarity, and scenes of devastation flickered to life within the cauldron's depths, each more catastrophic than the last. They were a dark symphony for Eryndor's twisted mind.

* * *

Times Square, New York City

The sky cracked open with a sound that could only be described as the world splitting at its seams. Billboards flickered and died, plunging Times Square into an eerie gloom. Tourists screamed, clutching loved ones as the ground trembled violently beneath their feet. Buildings swayed, windows shattered and a deep rumble grew beneath the asphalt. A sinkhole opened at the center of the street and swallowed cabs, pavement and people alike. Streetlights snapped, sparks raining down on the pavement.

* * *

Venice, Italy

Rivers of seawater gushed through the narrow streets, rising fast. Gondolas bobbed uncontrollably, smashing into marble facades. Tourists waded knee-deep, panic-stricken. The sky was a sickly green, above the swirling clouds, lightning branching like cracking glass.

* * *

Tokyo, Japan

Shibuya Crossing was a nightmare. Cars lay abandoned, alarms blaring, as terrified crowds surged for shelter. The ground rippled like ocean waves. From the bay, a colossal waterspout twisted upward, dragging ships skyward before hurling them into skyscrapers with horrifying precision.

* * *

Los Angeles, California

The Hollywood Hills crumbled, mansions sliding like toys as a massive sinkhole yawned open. Fires spread unchecked, painting the sky an apocalyptic orange. Families trapped in their cars on a highway that had become a river, sobbed prayers into the air. A news helicopter circled overhead, its camera capturing the devastation until a storm-surge wave rose impossibly high, slamming it from the sky.

* * *

Eryndor's lips curved into a satisfied smirk, as he continued to watch the devastation, in awe of the destruction he had caused.

One of his minions, cloaked in obsidian armor, stepped forward hesitantly, his head bowed. "My lord … the destruction … it spreads faster than we anticipated," he reported, his voice low and cautious.

Eryndor didn't even bother to look at him, instead his eyes were fixed on the scenes unfolding inside the cauldron. "Faster?" he drawled, tracing a finger along the cauldron's rim. "I would say it spreads precisely as intended. Does the sight of it frighten you, soldier?"

The minion flinched, a shudder running through him. "N-No, my lord. I live to serve you."

"Good," Eryndor murmured, his eyes narrowing as his vision shifted to a city bathed in blood-red twilight, its streets cracked and flooded with shadows. "Because this is only the beginning."

The cauldron's glow seemed to deepen, shadows writhing eagerly, as if tasting the terror rippling across the world. Eryndor watched, his eyes glittering with dark pleasure, as the chaos spread like wildfire—unstoppable and inevitable.

"Soon, there will be nothing left to stand against what I have planned," stated Eryndor, smirking. He watched a cathedral collapse in a cloud of dust, humans screaming, and forests withering to ash in a matter of breaths.

* * *

The air was cold and damp as the Griffins and Lepidopteras continued through the narrow tunnel system, walking beneath the Alps and into Norway. The walls were rough-hewn stone, slick with moisture, the flickering light that came off their torches casting eerie shadows around them. The air was thick with the scent of earth and ancient dust.

"It's a bit unnerving being this far underground. These tunnels were built to keep the world out, yet we're the ones who don't belong here," stated Bennett, as she followed her Griffin leader Garrick, deeper into the tunnels.

"We don't have the luxury of being comfortable. Let's just get through this," stated Garrick, as he moved through the tunnel, his Griffin senses on alert for anything unusual.

As everyone moved deeper into the tunnels, their steps echoed off the stone walls and the air grew colder. The further they went, the more everyone could feel the weight of the world pressing down on them.

Days passed as they navigated the twisting passages, relying on old maps and the guidance of those who had traveled these roads many moons before. The path was rough, at times narrow, and other times winding endlessly, but with each step, everyone grew closer to their destination.

On the fourth day of travel, they finally emerged unscathed from the tunnels at the Hollow of Winds, then travelled through the ley lines to Bouvet Island. The snow-capped mountains rose around them, the ancient landscape both foreign and familiar.

It was then that they all heard the loud, ominous thrum again, reverberating through the ground, almost like a heartbeat, but much slower and more mechanical. The earth itself seemed to tremble beneath their feet, causing small rocks and snow to shiver and slide down the mountainside.

"What in the Gods' names is that sound?" asked Bennett, her eyes narrowing against the biting wind, as she scanned her surroundings. The pulsing seemed to echo inside her chest, unsettling her, as if the world itself were struggling to hold on.

"It's coming from the north," stated Kael, his gaze fixed toward the horizon.

"That pulsing, it feels like it's trying to tear my skull apart." Grayson pressed a hand to his temple, grimacing.

"It's Eryndor," Garrick growled, his tone dark and his feathers bristling underneath his skin with agitation. He pointed toward the column of blinding white light erupting from the ground, spiraling violently into the sky. "That machine of his, whatever twisted purpose it serves, is ripping the world apart at its seams."

"We don't have time to marvel at the apocalypse," stated William. "Let's get moving, before we are noticed.

"Too late … it looks like we have been spotted," Bennett muttered, her voice tense as she gestured toward the glazed-eyed minions closing in, their movements unnervingly synchronized. With a sharp hiss of steel, Bennett drew her sword from its sheath on her back, the blade gleaming with lethal intent.

Before everyone could blink, Eryndor's minions were standing in a line in front of them, swords drawn and ready for a fight.

The leader of the minions stood tall and unflinching, sword in hand and shoulders squared with confidence. His eyes were cold and unfeeling as he snarled, "Leave now, or die."

"Humph!" Garrick shifted instantly, his human form giving way to scales and claws. As he transformed into his Griffin form, a snarl rumbled deep in his chest. With a powerful beat of his wings, he knocked two of Eryndor's minions aside, sending them sprawling into the dirt.

"Stay together!" William yelled, as he drew his blades with deadly precision. His eyes flickered with cold focus as he moved with lethal grace, blocking a strike aimed at Christian, retaliating with a swift, brutal cut to the throat.

Danielle's eyes narrowed, the butterfly tattoo on her neck glowing faintly, as she summoned her Lepidoptera powers. Shadows twisted and writhed at her command, ensnaring one of the minions, hurling him backward with bone-shattering force. "Take that, fucker."

"There's too many of them!" Stephen called out, blocking a blow that jarred his arm to his shoulder. "We need to push forward—get to that cauldron before it's too late!"

"Then let's clear a path," Bennett snarled, her eyes flashing with feral determination. She lunged forward, talons slashing through armor and flesh, a whirlwind of fury and feathers.

But for every enemy they cut down, more seemed to swarm from the shadows, eyes gleaming with malice, and loyal to Eryndor's cause. The battlefield became a blur of blades, wings and dark magic, the roar of combat drowning out all else, except for the hum of the cauldron.

"Hold the line!" Garrick roared, his wings flaring wide as he tore through another wave of minions, his claws shredding armor and flesh alike. The scent of blood and scorched earth hung heavy in the air as he flew over.

Christian and Danielle fought back to back, their blades singing, shadows coiling around them like living armor. Christian's eyes glowed with lethal focus, every one of his strikes precise and unyielding.

With a burst of speed, Bennett darted forward, her movements fluid and deadly. Her talons flashed in the dim light, cutting down enemies with ruthless efficiency. "We're wasting time!" she snapped, her voice tight.

"Then let's finish this," William growled. With a swift motion, he drove his blades into the ground, unleashing a shockwave of power that sent the remaining minions crashing to the snow. Silence fell abruptly, broken only by the crackle of dark energy dissipating into the air from the cauldron.

Breathing hard, Kael shifted back to his human form and wiped blood from his brow. His distant gaze settled on the dark mouth of a cave ahead, half-hidden by jagged rocks and shadowed by the eerie glow of the light pillar. "That's where it's coming from," he said grimly. "The cauldron must be inside."

Garrick's eyes narrowed. "We move out. Stay vigilant, everyone. I'm sure Eryndor won't make this easy."

Keep your wits about you, everyone, thought William, telepathically.

With their weapons drawn and senses sharp, the Griffins and Lepidopteras advanced toward the cave, where the ominous column of white light pulsed brightly into the sky.

CHAPTER THIRTY-THREE

Garrick, William and the others landed silently inside the faintly lit phosphorescent crystal ice cavern. The Griffins retracted their wings and resumed their human form, as they exchanged glances and looked around.

The silence was soon shattered by a slow clap echoing off the walls. "Well, well. Look who's come to join the party. I was starting to think you wouldn't show," said Eryndor, as he stepped out of the shadows.

"Your games end here, Eryndor. You've taken enough lives. Surrender and we will spare your life," stated Garrick.

A low sinister laugh came from Eryndor mouth. "Oh, Father, I've only just begun. But if you insist, let's make this entertaining." With a flick of his wrist, Eryndor wasted no time summoning his dark-armored minions. As they surged forward, a battle erupted in a storm of claws, steel and magic.

Garrick's eyes glowed with power as he met Eryndor's gaze and lunged forward. Their swords collided with a resounding crash, sparks flaring as their powers clashed.

Eryndor snarled, his dark magic coiling around his free hand, striking out with lethal intent. "You think you can stop me? You are fools, all of you!"

"You'll answer for what you've done. To the Fae Queen. To the world," stated Garrick.

"You will have to stop me first, Father," snickered Eryndor, as he swung his sword at Garrick's torso.

Stepping back, Garrick avoided Eryndor's sharp blade by only inches. "Is that all you have?"

"No …" and without warning, Eryndor sliced open Garrick's right shoulder. "Still think you are better than me?"

Garrick clutched at his shoulder as the agony seared through him, falling to his knees. "Ah, fuck … you will pay for this."

Eryndor stood over Garrick, sword drawn, prepared to do whatever it took—even if it meant beheading his own father. He was ready to end it all.

Draven, who had spotted Eryndor standing over Garrick, shifted to his Griffin form mid-leap and, with his talons outstretched, he flew toward them. "Eryndor … stop!" screamed Draven, as he watched Eryndor's sword slice through Garrick's other shoulder.

Eryndor looked up, only to find Draven flying toward him. As he swung his sword again, this time toward Garrick's head, he was stopped halfway by Draven, who knocked his sword out of his hands and to the ground.

As Draven came in to land, his back talons tore through Eryndor's armor and flesh and, with a single, brutal swing of his sword, he severed Eryndor's left hand.

Eryndor dropped to his knees in pain, clutching at his bloodied wrist. "You'll regret ever laying a claw on me!" Eryndor screamed.

"It is you who will answer for every sin you've committed, especially for what you did to our leader," stated Draven, his eyes ice-cold, as he held his own sword to Eryndor's throat.

Do not kill him, Draven. That honor is for the Fae Queen, thought William, telepathically, as he came to stand next to Draven.

Humph! It would be so easy, and I would relish it. I hope the Fae Queen kills him slowly and he suffers excruciating pain. That is what this fucker deserves, thought Draven to William.

Yes, I agree, thought William, as he knelt down behind Eryndor. Taking some mystical chains out of his backpack, he placed them on Eryndor's right wrist and around his body to stop him from creating any further havoc.

Eryndor strained against the bindings, twisting and pulling, but it was useless. Shadows flickered weakly at his fingertips, but his powers were slipping away, leaving him too drained to summon even a trace of dark magic. Gritting his teeth, he growled, "You won't hold me forever, Griffins … Lepidopteras."

"Ah, that's where you're wrong, Eryndor," William remarked, hauling him to his feet and tightening the chains. "I doubt you will live long enough to cause any more trouble, especially once the Fae Queen gets her hands on you."

Eryndor's eyes burned with hatred, as the battle raged like a symphony of chaos and blood around him. He watched his minions with anticipation, but was disappointed as one by one they fell, cut down by the lethal precision of the Griffins and Vampires and their unbreakable line of defense.

"What can Aevyressa possibly do?" Eryndor sneered. "You really think a Fae Kingdom cell can hold me? I don't think so. In fact, the Fae Queen should be thanking me, I cleansed their pathetic bloodline!"

Handle your son, Garrick, thought William, disgust twisting in his gut at the sight of the creature before him.

But there was no answer from Garrick, only moans.

Where are you, my friend? thought William, as he glanced around, panicked.

Here! a quiet voice called out.

William's eyes swept over the chaos and carnage of blood that stained the ground. That's when he spotted Garrick, curled into a fetal position. "Shit!" he cursed, sprinting toward him.

Danielle … I need you to do some healing. Where are you? thought William, as he got to Garrick's side and checked his wounds.

There was no answer from Danielle, until William heard Christian's voice inside his mind.

She is over here, Sire. On your right, thought Christian, looking in William direction.

Is she okay? thought William, as he spotted Christian, then Danielle, who was lying on the ground, injured.

She will be. I have given her some of my blood. We need to regroup and get her home, though! thought Christian, as he picked Danielle up in his arms.

Unless we can get this cauldron turned off, we won't be going anywhere, thought William, telepathically.

Then we need to find a way to shut it down, thought Christian.

William's eyes narrowed as he scanned their surroundings. *Agreed. Stay close and protect her. I'll handle the cauldron.*

I will, Sire, thought Christian.

Christian looked down at Danielle and kissed her forehead. "I will protect you, my love, with my last breath, until we can return home."

"Thank you, Christian. I can feel my body healing already," Danielle lied, forcing a faint smile. She knew that without portal travel, the journey home would take at least four days and in her weakened state, she doubted she'd survive long enough to get blood or be healed.

"Garrick, are you able to stand?" asked William.

"No … both my shoulders have been severed, and I have lost a lot of blood. I am too weak to walk or fly," Garrick replied, his voice frail. As the last word left his lips, his eyes fluttered and he slumped into unconsciousness.

William stood tall and looked around for some of Garrick's soldiers. *Kael … Bennett, where are you? Your leader needs help. He is hurt badly.*

Kael and Bennett were by Garrick's side within seconds.

"What can we do?" Bennett asked, kneeling beside Garrick's unconscious body.

"Do Griffins have healing properties in their blood?" asked William.

"No," replied Kael, as he knelt beside Garrick's body.

"Pity!" said William.

"Is he going to be okay?" asked Bennett, trying to assess Garrick's wounds.

"I don't know," William stated, feeling cautiously optimistic. "I have a solution I would like to try, but you will both need to move back."

Kael and Bennett did as they were asked.

William sank his fangs into his forearm and drew some blood to the surface. He then placed his forearm over Garrick's lips and watched the blood trickle slowly into Garrick's mouth.

After a few seconds, Garrick's eyes opened slowly and William pulled his arm away. "William!"

"Ah, back in the land of the living, I see," stated William. "Can you stand, if Kael and Bennett help you?"

"I can try," replied Garrick. He watched Kael and Bennett kneel either side of him, felt them place their arms around his back and sit him up.

"Ah, shit," Garrick muttered, his face twisting in discomfort.

"Are you okay to stand?" asked Bennett.

"I'm not sure," replied Garrick.

"I can carry you, my lord," said Kael.

"Thank you, Kael. Both my shoulders have been severed, so be careful when you hoist me up," said Garrick.

Kael and Bennett nodded and helped Garrick to his feet.

"Can I leave Garrick with you both to look after?" asked William.

"Yes, Sir," they both said in unison.

William watched Kael pick Garrick up in his arms and walk over to where Danielle and Christian were standing.

Stephen, Grayson ... where are you both? thought William, as he looked around the ice cavern.

We are beside the cauldron, trying to figure out how to stop it, thought Grayson, who was standing beside Stephen.

Where exactly? thought William, impatiently.

Where we came in, there is a tunnel to the left. Take that, it leads you directly to it, thought Grayson.

William was standing beside them within seconds.

"We need to shut this thing down, now! What seems to be the problem?" asked William, as he looked from Grayson to Stephen.

"The cauldron won't let us touch it. It seems to have some sort of electrical force stopping us," replied Grayson.

You can't turn it off, you senseless Lepidoptera, Eryndor's smug thoughts echoed into William mind. *Only I have the power to do this.*

We will see about that, fucker! thought William, his nostrils flaring with rage. He tried to boot the cauldron over with his powerful Lepidoptera ability, but instead was knocked to the ground by an electrical force.

The cauldron thrummed with dark energy, its crimson light spilling over the edges in pulsating waves. Shadows twisted in the air above it, feeding off its power.

William got to his feet and approached the cauldron cautiously, his eyes narrowing at the dark runes etched into its surface—runes, he now knew, that only Eryndor's blood could command and control.

"How are we going to stop the world from imploding, Sire?" asked Grayson, standing next to William.

"I have another idea," William replied, his voice uncertain. "I'm not sure if it'll work, though." He stepped back, drawing a blade from inside his jacket pocket. The silver edge of the blade gleamed with ancient symbols, as it caught the light.

"This is the Blade of Severance," stated William, holding it out for Stephen and Grayson to have a look. "It's a weapon designed to sever magic at its source. Talitha told me of its power and gave it to me just before we left Bagnolet."

"Right! How does it work?" asked Stephen, who was thirsty for knowledge.

"I'll show you." William slashed his palm, letting his blood drip onto the blade, imbuing it with his Lepidoptera power. With a swift motion, he plunged the blade into the heart of the cauldron, to disrupt its connection to Eryndor's magic.

The runes along the cauldron sparked violently, with colors of crimson flickering to sickly green, as the dark magic was forced into conflict with William's power.

The cauldron shuddered violently, cracks webbing across its surface. And a razor-edged scream burst from the magic, thrashing in resistance. But William gritted his teeth, pouring his energy into the blade, forcing the dark power to unravel.

Your corruption ends here, thought William telepathically to Eryndor.

What have you done? No ... thought Eryndor, as he felt the power of the cauldron diminish. He struggled to free himself from the binding chains, but to no avail.

In a final surge, light burst from the cauldron, silver overwhelming crimson, until all fell silent. The dark liquid within hissed, evaporating into nothingness and, as the shadows receded, the oppressive weight in the air eased.

"Looks like you have severed its power, Sire," said Grayson.

"Yes, but it won't hold forever. We need to destroy it permanently," stated William.

"I see what you mean, Sire," said Stephen, noticing that the cauldron was cracked, but still ominous. He watched as the dark residue clung to its edges and felt the air was heavy with the lingering stench of corrupted magic. "How do we go about doing this?"

"According to Talitha, we'll need the Starfire Crystal from the Fae Kingdom," William said, his tone measured but urgent. "Apparently, there's a ritual that must be performed with it. Only then can we destroy the cauldron for good."

Grayson arched an eyebrow, with a glint of dark humor in his eyes. "Well, that's convenient. We can kill two birds with one stone, deliver Eryndor to the Fae Queen, and pick up this Starfire Crystal, along with the ritual."

"Precisely," William replied, already turning on his heel. "Now that Eryndor's power has been severed from the cauldron, we should be able to portal back to Bagnolet and the Fae Kingdom. Let's gather the others and get the hell out of here."

Stephen and Grayson exchanged a glance, nodding in agreement. Without wasting another moment, they followed William back through the icy passageways, toward the chamber where Eryndor was bound.

CHAPTER THIRTY-FOUR

The air was thick with the lingering scent of ash and magic. In the aftermath of the battle, the Griffins and Lepidopteras moved cautiously throughout the icy cavern, their weapons still drawn, their eyes sharp for any sign of surviving minions. The shattered remains of Eryndor's soldiers lay scattered, their dark armor glinting dully in the faint light.

As they reached the exit, a burst of silvery light flared before them, without warning. It was soft, ethereal, yet blinding.

The Lepidopteras shielded their eyes instinctively, swords raised.

As the light dimmed, a figure stood in its place, regal and radiant—Fae Queen Aevyressa. Her gown was woven from threads of starlight and moonbeams that seemed to ripple with its own luminescence. In her hands, cradled like a delicate flame, was a crystal that pulsed with prismatic light—the Starfire Crystal.

"Queen Aevyressa," said William, lowering his sword.

"Well, that's one way to make an entrance," muttered Stephen, in a low voice.

"Your Majesty ... how—" said Grayson, his voice tense, with his grip tight on his sword.

"I see the Blade of Severance has done its work," said Queen Aevyressa, interrupting. She had previously been watching the cauldron of chaos's light illuminating the sky, and had witnessed its demise. "With Eryndor's dark bonds severed, the paths between realms are open once more." She glided forward, her eyes like molten silver fixed on William.

"How did you know we needed the Starfire Crystal?" questioned William, cautiously. He had noticed it in her hands.

"Once the blade severed the connection, Queen Talitha was able to contact me," replied Aevyressa.

"Right! Anyway, we are thankful that you are here to help us, Aevyressa," stated William.

"This is what you need to destroy the cauldron permanently." She held the Starfire Crystal out in front of her. "But, be warned, its power is unstable. The last time it was wielded, it nearly brought down half of my kingdom," stated Aevyressa. She watched the Starfire Crystal glow brighter and cast fractured rainbows across the icy cavern walls.

"Unfortunately, we don't have a choice. If we leave the cauldron intact, Eryndor's corruption could still spread," said William.

Aevyressa sighed softly, her fingers flexing around the crystal. "You must use the Ritual of Unmaking, as well. This is a forbidden spell designed to unravel dark artifacts. It will demand a heavy cost ... energy, sacrifice, or worse."

"Sacrifice?" said Stephen, raising an eyebrow.

"Is there no other way?" asked Grayson, his brow furrowed.

Aevyressa shook her head. "None that would leave this world standing. The ritual will sever the dark magic at its core, unravelling it to a raw energy. But be warned, once it begins, there is no turning back."

"We must proceed with caution," said William, as he took the Starfire Crystal from Aevyressa and felt its warmth pulsing through his fingertips with an almost sentient awareness.

Taking a piece of parchment paper out of her gown's pocket, Aevyressa handed it to William. "Here ... this is the ritual you will need to chant, once you place the Starfire Crystal inside the cauldron."

"Thank you!" William took the ritual from her. "Come!" He walked back into the icy cavern, toward the cauldron, with Aevyressa by his side. Grayson, Stephen, Kael and Bennett followed.

* * *

"Are you ready?" asked Queen Aevyressa.

William nodded and approached the cauldron with anticipation and caution. As he placed the Starfire Crystal at the heart of the cauldron, its surface crackled and the dark residue inside hissed, recoiling from the pure light.

Standing back, he took the parchment paper out of his pants pocket and, with a steady, commanding voice, he began to chant in an ancient tongue, words long forgotten by most, that had been carved into the walls of lost temples, and whispered by those who dared.

> *By the light that undoes the dark,*
> *By the stars that silence shadows,*
> *By blood and bond, by will and wrath,*
> *I sever thee—be unmade.*

William continued to chant these words over and over, until he witnessed the Starfire Crystal flare, and beams of pure energy lancing into the cauldron. The runes on its surface ignited, clashing crimson against silver. Shadows screamed—high, piercing—as if resisting, and the cavern trembled violently, bringing glass-like shards of ice raining down on them.

Everyone placed their hands over their ears, as they waited for the high-pitched screams to stop, then moved to stand next to the cavern walls.

"Let's get the fuck out of here. This whole place is coming down!" yelled Stephen, over the roar of the cauldron.

Griffins, Lepidopteras ... Get to the surface, commanded William, telepathically.

Everyone did as they were instructed, except for Grayson, Stephen and Queen Aevyressa. They all waited with William, to see what was going to happen.

The cauldron shuddered, its cracks widening, as raw energy flooded its core. With a final, deafening crack, the cauldron imploded, collapsing in on itself with a surge of blinding light, the dark magic consumed within. The silence that followed was deafening, but beneath it lay a whisper of hope for the whole world.

"It is done," said Aevyressa, softly. She breathed a sigh of relief.

"Finally, it's been destroyed," stated William, his voice steady, as he walked toward the mangled cauldron.

"Hmmm, what do we have here?" queried William, as he reached into the cauldron. His eyes narrowed, as he carefully lifted each item from the Cauldron of Chaos—the Starfire Crystal, the Twin Icefire Blades, the Golden Chalice, the Fae's Golden Ring and the Ethereal Nexus Amulet—all miraculously undamaged. "These don't belong here," he muttered, a spark of determination flickering in his gaze. "We need to return them to their rightful owners—intact." Turning to Grayson and Stephen, he added, "Secure these. We can't risk them falling into the wrong hands, again."

"Yes, Sire," said Grayson, as he took each one from William and placed them in his backpack.

"Now … let's get the hell out of here," ordered William. He placed his arm out for Queen Aevyressa to take, and escorted her back to the surface, with Grayson and Stephen following closely behind them.

* * *

Icy winds howled across the barren expanse of Bouvet Island and the sun barely pierced the thick clouds above, as William, Aevyressa, Grayson and Stephen stepped out of the cavern and onto the snow.

Aevyressa's gaze immediately locked onto a dark figure standing atop a ridge of ice—Eryndor. Cloaked in black, his crimson eyes glinting with malice, despite the chains binding him, a smirk twisted on his face when he spotted her.

Aevyressa's lips curved, cold and mocking. "Well, well," she drawled, her voice smooth and deadly sweet. "If it isn't the Fae Kingdom's soon-to-be trained monkey. Are you prepared to grovel, Eryndor? Or would you rather just die?"

Eryndor chuckled, the sound dark and grating. "Bold words for a queen without her crown," he sneered. "Or are you still clinging to dreams of vengeance for that weakling sister of yours?"

William's jaw tensed and his fingers flexed around the hilt of his blade, but Aevyressa's hand on his arm held him back. Her gaze remained fixed on Eryndor and her eyes gleamed with starfire.

"Oh, it's no dream," she purred, stepping forward. "I simply wanted to see for myself how pitiful you've become. A dog pretending to be a wolf." Her smile sharpened. "But don't worry, your suffering won't last long. Myrrathen, Thalara and I will see to that. Consider it justice for Elyndra."

Eryndor's eyes flashed with rage and shadows rippled around him. "I'll see you kneel yet," he spat, his voice laced with venom.

Aevyressa arched a brow, unfazed. "Promises, promises," she sighed. "Though I must admit, I didn't expect you to make this so easy."

Before Eryndor could react, Aevyressa's eyes flared with blinding light. Threads of starlight shot from her fingertips, weaving around Eryndor faster than shadows could gather. He snarled, fighting against the bonds, but the light only tightened, pinning his arms to his sides.

"You ... wretched ..." he growled, struggling as the light seared his skin.

"Save your breath," Aevyressa interrupted, her voice cold as winter. "You'll need it to beg for mercy at your trial."

She flicked her wrist and Eryndor was dragged forward, crashing to his knees in the snow before her. His crimson eyes burned with hatred, but the bindings held fast, gleaming with magic that even his shadows could not unravel.

William stepped forward, his gaze steely. "Are you certain about this?" he asked quietly. "Bringing him back alive might pose a risk to your kingdom."

Aevyressa's eyes never left Eryndor's face, her expression unyielding. "Thank you for your concern, but he needs to face justice for Elyndra's blood," she replied. "Death is too kind a fate."

She leaned in closer to Eryndor, her voice a whisper laced with ice, as she said, "The Fae Kingdom will watch you kneel, Eryndor. And when you've sung every secret, Myrrathen, Thalara and I will see you pay for every drop of blood you spilled."

Eryndor's snarl faltered and a flicker of fear broke through his fury.

Aevyressa stepped back, lifting a hand. Threads of starlight twisted in the air, expanding into a swirling portal shimmering with hues of silver and violet. From within its depths, two figures emerged—Myrrathen and Thalara.

Myrrathen's eyes were cold, a stormy silver, and her midnight hair flowed like dark water. Thalara's gaze blazed with a fiery wrath, her faint green curls framing a face set with grim determination. They moved with lethal grace, eyes locking onto Eryndor with unspoken promise.

"Ah," Aevyressa smiled, wicked and satisfied. "Right on time."

Eryndor's defiance flickered again, replaced by a flash of genuine fear. "You think chaining me will change anything?" he spat, thrashing against the starlit bonds. "Your kingdom will burn before I beg!"

Thalara's smirk was savage. "Keep talking," she sneered. "It'll make watching you squirm that much sweeter."

Myrrathen stepped forward, her voice smooth and lethal. "The only fire here will be yours, Eryndor. And I intend to watch every second."

Aevyressa released her hold and Myrrathen's magic seamlessly took its place, the bindings tightening with an audible crack.

Eryndor hissed and bared his teeth.

"Take him," Aevyressa commanded, eyes glinting with finality.

Myrrathen and Thalara nodded, their grips unyielding, as they dragged Eryndor into the portal, his curses swallowed by the shimmering light.

Aevyressa turned to William and said, "Your debt has been repaid. My kingdom thanks you."

William nodded once and watched Aevyressa gracefully walk into the portal.

When the portal closed, silence settled once more, broken only by the howl of the wind.

William exhaled slowly, his dark brows arched. "Remind me never to get on her bad side," he muttered dryly. Taking his satellite phone out of his pocket, he dialed the Gramaze mansion.

"Violette … bring us home, and have blood ready for Danielle. You will also need to help heal Garrick, as he is badly hurt," instructed William.

"Yes, Sire," replied Violette.

Within minutes, a portal materialized, beckoning the Griffins and Lepidoptera Vampires to step through. Their mission to save the world from complete destruction had been victorious, but a lingering unease tightened in William's chest. He couldn't shake the feeling that it wasn't truly over yet.

CHAPTER THIRTY-FIVE

It had been two days since the Ironclaw Griffins and the Gramaze Lepidoptera Vampires had returned from their perilous mission to save the world from destruction. Amidst the icy desolation of Bouvet Island, they had succeeded in destroying the Cauldron of Chaos, a dark artifact capable of unravelling the very fabric of their world. With Eryndor subdued and bound, they had delivered him to Queen Aevyressa, fulfilling their debt to her and restoring a fragile balance to the realms.

In the days that followed, whispers spread rapidly through hidden networks and shadowed corners of the supernatural world. Rumors spoke of Eryndor's fate—that he had been made to suffer greatly at the hands of Queen Aevyressa herself, who sought to extract every secret and sin from his blackened soul. The grapevine buzzed with tales of vengeance and justice, each more chilling than the last. By now, the consensus was clear: Eryndor was dead and his dark ambitions had been extinguished, alongside the cauldron he had sought to wield.

* * *

"Good morning, William, Renee," Danielle greeted, with a respectful nod, as she stepped out onto the patio, with Christian walking beside her.

Christian also gave William and Renee a respectful nod as he walked toward them.

"Good morning, my dear. How are you feeling today?" Renee asked, her eyes following Danielle and Christian as they settled onto the lounge across from her.

"A lot better today. Actually, I was thinking I would be able to return to duties today, if that is okay?" queried Danielle.

"I am sure that can be arranged," stated William. He cleared his throat softly, drawing Danielle's attention. His eyes were steady, but there was a hint of something else, something almost tender. From the inner pocket of his coat, he withdrew a small, cream-colored envelope, which was sealed with a delicate wax emblem. "Danielle," he said, extending it toward her. "There's something I need to return to you."

"What is it?" asked Danielle, her brows knitted with curiosity as she accepted the envelope.

"Open it and you will find out," stated William.

Breaking the seal with careful fingers, Danielle reached inside and her breath caught. There, nestled against the soft paper, was the golden ring her mother had left to her. She marveled at the intricate symbols winding around the delicate band as they glinted warmly in the sunlight. It was unmistakable, the very ring she had believed lost forever, destroyed when the cauldron imploded at Bouvet Island.

"How … how is this possible?" she whispered, her voice tight with emotion, her eyes wide with disbelief.

"I found it inside the cauldron," William explained, his tone steady yet gentle. "I couldn't leave it behind."

Danielle's eyes glimmered, tears threatening to spill onto her cheeks. She glanced from the ring to William, words faltering on her lips. "I thought it was gone," she managed, her voice breaking. "I can't … I don't even know how to thank you."

"There's no need," William assured, a rare warmth softening his features. "It belongs with you."

Renee's eyes shone with soft affection as she watched Danielle slide the ring onto her finger.

Christian reached over, his hand settling comfortingly on Danielle's back. "Beautiful … like the owner."

Danielle twisted the ring slowly, a tear slipping down her cheek. "Thank you," she whispered again, her voice raw with sincerity. "Truly."

William's lips curved in a faint, but genuine smile. "You're welcome," he replied simply.

As they discussed the items William had discovered within the Cauldron of Chaos, the sound of approaching footsteps caught their attention. William looked up to see Garrick and Elara emerging from the mansion.

"Good morning," greeted Garrick, his stride strong and sure, a stark contrast to the battered state he had been in only days ago. The brutal slashes Eryndor had inflicted across both his shoulders were now fully healed, thanks to Violette's healing abilities. His eyes were clear and steady, though a shadow of weariness lingered beneath.

"Morning," greeted Elara. Her arm was linked loosely with Garrick's, her expression serene but warm, as her gaze swept over the group.

"Garrick, Elara," William acknowledged with a nod, rising from his seat. He placed his hand out to shake Garrick's. "It's good to see you back on your feet, Garrick."

Garrick smiled and shook William's hand. "Violette's talents are … unparalleled," he admitted, flexing his shoulders subtly, as if testing the smoothness of the healed wounds. "I owe her more than I can say."

Elara's eyes softened, her hand giving his arm a gentle squeeze. "We both do," she added warmly.

"Please, sit," Renee urged, motioning to the empty seats across from them.

Danielle and Christian smiled and nodded respectfully to the Griffin leader and his partner.

"We should take our leave, Sire, and give you some privacy to discuss matters with Garrick and Elara," Christian said, rising to his feet and offering his hand to Danielle.

"Very well. I'll catch up with you both later, to go over your return to duties, Danielle," William replied.

"Yes, Sire. And thank you, again. I truly appreciate having my mother's ring back," Danielle said gratefully.

William gave a nod and watched as they made their way into the mansion.

Garrick took a seat beside Elara; his gaze fixed on William. "From what my soldiers have told me this morning, I believe that your family and mine have traveled to numerous countries in the past few days, to address the destruction caused by our adoptive son. Is that correct?" he inquired.

"That's correct," William replied. "Some of the damage was minor, but some will take years to repair. There's still a lot to be done, but we're making progress." His gaze shifted from Garrick to Elara. "Have you been informed about Eryndor and what became of him in the Fae Kingdom?" he asked.

"Yes," Garrick said, his eyes flicking to Elara before returning to William. "It saddens us, but we're also relieved that he's been dealt with. The shame he's brought to our family is not something that can be mended quickly."

"Agreed," William said. "While we are sorry for your personal loss, we have no doubt that handing him over to Queen Aevyressa was the right decision."

"You're right, William," Elara admitted. "But it doesn't ease the pain of knowing that, as parents, we failed Eryndor."

"I don't think there was anything more you could have done," Renee said, gently. "You gave Eryndor a good upbringing. I believe he was destined for darkness, no matter what."

Garrick placed his hand in Elara's and they glanced at each other, nodding in agreement.

After a moment, Garrick's expression grew less serious, though not unkind. "We will be leaving for home, today," he said. "Now that I've recovered, Elara and I must return to Olden Fjord. There's much to prepare for."

Renee tilted her head, curiosity brightening her gaze. "Oh? For what, if you don't mind me asking?"

Elara's eyes glimmered with a mix of pride and fondness. "It's our village's day of commemoration," she explained. "There will be a grand celebration this evening, ceremonies, feasts and … well, quite a lot of chaos, I expect." Her smile turned slightly teasing, aimed at Garrick.

He chuckled, shaking his head with a mock-weary sigh. "Far too much chaos," he agreed. "But it wouldn't be right to let such a milestone pass unmarked." His gaze shifted to William and Renee, a spark of sincerity lighting his eyes. "We'd be honored if you would join us. Consider this an official invitation to Olden Fjord for the celebrations."

William's brow arched slightly and a smile tugged at his lips. "It would be an honor," he replied, inclining his head. "We wouldn't miss it."

Renee's face brightened with genuine delight. "That sounds wonderful. Thank you for inviting us."

"You're welcome," Garrick said, his gaze shifting from William to Renee. "However, there's one more matter we need to discuss. Our son, Hawk. We need him to return to Olden Fjord. He has a significant role to play in the ceremony we have planned."

"Right! Will Hawk be returning to the academy, once the ceremony and celebrations have finished?" asked William.

"No, he won't," Garrick replied. "We've seen how much he's grown since attending the academy. Being here has matured him in ways our own culture couldn't have. We're truly grateful for the opportunity it has given our kingdom, especially as he prepares to take the throne." Garrick's eyes met William's. "You do know that he is next in line for the throne, don't you?"

"Yes, we were aware of that," William replied. "So, you believe he's ready?" He paused for a moment before continuing. "Will he be returning to Olden with you today?"

"Yes, we've already spoken with him this morning," Garrick replied. "He's not pleased about it, but he understands that this is where his future lies."

Renee nodded thoughtfully. "I don't think Sully will take it well, especially since she won't be going with him." She paused before adding, "You do realize they're life partners, right?"

"Yes, but the future king of our kingdom is far more important than a life partner," Garrick stated, his arrogance evident in his tone.

"Humph, that's where you're wrong, Garrick," Renee said, her brow furrowing. "What you fail to understand is that once their bond is confirmed—and it has been confirmed—they are, and will remain, inseparable. Forever." She turned to William, seeking his support.

"I'm afraid Renee is right," William said, his tone firm. "Hawk and Sully have already consummated their life partner bond. No matter what any of us do," he gestured to everyone seated on the patio, "we won't be able to stop them. I think we need to give this more thought before we, as their parents, make any decisions, don't you? Especially after what happened last time, when they ran off to Saint Lucia."

"Hmm, you might be right there, William. What are we supposed to do?" Elara asked, her voice tinged with uncertainty.

Garrick raised his eyebrows in a deliberate motion and let out a heavy sigh. "For now, Hawk will return with us to Olden. After the ceremony, we can decide what's best for both him and Sully. It will give us more time to consider their futures. What do you think?" he suggested.

"Agreed!" replied William, as he glanced at Renee.

"Now that we have this sorted, we will need to return home. Could you ask Violette if she could portal us home to Olden?" asked Garrick.

"Yes, but before you go … there is something else we need to discuss," said William.

"And that is?" stated Garrick.

"Do you remember much about the visit to Bouvet Island?" asked William to Garrick.

"A little …"

"Did you know that once the Cauldron of Chaos imploded, there were items left inside?" asked William.

Garrick frowned. "What items?"

"The Twin Icefire Blades, the Golden Chalice, the Ethereal Nexus Amulet, the Starfire Crystal and Danielle's ring."

"No, I didn't know that these items even survived. Where are they now?" asked Garrick, eager to take them back to Olden.

"We brought them back with us. I have stored them in our safe, here at the mansion. That is until you were well enough to take them back to Olden," stated William.

"I thank you, my friend. These ancient artifacts hold great cultural significance to our kind," Garrick stated. "They must be returned to Glittertind. I'm sure the councillors will be pleased about this."

"I gathered as much. I'll have them ready for when you depart, all except for the ring and the Starfire Crystal. I need to return the crystal to the Fae Queen," William stated.

"That would be most appreciated, William," Garrick replied. "Well, we should gather our things and start making our way back to Olden," he said, rising to his feet. He extended his arm to clasp William's in a forearm shake. "Thank you, my friend, and thanks to your family as well, for your hospitality and for helping us save our world."

"Anytime, my friend," William replied, returning the forearm shake firmly.

"Thank you, Renee, for having us, and looking after us, in your beautiful home," said Elara, standing. She walked over and gave Renee a warm hug.

"You're welcome," said Renee, hugging her back.

Garrick turned to Elara. "Come on, let's get our things and make sure everyone is ready to portal home."

Elara nodded and they walked toward the open doorway.

CHAPTER THIRTY-SIX

"Knock, knock," said Albinus, as he and Xanthia stood on the other side of the wooden door to William's office.

"Come!" William called out.

"Do you have a few minutes, William?" asked Albinus, as he and Xanthia walked into the room.

"Yes, of course. Come in," said William, looking up. "Take a seat." He gestured to the two chairs in front of his desk. "What can I do for you?"

"The probate solicitor contacted Xanthia this morning. He finally traced what happened to our house after the bank sold it. It went to a prominent public figure who paid in full, in cash, well above its value. So … once all the debts were cleared, there was still a considerable sum left over, which has now been transferred to Xanthia's bank account," said Albinus, as he and Xanthia sat in the chairs across from William, their expressions a mix of surprise and curiosity.

"That was fast! And that's fantastic news about getting more than you asked for. Well done!" William replied, with a pleased smile spreading across his face.

"Yes, it is," Albinus agreed, relief evident in his tone. "Actually, that's what I wanted to discuss with you. We should have at least three hundred thousand euros remaining, and … well, we'd like to give that money to you and your family. Xanthia and I are incredibly grateful for the home you've provided here and for taking us in. We feel it's only right to give something back."

"That's incredibly generous of you, but it's not necessary," William replied warmly. "My family and I are more than happy to have you both move in. Besides, you'll certainly be contributing, especially with your help around the grounds and in our operations room. Your expertise in security and intelligence will be invaluable to us."

Albinus offered a modest smile, inclining his head slightly. "I appreciate your kindness, William, truly. But I insist. You've opened your home to us, without hesitation, and I would feel better knowing I could repay that generosity in some way."

William chuckled, shaking his head. "Your expertise is more than enough repayment, Albinus. We could use someone with your skills to keep an eye on things."

Xanthia, who had been quietly listening, spoke up with a soft smile. "And it's not like Father to take no for an answer."

Albinus gave her an amused look, with a hint of pride in his eyes. "She knows me too well," he remarked. Turning back to William, he added, "Consider it a contribution to the cause, then. For everything you've done and for giving Xanthia and me a fresh start."

William's expression softened and, after a moment, he extended a hand. "In that case, I won't argue. And for what it's worth, we're glad to have you both live with us."

Albinus clasped his hand firmly, with a glint of determination in his eyes. "We won't let you down."

"I'm sure you won't. And thank you for the money. My family and I are most grateful," said William, graciously.

"You're welcome." Albinus turned to Xanthia and said, "Now that we are free to enjoy the rest of our lives, why don't we enjoy a day at the movies?"

"That sounds nice, Father. I would love to," replied Xanthia.

"Thank you for your time, William," said Albinus, standing.

"No problem," said William, as he watched Albinus and Xanthia walk toward the doorway.

When the time is right, I will reveal to Albinus and Xanthia that I'm the one who bought their home. Once things settle, I plan to return it to them as a gift. I'm sure they'll be overjoyed to have a place of their own again, thought William to himself, as he watched his office door close.

* * *

William, are you free? thought Kura, telepathically, who was still living at the Gramaze residence with Alessia.

Yes, I can meet you in the operations room, in say, five minutes, if that suits, thought William.

Great! Thank you, thought Kura, as she walked out of her room, toward the operations room.

The heavy glass doors to the operations room slid open and Kura stepped inside. The room was bathed in dim light, screens showing data and reports from various locations.

William sat at a table; his eyes fixed on one of the screens, as he reviewed a map of the Bagnolet area. The air hummed with energy and a sense of urgency, which always seemed to linger in the aftermath of a mission.

Kura's presence caught William's attention and he turned to greet her. "Kura … what's on your mind?"

She smiled, though her expression was a mixture of determination and concern. "I wanted to speak with you about Alessia. The time has come for her to return to the River of Whispers."

William raised an eyebrow and folded his arms over his chest. "After everything that's happened, I thought you'd wait longer."

Kura shook her head. "Now that everything is back to normal, I feel it's time. The River of Whispers is peaceful again and, now that Eryndor has been taken care of, it's one of the safest places for Alessia. I've spoken with Parker and TJ this morning, and they have agreed to let Alessia return, but they asked for something in return."

"What's that?" William's tone was cautious, his eyes narrowing.

"They asked if they could come visit Alessia sometimes, or if Alessia could return to the farm occasionally. They want to ensure that they are still part of her life, and that she is happy."

William considered this for a moment. "I understand their request. Family is important. But how does Alessia feel about it?"

"Of course she will miss her parents, but she wants to return to the River of Whispers," Kura answered, her voice softening. "Alessia has grown stronger since she left the farm, and I know she feels at peace in the River of Whispers."

William nodded. "And you? Are you ready for this? You've been through a lot, too."

Kura's smile was small, but knowing. "I am definitely ready for this, William. It's time for both of us to find balance again." She gazed off in the distance. "Alessia reminds me so much of my granddaughter, Stjernefrída."

"Then I'll make sure the necessary arrangements are in place. You and Alessia will be safe there. And I'll respect the McCrindles wishes, too. I know how important family is."

"Thank you, William," Kura said, her voice filled with gratitude. "We will leave today, if that's okay with you."

"Yes, that is fine with me. Was there something else?" enquired William.

"No, that's everything. I will go and get Alessia ready, and then we will depart. I also would like to say thank you for keeping us safe. I won't ever forget your kindness," said Kura, placing her hand out to shake William's.

William pushed his chair back and stood tall. "You are most welcome," he shook her hand and smiled. "If you need anything in the future, or if my family and I can be of any assistance, please don't hesitate to ask."

"Thank you, William. That means a lot. Well, I will leave you to your business, and we will chat again, soon," said Kura.

"Yes, we will," replied William. He watched her walk toward the sliding door.

William turned to Brock, who was seated at the operations room computer, and said, "We can't afford to see a repeat of the tragedies unfolding around the world ever again, so I want you to organize for a full-time guard to be positioned at the River of Whispers."

"Yes, Sire. Was there anything else?" asked Brock, turning around.

"Not at the moment. I need to go and get ready, as Renee and I, along with some of our family, will be leaving for the Fae Kingdom, to return the Starfire Crystal, and then on to Olden for the commemorations, in the next hour. Keep an eye on things while we are away," stated William.

"Yes, Sire," said Brock. He watched William walk toward the sliding glass door.

* * *

The forest was alive with the sounds of birds chirping and the rustling of leaves in the wind, as Alessia walked beside Kura and felt the pulse of the River of Whispers.

"This place always makes me feel like I'm home," said Alessia. It felt like a long time since Alessia had last been there. The air smelled of fresh earth and water, and the familiar whispers of the river were beckoning her.

"That is exactly how I always feel, my dear," said Kura.

As they neared the heart of the river, the three guardians appeared before them, emerging from the mist. "Welcome, Kura. And welcome, Alessia. It has been too long," said the Guardian of the River's Source, warmly.

The Guardian of the River's Flow bowed his head in acknowledgment and said, "It is good to see you both again."

"The river is happy to have you both back, Alessia and Kura!" said the Guardian of the River's Destination.

"Thank you, guardians. I have missed each of you, too" stated Alessia, as she glanced at each of them and smiled. A warm sensation filled her heart.

Kura also smiled, and a sense of peace settled over her as she addressed the guardians. "We are home now. Alessia has grown stronger, and the river will help her continue her journey."

The guardians nodded, understanding the weight of Kura's words. Taking their bags from them, the three guardians moved to flank the two women, walking with them through the misty landscape, their steps silent and steady.

As they approached the stone house nestled by the river, Kura said, "You go in, my dear, and make yourself comfortable. I need to speak with the guardians and then I will join you." She gestured for Alessia to enter.

"Okay," replied Alessia. She walked up the steps and into the house. When Alessia opened the door, she noticed that it was just as it had been when they left—quiet, serene and full of energy. The soft glow of the river's light bathed the interior, creating a peaceful ambience.

When Alessia closed the door, Kura turned to the guardians and said, "You will notice that we have a guard," she gestured to the Lepidoptera Vampire standing in the shadows.

The three guardians turned and spotted the male figure, who was dressed in full battle armor, standing to attention, and ready to fight, next to a tree. "The Gramaze family will be guarding Alessia for the next couple of months. I want you to make anyone they send feel welcome. Am I making myself clear?"

"Yes, Kura," said the three guardians in unison.

"Is there anything we need to discuss?" asked Kura.

"No. We have everything under control," said the Guardian of the River's Destination.

"Great! Now … go and make yourself known to the Lepidoptera guard," said Kura.

They nodded in agreement and Kura watched them walk toward the Vampire and greet him, before she headed to the cabin.

"Alessia," Kura called out.

"Yes, great-grandmother," said Alessia, as she walked out of the bedroom.

"Come here, my dear. Take a seat. There is something I wish to discuss with you," stated Kura, as she walked over to the lounge and sat.

Alessia nodded and also walked over to the lounge. "What would you like to chat about, great-grandmother?" asked Alessia, as she sat next to Kura.

Kura turned to Alessia and pulled a small wooden box out of her bag. The box was old, carved with intricate symbols and patterns that seemed to shimmer in the light. Kura opened it carefully, revealing a beautifully carved wooden amulet on a chain. It was delicate but strong, radiating a quiet power.

"This," Kura said softly, holding out the amulet, "was your mother's. Stjernefrída's. It's a guardian charm, and it will protect you from harm, Alessia. She gave it to me for you, and now it's time for you to wear it."

Alessia's fingers trembled as she took the amulet, her heart swelling with emotion. "I … I don't know what to say."

"You don't have to say anything," Kura reassured her, brushing a strand of hair from Alessia's face. "It's a symbol of your strength and of the protection that the river will always offer you. You are never alone here."

Alessia slid the necklace over her head and felt the warmth of the amulet against her skin. A quiet surge of power flowed through her and, for the first time in a long while, she felt truly at peace. The River of Whispers was her home and she would grow stronger here, protected by the legacy of her mother and the guardians who watched over her.

With a soft sigh, Alessia smiled at Kura. "Thank you … for everything."

Kura's eyes softened as she returned the smile. "You're welcome, Alessia. Welcome home."

CHAPTER THIRTY-SEVEN

A shimmering portal of pink, purple and white hues materialized before the Ironclaw estate in Olden Fjord, Norway, and William, Renee, Grayson, Sully, Danielle, Christian, Kelan and warlock Adrian stepped through. They had just visited the Fae Queen to return the Starfire Crystal, and were now ready to spend a night of celebration, marking the commemoration of the Fjord.

"Good evening, William, Renee and family," greeted Griffin Zephyrion, nodding to each of them.

"Good evening, Zephyrion," said William.

"This is my brother, Rhydian," he gestured to the Griffin standing beside him. "We will be your attendants for the night. Come this way and we will take you to your table."

Everyone nodded respectfully to Zephyrion and Rhydian.

"Thank you," William said, as they all followed the two Griffins toward the celebrations.

As the Lepidopteras reached the castle, they were greeted by a massive arched doorway, with iron-bound wooden doors adorned with banners bearing the Ironclaw crest. The floors were a polished stone, reflecting the golden glow of torches that were mounted along the walls. A long, crimson carpet led the way deeper into the castle, flanked by marble statues of past rulers and legendary warriors, each illuminated by soft candlelight.

Overhead, chandeliers that were crafted from dark iron and crystal hung, their candle flames dancing and casting intricate patterns across the high, vaulted ceilings. Fresh flowers in deep reds and golds filled tall vases along the corridor, their fragrance subtly wafting through the air.

As they entered the grand hall, music drifted from where a small orchestra played on a raised platform. Harps, violins and flutes blended into a melody, complementing the lively chatter of the many guests.

Round tables for honored guests, which were crafted from dark wood with intricate carvings of Griffins and ancient symbols along their edges filled the grand hall. "Wow, this sure is beautiful," stated Sully, as she noticed the silver goblets that were polished to a mirror shine and plates with detailed patterns of vines and stars that sat ready. Tall candelabras cast a warm glow, their light reflecting off gold-rimmed dishes and crystal decanters filled with rich wines and mead.

"Grand, isn't it? The Griffins really know how to throw a party," stated Renee, looking at Sully.

"This isn't just a party, it's a celebration of our lives," stated Zephyrion, who had overheard Sully and Renee's compliments. "Despite the grandeur, there is a sense of camaraderie—friends reuniting, alliances reaffirmed and laughter that spills freely amongst our guests."

"I couldn't agree more," said William, his gaze sweeping over the hall.

"Now, that's a feast," stated Grayson, his gaze roaming over the tables that were overflowing with platters of roasted meats, spiced vegetables, honeyed breads and crystal bowls of fruits and nuts.

"Please … take your seats," said Rhydian, stopping at their table and pulling the chairs out for the ladies.

"Thank you," said William, pulling out his chair, noticing attendants in dark uniforms who moved gracefully amongst the guests, filling goblets and offering trays of hors d'oeuvres. As he sat in his chair, William adjusted the cuff of his sleeve, his eyes scanning the hall with guarded composure.

Renee smirked and nudged him. "You look like you're about to start an interrogation," she teased.

William's mouth twitched. "Old habits," he replied dryly.

"You look beautiful tonight," said Hawk, who was now standing behind Sully. He had noticed her slender body, which was dressed in a full-length, emerald-green gown, made of satin and tulle, when she walked into the grand hall.

Sully smiled when she heard his voice and turned to find Hawk behind her. He was dressed in a finely tailored, midnight-blue tunic, adorned with intricate gold-threaded embroidery, that showcased symbols of the Ironclaw house, intertwined with a motif representing his lineage and the kingdom's history. "Thank you. You're looking handsome tonight, too."

"May I have a dance later, with Sully?" asked Hawk, looking at William.

Sully looked to William for his approval.

William nodded once. "I can't see why not!"

Hawk smiled and nodded respectfully to William. Before he could respond, the crowd stirred, parting to reveal his parents approaching. As he took his seat beside Sully, he slid his hand into hers beneath the table and they exchanged a warm, loving smile.

"William, Renee," Garrick greeted, his deep voice carrying an unmistakable authority. "It is good to see you here."

William stood, clasping Garrick's forearm firmly. "The honor is ours, Garrick, Elara," he replied.

Elara's gaze softened as she looked over the group. "We are grateful for your presence. Tonight is a celebration of unity as much as tradition."

"Thank you for inviting us. You have outdone yourselves; the grand hall looks lovely," stated Renee.

"Thank you," replied Elara.

"I trust you are being looked after?" asked Garrick, as he looked at everyone seated at the table.

"Yes, without question," replied William.

"That's good. Well, I can see they are calling me over to do a speech. Enjoy the evening … I will chat with you all later on," said Garrick.

"Thank you, Garrick, Elara," said William. He watched them walk toward the podium.

As Garrick and Elara moved away, the room gradually quieted and the hall stilled. Once they reached the raised platform at the far end, all eyes turned to where Garrick now stood, his silhouette strong and commanding. Behind Garrick hung a tapestry depicting the history of the Ironclaw line, and a scene of battles fought and victories won, with threads of silver and gold woven into the fabric.

Garrick surveyed the room and a moment of silence stretched before he spoke. "It's been more than ten thousand years since the creation of the Fjord," he began, his voice resonating with a timbre that demanded attention. "Tonight, we celebrate not just the endurance of the Ironclaw line, but the unity forged through sacrifice and alliance, and the friendships forged through battle and peace alike."

A murmur of agreement swept through the hall.

"The world shifts and darkens," Garrick continued, his gaze unwavering. "Whispers of threats yet unseen grow louder. But we—Griffins, Lepidoptera Vampires, Fae, and allies—stand together. Our strength is in our unity, and our resolve is unbroken."

Applause rang out, with a steady thunder of approval.

"Let this night be a reminder," Garrick declared, his voice rising, "that no matter what shadows threaten our world, we will face them, together."

The room erupted into cheers and goblets were raised high.

"Now … let's celebrate!" Garrick called out, as Elara joined him on the podium and they raised their goblets high in the air, to commence the celebrations.

As the cheers died down and Garrick and Elara stepped off the podium, the music swelled in the grand hall again, carrying a note of defiance and a hope that lingered in the air.

*　*　*

Hawk leaned into Sully's side and asked, "Can I have this dance?" He stood tall and placed his hand out for her to take.

Sully looked up and said, "I would love to, kind Sir." She smirked and pushed her chair back, placing her hand in his.

As they stepped onto the dance floor, Hawk took Sully in his arms and they joined the many other guests, who were dancing to the symphony of the orchestra's beautiful sound.

"Remember us dancing like this in Saint Lucia?" asked Hawk, looking into Sully eyes lovingly.

"I remember those days well. It was you and me against the world, and we were happy." She paused, then continued, "If it wasn't for Eryndor, we might still be there, living our lives to the fullest," stated Sully, remembering the day Eryndor turned up and spoiled everything.

"You are not wrong. And now … you live in Bagnolet and I'm back in Olden. Do you think our parents will ever let us live together, like Saint Lucia?" asked Hawk.

"I don't know. All I do know is that I love you, and will miss you and what we had. It's doesn't seem fair, does it?" stated Sully. She placed her cheek on his chest and closed her eyes, savoring every moment.

Hawk placed his arms around Sully and they continued to dance. "No, it isn't fair."

"Garrick …" said Elara, leaning into him. "Look at how happy, yet miserable, Hawk and Sully are. We need to fix this."

Garrick turned around and watched them dancing together in a loving embrace. "Maybe it's time we speak with William and Renee. Do you think they would be happy for Sully to move here with Hawk, to live out a happy life, with her life partner?"

"There is only one way to find out … let's go and ask them," said Elara, looking over to where William and Renee were sitting.

Elara placed her arm through Garrick's and they walked over to William and Renee's table.

"How has your evening been, William, Renee?" asked Elara, as she and Garrick sat across from them.

"We have enjoyed every moment," said William, graciously.

"Do you have time for a chat?" asked Elara.

"Sure … but first, I wanted you to have a look at how comfortable Hawk and Sully are on the dance floor. We can't possibly leave them like this. It's not fair for life partners to be kept separated," said Renee, as she looked to William for support.

"We agree," replied Elara. "Actually, we have come to ask you … if you both wouldn't mind Sully moving to Olden. We figured, this way, Hawk and Sully, can be together, as life partners. What do you think?" asked Elara.

Renee looked at William and silence filled the conversation.

"We could always start with a trial period," suggested Garrick. "And of course Sully will always be treated as part of our family, especially as she is part Griffin."

"How long of a trial period are we talking?" asked William.

"What about three or six months? And if, before then, Sully wants to return home, that won't be a problem, either," replied Garrick.

"That sounds fair enough. Let's call them over and let them know," stated William.

Garrick and Elara nodded in agreement.

Sully ... Hawk, you are required to attend a discussion we have had. Join us at the table, thought William, telepathically.

Yes, William, thought Sully, as she looked into Hawk's eyes and gulped hard.

"I wonder what this is all about? Sounds serious," said Hawk, as he placed his hand in Sully's and they walked toward their parents.

"Sit," stated William.

As Sully and Hawk sat next to each other at the table, Renee said, "We have a question for you, Sully, but it will affect you both."

Sully and Hawk glanced at each other, and Sully said, "Before you say another word, I would like to ask something first."

"Okay ... what is it?" asked Renee.

"Hawk and I ... we don't want to be separated. Is there any chance we can still be together?" asked Sully.

"This is exactly what we wanted to discuss with you both," said Garrick. "I ... we" he gestured to Elara, William and Renee, "We think you shouldn't be separated either."

"Really?" Sully replied, excitedly.

"Yes. What we propose is that you have a trial period, of either three or six months, where you," he gestured to Sully, "move to Olden and live with Hawk, in our home," stated Garrick. "Of course, if it doesn't work out, you can return to Bagnolet at any time."

"For real?" asked Hawk. He glanced at Sully and smiled, then back to Garrick.

"Yes, but it's under one condition," stated William. "That you keep up your studies and your combat training, Sully. You have come a long way, so we don't want you falling behind in either."

"You have my word, William, Renee," said Sully, as she looked at them both.

"Thank you, William, Renee. And don't worry, I promise that I will look after Sully, until my last dying breath," said Hawk.

"I will keep you to that promise, Hawk," stated William.

"So … when can I move in?" asked Sully, looking at Garrick and Elara.

"Whenever you are ready, my dear. And if you're here by Thursday, you will be able to help celebrate Hawk being declared heir to the throne. He is to be named Garrick's successor when he steps down," stated Elara.

Sully looked at Hawk and smiled. "You're the next king of Olden? Wow … how lucky am I?" said Sully.

Hawk laughed and shrugged his shoulders. "You lucked out there, didn't you? Anyway, I am the lucky one, to have such a wonderful life partner."

Sully leaned in and kissed Hawk's lips softly.

"Would you like to attend the ceremony on Thursday, William and Renee," asked Elara.

"It would be our pleasure," replied William.

"Well, we had better get back to our guests. We will see you all Thursday for the ceremony, which is around one o'clock in the afternoon," said Garrick, standing, with Elara by his side.

"Yes, we must be going, anyway," said William, standing with Renee. "We have a few issues at Bagnolet to deal with when we return. Say your goodbyes, Sully."

"Yes, William," said Sully standing. She leaned in and gave Hawk one last kiss and said, "See you Thursday, if not before."

"I look forward to it," said Hawk, as he slowly pulled away from her embrace.

"Zephyrion and Rhydian will escort you all out of the castle," stated Garrick. He held his hand out to shake William's. "Thank you for coming."

"Wouldn't have missed it for the world," replied William, shaking his hand.

"I have enjoyed the evening," said Renee, as she leant in and gave Elara a hug.

"I'm glad," said Elara, returning the hug. "We will chat again soon, I am sure."

Renee nodded in agreement.

"Come, this way," offered Zephyrion, as he gestured toward the large wooden door.

"Thank you," said William. He placed his hand in Renee's and they walked toward the doorway.

Adrian ... Can you create a portal to take us back home, thought William, telepathically.

No problem, thought warlock Adrian. He placed his hands out and a shimmering portal appeared, to take them back to Bagnolet.

EPILOGUE

The grand hall of the Olden Fjord palace, packed with seated guests, stood in solemn silence, its high, vaulted ceilings carrying only the soft whisper of the wind outside. At the center of the room, Hawk stood tall, draped in a ceremonial cloak of dark fabric, its intricate silver embroidery catching the dim light. Feathers from rare Griffins were woven into the hem, a mark of his lineage and destiny. The ancient stone walls, steadfast through centuries of tradition, had witnessed many ceremonies, but none like this. Today, they bore witness to the naming of Garrick's successor.

Before him, Garrick, the current King and Hawk's father, stood tall and imposing, his gaze as piercing as ever. The elder Griffin wore his own regal attire, though there was an air of quiet solemnity around him today.

"Hawk," Garrick's deep voice reverberated through the hall, drawing the attention of the gathered members of their kingdom. "As your bloodline before you, I stand here today to acknowledge you as my successor. The throne of Olden Fjord is a mantle not taken lightly. It is both a privilege and a burden."

Hawk's eyes met his father's and he felt the full weight of his gaze. The years of training, of sparring, of lessons in leadership all led to this one moment. The air was thick with anticipation, and Hawks hands, though steady, gripped the edges of his cloak as if to ground himself.

Garrick stepped forward, his eyes softening for the briefest of moments. "I have watched you grow, Hawk. I have seen your strength, your courage, and the way you protect this kingdom. But more than that, I have seen your heart." He placed a hand on his son's shoulder, his grip firm but reassuring. "You are ready for this."

Hawk's voice was low, but the words carried the weight of generations. "I accept, Father. I will carry the mantle when the time comes." His throat tightened, but he held his composure.

Garrick's gaze never wavered. With a slow movement, he reached for the silver crown that rested upon the pedestal behind him—a crown passed down through the centuries; its sapphire jewel glowing faintly with an ancient, enchanted light. The crown represented not just rulership, but the legacy of their people.

Hawk could feel the eyes of the kingdom upon him, but the moment seemed to stretch, timeless, as his father placed the crown gently upon his head. The weight of it was both an honor and a responsibility, a reminder of everything that came before him and everything that would be his to protect, when his father stepped down or passed beyond this world.

"This crown," Garrick's voice was soft, but filled with conviction, "is a symbol of the throne, of the kingdom, of our people. Let this be a sign that you are the future of Olden Fjord. When the time comes, you will lead us. And until then, you will walk this path with me."

The crown settled into place and Hawk felt the cool metal against his brow, the pulse of the sapphire sending a faint shiver through his body. The cloak seemed heavier now, the weight of it settling onto his shoulders like a mantle that had always been meant for him.

"Together," Garrick added, his voice thick with emotion as he placed a hand on Hawk's shoulder, standing side by side with his son, "we will protect Olden Fjord. You will not walk alone in this."

Hawk bowed his head slightly, the emotion rising in his chest, though he kept his face calm and composed. "Together."

For a long moment, neither spoke. The silence between them was a bond forged over the years and their shared history connected them in ways that words never could. The kingdom's people had watched the ceremony unfold, their future king now standing before them, ready to face the challenges that awaited.

The moment Garrick's hand lifted from Hawk's shoulder, a silence hung over the grand hall, thick with anticipation. And then, like a dam breaking, the chamber erupted into applause. The sound echoed off the high stone walls; a thunderous wave of approval rolled through the gathered nobles, warriors and citizens of Olden Fjord.

The Griffin elders, draped in ceremonial robes, raised their staffs in salute. Warriors, some bearing old battle scars, clapped their fists against their chests in a gesture of loyalty. The nobles bowed their heads, acknowledging the future king with deep reverence.

From the balcony overlooking the great hall, voices rose in unison, chants of *"Hawk! Hawk! Hawk!"* filled the air, a chorus of devotion and expectation. Outside, in the vast courtyard, the gathered citizens of the kingdom, too many to fit inside the hall, echoed the cheers. The sound of celebration carried into the cold Norwegian winds, a declaration to the world that a new era was beginning.

Hawk stood tall beneath the weight of the silver crown, the shimmering cloak settling around his broad shoulders. His chest tightened, not with nerves, but with the sheer magnitude of the moment. He had spent years fighting to prove himself, resisting this destiny at times, but now, as he looked out at the sea of faces cheering for him, he felt something different. He *belonged* here.

Garrick, still standing beside him, nodded approvingly, leaning in just enough for only Hawk to hear and said, "They believe in you. Let them see why they should."

Hawk swallowed, then took a slow step forward. As he did, the crowd hushed, waiting. The weight of expectation hung in the air, but he did not falter. He raised his hand, not to silence them, but to acknowledge them.

"I stand before you today," Hawk began, his voice steady, "not just as the chosen son of Garrick, not just as his heir, but as a warrior of Olden Fjord. As one of *you*."

A murmur of approval rippled through the hall.

"I have trained alongside you. I have fought beside you. I have made mistakes, and I have learned from them." He took a breath, his gaze sweeping over the faces before him. "And now, I vow to lead you. To protect this kingdom. To uphold the honor of our ancestors and guide us into the future, when the time comes."

The crowd roared, fists rising into the air, wings flaring from those in their half-shifted Griffin forms.

The energy of the moment sent a charge through Hawk's blood, setting his pulse racing.

Garrick stepped forward once more, lifting his voice above the cheers. "Then let it be known! From this day forward, Hawk stands as the heir to the Griffin throne. He is your future king!"

The crowd erupted again, louder than before, and the walls of the great hall trembled with the sheer force of their loyalty. From above, the torches lining the hall flickered wildly, their flames dancing as if even the elements recognized the importance of this moment.

Hawk clenched his jaw, his heart steady. The path ahead would not be easy. He knew there would be battles, challenges and sacrifices. But tonight, as the kingdom roared his name, he let himself take in the moment.

For the first time, he wasn't just the reckless son of a king. Instead, he was their future. And he was ready.

* * *

As Sully looked around and heard the kingdom's people cheering and chanting Hawk's name, she felt a sense of pride.

Congratulations, Hawk. You certainly are loved by your people, thought Sully to Hawk.

Hawk looked down in the crowd and, as he spotted her, he smiled. *Thank you*, thought Hawk to Sully.

He sure has changed from the Hawk I first met, at the academy, that night on the basketball courts, with Kiplin, Samuel and Elsie. He was arrogant, reckless, defiant and thought the world owed him a favor. Now he's someone who carries the weight of his lineage with strength and dignity, and is the sweetest guy I know, thought Sully to herself.

Beneath her pride, there was something else, a flicker of something she wasn't ready to name. Watching him now, standing tall beneath the glow of the ceremonial torches, she realized that this moment wasn't just his. It would be theirs.

* * *

As Garrick stepped back from the podium, Elara was there to greet him. "You gave a wonderful speech," she said, leaning in to press a gentle kiss to his cheek.

"Thank you," Garrick replied, his gaze lingering on hers as he pulled away. A quiet warmth filled his voice. "Right now, I am a very proud father. It's hard to believe that just months ago, we struggled with Hawk, questioning whether he was truly ready to take on this role. We wondered if he was fit to be my successor, or if he could handle the weight of the throne, when that time came. Sending him to the Bagnolet Academy to learn and grow … it changed him. He has become the leader we have always hoped he would be."

Elara smiled, her eyes shimmering with pride as she glanced toward Hawk, standing tall before the kingdom. "He has," she agreed softly. "I always knew there was greatness in him, even when he was reckless, even when he defied us at every turn. He just needed to find it for himself." She reached for Garrick's hand, squeezing it gently. "Watching him now, standing where he belongs, I see not just our son, but a future king in the making."

She let out a quiet breath, as if releasing all the worries she had once held. "No matter how much he tested us, no matter how many times we doubted him, this moment proves it was all worth it." Her lips curved into a knowing smile. "And I suspect he has Sully to thank for part of that, too."

"I think you are correct, my love," replied Garrick, noticing Sully in the crowd, walking toward them, with William and Renee.

William approached Garrick with an approving nod, his sharp gaze briefly sweeping over the crowd still buzzing with excitement.

"That was a speech befitting a king," William said, clapping a firm hand on Garrick's shoulder. "You spoke with strength, but more than that, with pride, and rightfully so. Hawk has proven himself worthy. He's come a long way from the rebellious young Griffin who once gave us all headaches." A smirk tugged at the corner of his lips before his expression turned more serious. "You and Elara should be proud. He's ready."

"Thank you, William. We think so, too," said Elara.

"Are you sticking around for the celebrations later," asked Garrick.

"No, sorry, my friend, we won't be able to. I have business to attend to, back in Bagnolet, with a new member of our household. And I do need to follow up with Kura and Alessia, at the River of Whispers," stated William.

"Right! How is Alessia settling into her new role?" asked Garrick.

"Alessia and Kura returned home to the River of Whispers a few days ago. Apparently, the transition hasn't been easy for Alessia, but with Kura's guidance, she's adapting as well as can be expected. She's stronger than she realizes." He paused, with a thoughtful look in his eyes.

"Kura has been a steady support for Alessia, helping her understand not just her power, but her place in all of this." He let out a quiet breath. "It's reassuring to see her finding her footing. After everything she's been through, she deserves a chance to heal and grow." William's gaze flickered back to Hawk. "Much like your son. Change comes for all of us, whether we're ready or not."

"I agree. It's good to hear that Alessia is adjusting," Garrick said, his voice steady. "Kura was always meant to guide her. There's no one better to help Alessia find her strength. She's been through more than most could endure and, yet, she rises despite her youth and her limited knowledge of her heritage."

"She has, but I'd say she'll get through this. I believe Alessia has her parents visiting this coming week, so that will be a significant moment for her."

Garrick's brow lifted slightly. "That will be good for her," he agreed. "Reconnecting with them after everything … it won't be easy, but it's necessary."

William nodded. "It is. From what I've heard, she's nervous but also eager. Parker and TJ have been waiting for this moment, too. They've always been her family and, despite everything she's learned about herself, that hasn't changed."

Elara smiled softly. "Having them there will remind her of who she's always been, even as she steps into who she's becoming."

Garrick exhaled, crossing his arms. "It sounds like she's in good hands—with Kura, with her parents." His gaze flickered toward Hawk once more. "Much like our own son."

William followed his line of sight and smirked. "Yes, though I suspect Hawk will still need a few more reminders to keep that ego of his in check."

Garrick chuckled. "No doubt. But at least now he's wearing it like a leader, rather than a reckless fool."

Sully rolled her eyes at the mention of Hawk's past behavior. She knew all too well how reckless he had once been, but she didn't appreciate anyone dwelling on it, especially when he had come so far. He was her life partner and she wouldn't listen to anyone belittling him, even in jest. "Would I be able to go and see Hawk?"

"That should be fine, my dear. Looks like he has finished, anyway," said Elara, looking from Sully to Hawk.

"Thank you. Will you be staying for a while longer, or leaving soon?" asked Sully to William and Renee.

"I would say we will be leaving in about five minutes. But we will come and say goodbye before we leave," replied Renee.

Sully nodded in acknowledgment, a small smile playing on her lips. "Alright. I'll see you before you go, then."

Without wasting another moment, she turned toward Hawk, her steps quick but graceful. The cheers had begun to quieten, but the warmth of celebration still lingered in the air.

As she approached, Hawk caught sight of her and his expression shifted, first to relief, then to something softer, something just for her. Without hesitation, she reached for his hand, squeezing it firmly.

"You did well," she murmured, her gaze steady on his. "I'm proud of you."

"Thanks," replied Hawk. He pulled her in tight for a cuddle.

Sully could still hear the echoes of the crowd chanting Hawk's name, but in that moment, it was just the two of them.

* * *

The crisp evening air of Olden Fjord carried the distant echoes of celebration as William and Renee stood near the shimmering portal, preparing to depart. The festivities had begun to wind down, but the warmth of the occasion lingered. The ceremony for Hawk had been a momentous event, marking the dawn of a new era for the Ironclaw Kingdom.

Sully stood with William and Renee, her hands clasped tightly in front of her, as she tried to keep her emotions in check. She had known this moment would come, but now that it was here, the weight of it pressed on her heart.

William looked at her with a rare softness in his eyes. "You've come a long way, Sully," he said. "We're proud of you. You know that, don't you?"

Sully swallowed against the lump forming in her throat and nodded. "I do. And I'm grateful for everything. For saving me from the Debauched, for taking me in and raising me, for training me, for always being there when I needed you." She glanced at Renee, her voice thick with emotion. "I wouldn't be who I am, without you both."

Renee stepped forward, pulling Sully into a warm embrace. "You'll always be a part of our family," she whispered. "And you're welcome to return to Bagnolet anytime. If things don't work out here …" She pulled back slightly, giving Sully a knowing look. "You always have a home with us."

Sully exhaled a shaky breath and nodded. "Thank you. But this is where I need to be." Her eyes flickered toward Hawk, who stood a few paces away, watching the exchange in respectful silence. "With him."

William gave a small, approving nod before turning to Hawk. "Congratulations, Heir of Olden Fjord," he said, his tone half-formal but carrying an edge of familiarity. "You've earned this and I have no doubt you'll lead well, when the time comes."

Hawk smirked slightly. "I appreciate that, William. And don't worry, I'll try to keep myself out of trouble."

William chuckled. "That would be a first." Then his expression turned serious as he shifted his attention to Garrick, who had joined them. "Garrick, I welcome the alliance between our people. The Gramaze Lepidoptera

Vampires will stand with the Ironclaws. If you ever need anything, don't hesitate to reach out. We will be there."

Garrick extended a hand and William clasped it firmly. "That means a great deal, William. And know that the same goes for you."

"Thank you," replied William, shaking his hand.

With a final glance at Sully, William and Renee stepped toward the portal. Renee gave her one last smile. "Don't forget to visit. We'll miss you."

"I'll miss you, too," Sully said, her voice quiet, but certain.

As William and Renee stepped through, the portal shimmered for a brief moment before vanishing, leaving only the night air in its wake.

Sully stood between Hawk and Garrick, staring at the space where they had been. As a breeze rolled through the Fjord, it carried with it the scent of the sea and the promise of a new chapter.

Hawk reached for her hand, intertwining his fingers with hers. "Are you okay?"

Sully squeezed his hand gently and let out a deep breath. "Yeah, I will be," she said, turning to face him. "I'm exactly where I'm meant to be: with you, Hawk."

The End

A NOTE TO ALL MY READERS:

Thank you from the bottom of my heart for joining me on this journey with the Empire of the Legacies Academy series. Whether you've been with the Griffins and Vampires from the very beginning or have just discovered their story, I'm so grateful you've shared in their adventures. I poured my heart into this world, and your support truly means everything.

With all my love and appreciation, Susan.

CATCH UP ON ALL THE LATEST NEWS AND UPDATES FROM SUSAN HODDY

Facebook: Susan Hoddy–Author
Instagram: susanhoddy
LinkedIn: Susan Hoddy
TikTok: Susan Houston 478
Threads   Susan Houston (Hoddy) (@susanhoddy)
Website: https://www.susanhoddy.com/

All readings, discussions, signings or appearances are done by appointment only.

If any libraries, schools, daycares, book stores or book clubs would like Susan to come along and do a reading of some chapters and/or a discussion about her books to their group of passionate readers; you can contact Susan via her website and fill in the **Contact Us** form.

https://www.susanhoddy.com/contact/

For rights availability inquiries, including film and television options, please inquire directly with the author using the **Contact Us** form at her website.

https://www.susanhoddy.com/contact/

ACKNOWLEDGMENTS

This book would not be here, resting in your hands or on your e-reader if it weren't for the following people. I owe all of them my deepest gratitude and love.

My book cover artist, Ammonia Book Covers, who worked tirelessly on three covers of the Empire of the Legacies Academy. Thank you, your covers are overwhelmingly beautiful, and I am so lucky to have found you.

My editor, Debbie Phillips from DP Plus, whose continued knowledge, advice and support has provided me with a much-needed calming strength to keep going. I am extremely grateful to you. Thank you, Debbie.

My formatter, Debbie Phillips from DP Plus. Thank you, Debbie, for a wonderful job of making my book look awesome on each page.

My wonderful husband, Michael, for putting up with me, when all I spoke about for months was the characters, plotlines and storyline of the three books in this series. Thank you for your patience and for everything you do for me.

My beautiful daughter, Samantha, who has always given me her advice, support and love. Thank you, Sam. As an avid reader, I think one day you, too, might become a writer.

My many friends and associates, for all their support, feedback and suggestions. I appreciated each and every one of you. Many thanks to you all.

ABOUT THE AUTHOR

Susan Hoddy is an award-winning author celebrated for her captivating blend of fantasy, romance and young adult fiction. Best known for her Lepidoptera Vampire series, she brings a fresh and imaginative take on the vampire genre, weaving together supernatural intrigue, rich world-building and compelling characters. She has also ventured into contemporary romance with her novel Security, showcasing her versatility as a storyteller.

Expanding her creative horizons, Susan recently embarked on a delightful new journey—writing and publishing a fully illustrated children's book series, The Adventures of Georgia and Cash, inspired by the joy of friendship and adventure.

Born in Perth, Western Australia, Susan has always been a dreamer at heart. She cherishes lively conversations with family and friends, spontaneous road trips with her husband, and quiet moments with a good cup of tea and a book.

After spending years working in various office roles, Susan decided in 2012 to follow her passion for storytelling. Earning a novel writing diploma from the Australian College of Journalism, she hasn't looked back since—continuing to craft enchanting tales where fantasy and romance collide.

AWARDS

In 2022 Susan won two book awards for *Attraction* and *Awakened* in the Lepidoptera Vampire series.

***Attraction*, book one in the Lepidoptera Vampire series** was chosen as the 'Silver Winner' in the Fiction Romance category from MMH Press Book Awards.

***Awakened*, book two in the Lepidoptera Vampire series** was chosen as the 'Bronze Winner' in the Fiction Romance category from MMH Press Book Awards.

In 2019 Susan won two book awards for *Attraction* and *Awakened* in the Lepidoptera Vampire series.

***Attraction*, book one in the Lepidoptera Vampire series**, was chosen as the 'Official Selection Winner' in the Young Adult General Fiction category from New Apple Literary Fifth Annual Indie Book Awards.

***Awakened*, book two in the Lepidoptera Vampire series**, was chosen as the solo 'Medalist Winner' in the Young Adult General Fiction category from New Apple Literary Fifth Annual Indie Book Awards.

OTHER SUPERNATURAL FANTASY BOOKS WRITTEN BY SUSAN HODDY

The Lepidoptera Vampire Series

Keep an eye out for news on Susan Hoddy's social media or on her website https://www.susanhoddy.com/ for upcoming book announcements and news.

www.ingramcontent.com/pod-product-compliance
Lightning Source LLC
Chambersburg PA
CBHW061057100726
47911CB00012B/275